Dream Chaser

Dream Chaser

NORMA SEELY

DOUBLEDAY & COMPANY, INC.

GARDEN CITY, NEW YORK

1987

All of the characters in this book
are fictitious, and any resemblance
to actual persons, living or dead,
is purely coincidental.

Library of Congress Cataloging-in-Publication Data

Seely, Norma.
Dream chaser.

I. Title.
PS3569.E345D7   1987   813'.54   86-29213
ISBN 0-385-23568-2

For
The Mile High Writers
With Thanks for Years of Encouragement

Dream Chaser

CHAPTER 1

The Olympic Mountains gathered like clouds on the horizon and sunlight dappled in squares across the brick floor of the Solarium as Rena Drake walked into Mitchell Johns's outstretched arms. It was an embrace shared by special friends who hadn't seen each other in a long time, but Rena wondered if it was wishful thinking that Mitch seemed reluctant to release her.

"It's been a long time, Mitch."

"Three hundred and ninety-four days to be exact."

"You've actually kept track?"

"When you walked out I lost the best gemologist around. As soon as I heard you'd returned to Seattle I called. I want you back, Rena. Enough of this independent appraiser business. I need you. Pacific Imports needs you."

Mitch made her feel incredibly special, but her chief importance was her value to his corporation. "But I like being free." Silently she added, *I like not having my heart broken each day by a man I can never have.*

She looked away to the baskets of flowers banked around the converted greenhouse that retained the uniqueness that had made it a Victorian treasure.

"Was I that stern a taskmaster?" Mitch's voice teased her. Rena found she couldn't keep her gaze away from this man she'd missed so much.

"Are you fishing for a compliment?"

He laughed and nodded.

"I'm not sure you deserve it, but you must know you're the best employer around."

"I know I try. But I failed with you."

"Mitch, you didn't! I needed to be on my own."

He cupped her chin. "I *know* you left for reasons other than a need to be self-employed. I've just never been able to figure them out."

And I hope you never do, she thought. She might not ever have his love, but she would do nothing to jeopardize their friendship. "Mitch, you know the main reason I went into gemology in the first place."

"You hoped to discover who had ruined your father's reputation as a jewelry appraiser. How is he by the way?"

Rena tossed her pink straw hat on a wicker settee and walked over to the windows that provided a sweeping view of Seattle. "He's fine. Actually, he's accepted what happened a lot better than I ever did."

"But you're no closer to finding the person responsible than you were when you worked for me."

"I thought being on my own and taking commissions around the world would give me a better chance of finding the real villain. But that hasn't been the case." It hadn't helped her to excise Mitch from her heart either.

"Have you ever considered," his voice was deliberately gentle, "that there might not be anything to prove?"

"My father is not a thief!"

"He could have made a mistake. Remember the authenticity of the stones was in question at the time."

"My father was one of the best gemologists around. He would never have identified paste as diamonds! Someone substituted those stones and as a result destroyed a fine man's career. I will never give up trying to find the culprit!"

"Revenge doesn't become the sweet girl I took a chance on."

"I don't want revenge—only justice."

"Then come back to work for me, Rena. You can have all the time off you want. In fact, you can have anything you want."

But I can't have you, she thought. Their worlds were too far apart. Mitchell Johns was able to move comfortably among the very wealthiest of the rich and Rena was just a working girl. She would not make the mistake that had ruined her sister's life. Yet she had been unable to resist his invitation to lunch. "Thanks, but I like being on my own."

"Your office is still waiting for you."

Rena felt her determination weakening. She should have refused his luncheon invitation. In fact, she should never have returned to Seattle. But she had wanted to see Shay, her sister, and their father. And, if she were honest, she had hoped to see Mitch again. "Mitch, can't we enjoy lunch and not talk about what can never be?"

"If you insist, but remember, if I had accepted anything as impossible I wouldn't be where I am today."

"Everyone knows how hard you've worked to expand your grandfather's company."

"Actually, no one has the faintest idea. But I don't want to discuss ancient history. I want to talk instead about how lovely you look. I'm glad you haven't cut that glorious raven hair."

"You don't know how close I came to shearing it off in Sri Lanka."

"How was your trip?"

"Interesting. It's hard to believe most of the country is potential gem-bearing land. One of the stones I appraised was a blue sapphire an old man was using as a scrubbing stone."

"I envy experts like you. I have a wide smattering of knowledge, but I'm expert at nothing."

How wrong he was! Mitchell Johns was an adept at lighting the fires that flamed within her. "Come, Mitch, you're proficient at being successful. What more could you want?"

"At the moment it's enough to be with a woman who makes me glad I'm a man. I approve the rose pattern of your dress."

"Thanks, it's going to do double duty at a wedding this afternoon." Rena was shy of admitting the dress had been specially purchased for this reunion luncheon. "Another of my friends has found her Prince Charming."

"And you, Rena, have you discovered yours in the past year?"

"Of course not! I'm a dedicated career girl, remember?"

"I'd be a dunce if I didn't. But then I remember most everything about you. Like the fact you enjoy chilled lobster salad."

"Is that what we're having?"

"Since you once told me it was your idea of a truly elegant lunch I thought it appropriate."

The Solarium was filled with masses of spring flowers and Victorian rattan furniture heaped with pillows. As far as Rena was concerned, it was the perfect room. Constructed from an old-fashioned greenhouse, it made her feel as if she'd stepped into another era when life seemed to be lived at a more leisurely pace. It was a room to curl up in with a good book and watch the changing pattern of the seasons. Right now it was late spring and a more glorious one she couldn't remember.

Lunch was served by a silent manservant. A small basket of pinkish violets sat in the center of a table set with pink-edged pottery and gleaming ruby stemware. "This is lovely."

It was soon apparent Mitch was more interested in watching her than in eating his meal. It made Rena hope she didn't dump her salad in her lap.

"I remember the first time we ever had dinner together. You hadn't worked for me very long."

"Why should you remember that?"

"You'd told me you were hungry for lobster so I took you to this restaurant where you select your own and then it's prepared for you."

Rena laughed. "I've always hoped you wouldn't remember that."

"I thought the incident rather charming. I'd never met anyone who felt selecting a live lobster too personal and subsequently like eating an acquaintance. I thought at the time it was a good thing you didn't live on a farm or you would probably starve to death."

"You're probably right. I really don't like my food to look back at me." Then she added in appreciation, "I only wish everything I ate was this delicious."

"Save room for dessert. It's strawberry trifle."

"How could you! How can I possibly refuse my favorite?"

"Why should you want to?"

"Desserts are fattening. This lunch is going to put pounds on me."

"I'm sure they'll all be in the right places." At that moment the silent servant again appeared. "We'll have dessert now, Mason."

"And the champagne, shall I bring it also?"

"Yes, please, and coffee."

"To think later today I'll be expected to eat wedding cake."

"Yes, but you know those pieces never amount to anything. I've always thought it ridiculous that people stand around waiting for a slice of cake they can eat in two small bites. When I'm married I intend to do things differently."

Rena felt her heart sink. "Are you contemplating such an event?"

"Only if the woman in question says yes."

"So there's someone special?" Had her heart really turned to lead?

"There has been for a long time."

No doubt the strawberry trifle tasted as marvelous as it looked, but it had no flavor as it melted in Rena's mouth. She felt curiously empty and filled with the desire to go home and cry her eyes out.

"Would you like some champagne?"

"Do we have something to celebrate?"

"We would have if I'd convinced you back to Pacific Imports. But since the bottle has been chilling for some time it would be a waste not to drink it —don't you think?"

Relieved that they weren't going to toast his impending marriage, Rena readily agreed. "Since you've had it chilling."

"Do you suppose I could get you to pour it for me?"

"Of course." As she pulled the bottle free, Rena noticed something strange about the ice surrounding it. With a thump, she set the bottle on the table and dipped her hand into the bucket. Perfectly shaped green and red "ice" slipped from her cupped hand. They caught the sun and shot dancing reflections of light around the room. Her voice shook. "What is this supposed to prove?"

"Beautiful, aren't they?"

"But they're not real."

"Now you know better than to jump to that conclusion. The world's leading gemologist would reserve her opinion for the proper tests."

"I have never fallen into the trap of thinking I'm the best. I'm assuming they're not real because—well—because nobody in their right mind would substitute real gems for ice."

"I thought it was rather a grand gesture."

"It's that, all right. I take it this was a last-ditch attempt at persuading me back to Pacific Imports?"

"Did it succeed?" Was the hope in his voice as sincere as it sounded?

Carefully, she laid the stones on the table where they sparkled like fire rather than ice. "Mitch, I can't."

"Can't or won't?"

"I suppose it's a little bit of both."

"Why? I could accept your refusal if I just understood why."

Her gaze searched his face. How could you tell your best friend you were in love with him, especially when it would undoubtedly bring about the end of your treasured friendship? Both of them would be embarrassed by such a confession. She blushed just thinking about it.

"I'm waiting, Rena."

"There's things I have to do, Mitch."

"Meaning your crusade to clear your father's name. How many years do you plan to sacrifice to this cause?"

"I don't consider it a sacrifice. My father was the best jewelry appraiser in the business. If he said the LaSalle diamonds were genuine—then they were."

"I know you've always maintained someone switched the jewels after your father saw them. But the LaSalles didn't feel that was possible."

"No, and they carried a great deal more weight than my father. The whole thing blemished his reputation and his business."

"He's very lucky they didn't prosecute him for theft—that they believed he was honest if not accurate."

"I know that. But either assumption doomed his career."

"Don't you think you could continue your search just as well if you worked for me?"

"I'd have to check with you every time I wanted to follow up a lead."

"What if I agree to free you at a moment's notice?"

"Mitch, you're making this very difficult for me."

"I'm trying to make it impossible for you to refuse. I want you back, Rena. And I don't give up on something I want."

She glanced at her watch, glad of the already mentioned wedding as an excuse for fleeing a dangerous situation. "I've got to go if I'm not going to be late. Thank you for a perfectly wonderful lunch."

"Can I see you again while you're in town?"

She intended to say no, but it didn't come out that way. "If you'd like."

"You'll be at your sister's?"

"Yes."

"Then can I pick you up there this evening?"

Rena blinked in surprise. She had thought his request to see her meant another day.

"There's a private party on the *Puget Sound Queen* tonight. I'd appreciate it if you'd go with me."

"Won't your fiancée mind?"

It was his turn to blink in surprise. "Fiancée?"

"You said you were thinking of asking someone to marry you. I wouldn't think she'd like you dating other women."

"Don't worry about her. This is a rather special event tonight and I'd like you there. Please."

"How can I refuse?"

"That's what I keep asking myself. Perhaps after tonight you won't be able to."

"Oh, Mitch, you're not going to put more pressure on me, are you?"

"No, I'm going to let a certain set of circumstances do that for me."

"Mitch, this isn't fair."

"All right, I'll give you a hint. Do you remember the Dressler Collection?"

"You've always wanted to buy it."

"Well, it has something to do with tonight."

"Is Dressler finally willing to sell?"

His eyes definitely danced with anticipation. "You'll see—if you go."

"Then I guess I'm doubly persuaded."

"That's all I ask."

Once outside in the spring sunshine, Rena decided against attending the wedding. She hadn't really been close to the bride and didn't think it would matter if she wasn't there. She didn't want to see two people joined in forever-after happiness, since the possibility of that now seemed beyond her reach.

Rena drove her rented car down to the waterfront, parked, and got out for a walk. The breeze that blew under Rena's dress threatened to seize her hat. Removing it, she let the wind play with her dark hair. The encounter she'd both dreaded and looked forward to was over. Mitchell Johns was just as devastating as she remembered.

Glancing at her watch, a round gold face attached to three strands of water pearls, Rena discovered she had no more time for dawdling. With reluctance, she permitted herself one last glimpse of Elliott Bay, its water made choppy by the wind even on this nice day. Islands dotted the immediate horizon and she longed for the time to take a ferry ride. The day was too far advanced and she'd have to hurry now or be caught in rush hour traffic. Then she'd never be ready when Mitch called.

Traffic was heavy and Rena tapped a pink-lacquered nail against the steering wheel. Each minute seemed an hour as she tried to weave her way through the streams of cars.

Shay was rattling pots and pans when Rena let herself into the apartment. With a stalk of celery in one hand and a scrub brush in the other, Shay greeted her. "How was lunch?"

Rena tossed her purse and hat onto a chair. "Mitch is considering marriage."

"Is that so surprising? He's what—thirty-seven?"

"Yes."

"Ten years older than you, little sister. Perhaps you should follow his lead."

"Oh, definitely. Which of my many suitors should I accept?"

"The only reason you don't have a line outside that door is because you can't see anyone but Mitch Johns and yet you discourage his every advance. By the way, who's the lucky lady?"

"He didn't say, but I imagine we'll know soon enough."

Shay frowned. "He wouldn't say who she was?"

"I didn't exactly ask."

"Rena, I don't think I'll ever understand you."

"There's nothing *to* understand. Mitch and I are from different worlds and no matter how much we might have in common, I don't think those two worlds can ever mix."

"Don't let my failed marriage spoil your chance at happiness, Rena."

"You've said yourself the difference in backgrounds was a part of the problem."

"I was a young, unsophisticated girl only a year out of high school when I married Bryan Windsor. He was thirty-eight, I was eighteen. He was patient with all my mistakes, but I was too stubborn to learn. Benefit from other people's mistakes, don't let them cripple your life. If I were you I'd go after Mitch hook, line, and sinker."

"You make him sound like a fish."

"He's certainly a prime catch!"

"You're forgetting, he's already been caught."

Shay folded her arms across her chest. "The ring isn't on his finger yet."

"Shay, he already belongs to someone else. I couldn't build my happiness by destroying someone else's."

"Well, at least see if you can get him to tell you who she is. It's well to know the identity of your adversary."

"It doesn't matter."

"Then why a two-day shopping trip to find the right dress?"

"I might know he's wrong for me, but that doesn't stop me from wanting to look my best."

Shay threw her hands up in despair. "And to think I'm responsible for this attitude. Haven't I made enough mistakes without you forcing me to feel remorseful?"

"Oh, Shay, I'm sorry. I didn't mean to make you feel bad. There are a lot of things keeping me from pursuing Mitch."

"I don't really believe you, but for the sake of my own conscience I'm going to try. Just remember, Rena, she who hesitates is lost."

"And you remember, big sister, that I really do know what I'm doing with my life."

"I certainly hope so. Now, I've got to get back to my spaghetti."

Rena wrinkled her nose. "It smells good."

"You're going to help me eat it, aren't you?"

"I'm sorry; Mitch is taking me out."

"For thinking he's not any good for you, you're certainly seeing a lot of him in one day."

"He used some unfair persuasion."

"Oh?"

Rena laughed at her sister's raised eyebrows. "You're awful to even think that. He's taking me to a private party on the *Queen*. Something regarding the Dressler Collection."

"No wonder you're willing to walk into the lion's den. He's tried several times to buy that collection, hasn't he?"

Rena nodded, "But Hugh Dressler wouldn't sell."

"I wonder who will inherit his estate when Dressler goes. I don't think he has a single relative and he's too cantankerous to have many friends."

"He'll probably leave his gemstone collection to a museum. Look, I'm going to be late if I don't hurry. I'm sorry about dinner. I've missed your spaghetti."

"Don't worry, I'll save you some. Run along and make yourself irresistible."

Pushing hangers along the rod, Rena pondered what to wear. Taking a champagne-colored silk from its hanger, she held it against her, and looked in the mirror. Its sequins and beads shimmered in the light and price tags dangled from the sleeve. She'd bought it for an occasion that had never happened.

There was only time for a quick shower, a liberal splash of rain scent, and a fresh application of makeup. Pulled away from her face and twisted into an elegant knot, her hair was just right for the dress. Fine strands of twisted gold slipped easily through her ears and she was ready except for her champagne evening sandals.

Shay stuck her head around the door and whispered softly, "Mr. Right, whether you know it or not, is here."

"Shush, he'll hear you. Do I look all right?"

"Very much so! This must be some soiree tonight."

Tall, blond Mitch always looked good. Tonight he looked fabulous. Sharply turned out in a perfectly tailored heather-blue pinstripe suit, a satin stripe blue shirt, and an elegant paisley silk tie, he almost took Rena's breath away. She couldn't help a proprietary proudness in the way he looked and he seemed equally satisfied with her appearance.

A smile crooked the corner of his mouth. "Another new dress?"

It was then Rena realized she hadn't removed the price tags. "Two years ago. This is the first chance I've had to wear it. Shay, do you have some scissors handy?"

"Just a minute."

Rena felt conspicuous standing there with dangling price tags. When Shay returned it seemed to take her forever to remove them because Mitch didn't take his eyes off her for one minute. "Well, I guess I'm ready . . ."

"You look flawless and self-assured. That and your reputation will have the competition shaking in their boots."

"Competition? What are you talking about? Don't you think you should tell me what's expected of me tonight?"

His forefinger traced the curve of her jawline, seriously denting her defenses. "And have you back out on me? Tonight is too important to risk that."

"Oh?"

"I prefer you approach the evening with no prior knowledge of what's going to happen. When it's over if you still want to tell me no, well, then I'll have to accept it. But I don't think you will."

"Don't you care what I want?" She could tell from his expression that her question was unexpected.

"Of course, I've always wanted what was best for you. But after tonight you'll have the opportunity to be known worldwide as the best gemologist

in the business. Your future will be secure and it may even help you smoke
out the criminal you've dedicated your life to finding."

"You certainly know the right incentives to offer."

"Because I always make a point to know my competition."

"Is that how you think of me?"

"That's what I consider your mule-headed refusal to come back to work
for me is."

"Even though I don't want to?"

"That's not it, Rena. You'd come back at the snap of my fingers if I could
just figure out what's bothering you."

"Don't try, it's only important to me." It would really spoil everything if
he knew what a hopeless crush she had on him.

"Someday I'm going to figure you out, Rena, and then you won't stand a
chance."

"Don't try, Mitch. I keep all of my secrets under lock and key. Anyway, I
won't be around long enough for you to even try. I've a job in Scotland
waiting. If my hunch is right, some long-lost jewels will soon be on the
market."

"After tonight you'll be putting your Scotland trip on hold."

"Don't bet on it."

"We'll see" was all he would offer in reply.

"If you weren't so intent on keeping me in the dark . . ."

"Because I want you to have the whole picture before you make a final
decision. I don't want you to form an opinion on only half the facts."

"I have to admit you've whetted my curiosity." Darn him, he really had
and she didn't need to be encouraged to hang around.

"Shall we go? We'll be late."

"I'll tell Shay we're leaving." Rena almost wished she hadn't when Shay
whispered for her to make the most of the evening.

"Let's be off. Shay says good-bye, but she's up to her elbows in tomato
sauce."

They were seated in Mitch's very comfortable Rolls-Royce before he
responded to her comment. "I ran into Bryan Windsor the other day."

"Oh?" She'd always liked Bryan. Even though she'd been just a child
when he'd married Shay, he had made Rena feel adult. "How is he? We
always seem to be in different places at different times, although I have
borrowed his beach house on Kauai." She hesitated, then added, "It's too
bad they didn't realize they were from different worlds before they married."

He said nothing and the silence became uncomfortable. "Mitch, did I
say something wrong?"

"I just wonder what you have against men with money."

"Nothing—if you happen to be from the same background."

"That's a rather chauvinistic attitude."

His answer startled her. "Why do you say that?"

"You don't even give men with money a chance. In your work you come into contact with wealthy people and priceless gems every day. I'd think it was a world you'd be comfortable in."

"I am on a professional level. I'm fascinated by gemstones and the value and importance people place on them."

"But you're not fascinated by men with money?"

Rena took a deep breath and lied, "That's right."

CHAPTER 2

Lights reflected off the dark water like ghostly moonstones. Rena stifled a sigh, knowing she had been too blunt and hurt Mitch.

"Mitch, I didn't mean that quite the way it sounded. I—I just don't think the rich and the poor can mix that successfully. Look at Shay and Bryan."

"Rena, your sister was still in her teens when she married a man twenty years older. If you must blame anything for the failure of their marriage, then blame the difference in their ages. Not the fact that Bryan Windsor had the knack of making money."

She had no rebuttal against his valid argument.

"But then I'm not convincing you, am I? You've already made up your mind and nothing I can do or say will change it."

"Well, what does it matter? There are no wealthy suitors on my horizon." Rena's words of bravado were hollow to say the least.

"You might be surprised."

Valet parking took care of the Rolls and they walked to the gangway of the *Queen.* It was lovely, an unusually-warm-for-the-time-of-year evening, and the party had spilled over onto the deck. Laughter, the hum of conversation, and a waiter with a tray of champagne greeted them. Mitch handed Rena a glass. Then raised his own in a toast.

"To the outcome of this evening."

She nodded and added one of her own. "And to our continuing friendship."

His eyes narrowed and he looked away breaking their visual bond. "It looks like most everyone is here."

"Have you seen the guest list?" It was meant as a joke.

"One was included with the invitation."

"So there would be no surprises?"

"Probably, and also as an enticement to those who thought they might give the gathering a pass."

She touched his arm as he moved to enter the saloon. "When are you going to stop being so mysterious?"

He was saved from answering when a florid-faced man stepped up to greet them. "Mitch, I was beginning to wonder where you were."

"Business made me a little late. You know how it is."

Always the gentleman, Mitch took the blame.

"Don't I. But then tonight is special and I was a little worried you had decided to bow out. It won't be much of a game if we don't have all the players."

"Well, I'm afraid whether or not you can deal me in is up to my companion here. Judson Kingsley, let me introduce you to Rena Drake."

"Ms. Drake, you have a well-known reputation among those who value precious gems. You recently saved an old friend of mine a lot of money."

Rena smiled and shook his hand. "I'm always glad when that's the case. Who are we talking about?"

"Valerie Lansing. I imagine you remember her."

"Definitely. I would hate to see anyone—whether they needed the money or not—be the loser on an unfair transaction."

"Well, Valerie needed the money."

Rena could sense Mitch's curiosity. It would serve him right if she didn't explain, simply as a payback for being so mysterious about the evening ahead. But she couldn't do that, and Valerie Lansing's story *was* an interesting one.

"Mitch, a year ago I was indulging in my favorite pastime of visiting pawnshops and secondhand stores looking for possible good buys in jewelry, when I met Mrs. Lansing. She was obviously nervous about being in the shop and didn't really want to part with the heirloom brooch she'd brought with her. I gathered she needed the money when I saw the look of dismay on her face at the small sum of money the pawnbroker was willing to pay."

Mitch interjected, "A familiar enough occurrence. I assume she was under the impression the piece was priceless."

Judson Kingsley affirmed his statement. "Valerie had always said if things got bad she could sell that brooch and live comfortably off the proceeds."

Rena nodded. "And she was being offered five hundred dollars for it. I put my two cents' worth in and offered to appraise the brooch for her. I know the importance of not making hasty decisions, but the cut of the stones hinted at more than five hundred dollars. I gave her my address and we agreed to meet later in the day. After she left, the dealer turned to me and said I was wasting my time, everyone knew her husband had gambled away all their money years before he died and had replaced her jewelry with inferior stones. But as you know, I have a weakness for emeralds and that pin looked special—call it intuition."

"And what was the brooch worth?"

"Three hundred and fifty thousand dollars."

Judson beamed his approval and Mitch whistled softly. "So, did she end up selling it?"

"Yes, to a jeweler who in turn sold it to an Arab millionaire and made a profit for himself. I believe it's now in the possession of a movie star. So everyone concerned is happy." She smiled at Judson Kingsley. "How is Mrs. Lansing?"

"Quite well. She also sold her huge old house, and those proceeds, along with the money from the brooch, have enabled her to buy a nice condo with a view. Without your intervention I don't know what she would have done."

"Well, good. We were both in the right place at the right time. Mrs. Lansing got what her jewelry was worth, and I received an unexpected commission."

Mitch sipped his champagne and watched her. "A happy ending for everyone concerned. Did I tell you, Judson, that Rena was one of the best?"

The older man smiled. "A case of beauty having an eye for beauty."

Rena blushed and protested, "Please, let's not get carried away. I enjoy what I do and I like being able to tell the difference between an exquisitely cut synthetic and the real thing."

Judson added to the mystery before bustling off. "Then this is the place for you. Enjoy yourselves. We'll be gathering in the main dining room in about fifteen minutes. You might want to go ahead and fill your plates with the assorted goodies available."

Mitch's voice was soft, like the breeze whispering across the water.

"Don't be so modest, Rena. You have an uncanny sixth sense where precious stones are concerned. A sixth sense that will be invaluable in handling what we're about to hear."

A bell sounded and they joined the crowd as it drifted toward the main dining room. The women, and many of the men, gleamed with jewels, making Rena thankful her dress captured and held the light. The tables were filling up, but when she would have joined Judson Kingsley at his, Mitch steered her toward one that would accommodate no more than the two of them.

"I don't want to share you tonight."

"That's very flattering, but why a table in the shadows?"

"It allows me to observe without being observed. You hold our table while I get us something to eat."

She watched Mitch as he joined the line of people waiting their turn at the buffet table. He was taller than most of the men and there were no signs of self-indulgence visible in his compact, well-kept body. She loved to be able to watch him without his being aware of it. Only at those moments could she be sure he wouldn't read between the lines and discover how very much she loved him. A prickling sensation warned Rena she was being observed and made her glance away. Her gaze was instantly intercepted by a man almost as tall as Mitch, but dark where Mitch was blond. He raised a champagne glass in silent toast as she puzzled to herself over the man's identity. So intent was she that Mitch startled her when he set an over-loaded plate in front of her.

"That's Randy Fletcher. He thinks he's as good as I know you are."

"He's a gemologist?"

"He'd like everyone to think so."

"You don't like him?"

"Let's say I don't trust him. I don't know him well enough to decide if I like him or not."

Rena nibbled at her food and then asked the question which had her almost bursting. "Is she here tonight?"

"Is who here tonight?"

"The woman you're thinking of marrying."

He looked at her oddly before responding and then his tone was guarded. "Yes, she's here."

Rena swept the room with her gaze and wondered which of the be-jeweled ladies was the lucky woman. "I don't suppose you'd enlighten me?"

"Under the circumstances I don't think it would be a very good idea."

His tone was clipped and his manner such that Rena decided not to press the issue. But it didn't keep her from wondering if each woman looking their way might be the one. "She must be very understanding."

"Why do you say that?"

"Well, here you and I are together and she doesn't even come over and say hello."

"We've spoken tonight."

"You have?" The interchange must have occurred while Mitch was filling their plates and she was watching Randy Fletcher. Darn, she'd taken her eyes off him for only a few minutes and look what happened. Still, she wondered at the odd note in Mitch's voice. Was there the possibility he was more involved than the woman? Rena envied her in a way, yet wondered if she'd be up to the globe-trotting and socializing that were the overwhelming life-style of the owner of Pacific Imports. Her wool-gathering was brought to an abrupt halt by Judson Kingsley blowing into the microphone. It was unexpectedly turned up full blast, causing almost everyone to jump in their chairs.

He grinned and apologized. "At least I caught your attention. I imagine everyone has enjoyed their meal by now and is ready to hear about the event that has brought us all together. All of you are familiar with the Hugh Dressler Collection. Many of you have tried to buy it at one time or another. Mr. Dressler has never forgotten those who've shown an interest. That's why you're here tonight. You're about to be invited to join in a most unique treasure hunt."

Rena glanced at Mitch and saw he was smiling.

"Mr. Dressler has decided to dispose of three pieces from his collection. *Which* three pieces will remain a mystery. Suffice it to say, each one exceeds in value the half-million-dollar entry fee."

Rena darted Mitch a look, but saw none of the surprise she felt on hearing the sum of money involved.

"In this game there can be as high as three winners and as few as one. Be warned before you get your checkbooks out. The hunt will not be easy. The clues are composed by experts and a thorough knowledge of the Dressler Collection is almost essential. It is on display under heavy guard in the ballroom. Each entrant will be allowed twenty minutes to study the twenty pieces. You must pay your entry fee before being allowed admittance. Are there any questions?"

A man with a thick foreign accent called from the front of the room. "Is there a time limit?"

"The hunt lasts as long as it takes for someone to find the treasures."

"Where will the treasure hunt be held?" This from a lady wearing a waterfall of diamonds.

"The clues, if you decipher them, will tell you that."

"Do you know where the treasures are hidden?" This from Randy Fletcher.

"No, I don't. No one person knows where all three are to be found. Not even Mr. Dressler. Everyone who enters will be given the first clue at the same time. Where you go from there is up to you."

A low hum of conversation buzzed around the room as Rena leaned over to capture Mitch's attention. "This is ridiculous."

"When you're as rich as Hugh Dressler it's eccentric."

"But to offer his collection as prizes in a treasure hunt."

"Very sporting, I think. He stands to make a profit even if only half a dozen people enter."

"You knew about this before we came?"

"Yes, a number of us were sounded out as to whether or not we would participate in such an event."

"And you said yes?"

"I wouldn't miss it for anything."

"But you stand to lose half a million dollars."

"I have great faith in you, Rena."

"Now wait a minute! I'm not going to get involved in this!"

"I don't believe you can walk away from the challenge."

"You'd better *start* believing, because that's what I intend doing."

"You're not the least bit tempted?"

"I'd have to be as crazy as Dressler not to be, but I don't want the responsibility."

"It's a responsibility you assume every time you appraise a stone."

"Then I'm being paid for my opinion."

"I intend to pay you."

"Along with the responsibility of half a million dollars resting on my shoulders? I'd have to be crazy to agree to such a scheme."

"Then there must be a lot of crazy people in this room." He nodded in the direction of Judson Kingsley.

People were lining up, more than willing to part with five hundred thousand dollars and laughing in the process.

"People enjoy a sporting chance at the wealth, Rena."

"But think of what people have to lose!"

"Think of what people have to gain—what I'll gain if you agree."

"Mitch, I refuse to be a part of this. I may know a lot about gems, but every treasure hunt I've participated in I've come in dead last. The clues will be hard. What if I couldn't figure them out?"

"I'd help. There's nothing against it in the rules."

If she weren't so crazy about him she might be tempted. But a summer in contact with him would send her heart into a tailspin. "No, Mitch!"

"Then you want me to settle for someone not near as good as you?"

"I don't want you to become involved at all. I thought it was crazy the first time I heard it and my opinion hasn't changed one bit."

"I'm afraid it's a little too late for me to back out now."

"Why?"

"I've already paid my entry fee."

"Mitch, how could you?"

"Easily. I didn't think you could resist the challenge."

"Mitch, you're making me feel guilty and that's the worst kind of coercion. There's got to be someone besides me who can help you. Besides, you don't need a gemologist. You need a cryptographer or someone who's good at puzzles."

"I want your expertise with gems and your sixth sense."

"Maybe you could get your money back."

"No refunds allowed."

Rena closed her eyes and leaned back in her chair. It both pleased and dismayed her that he had counted on her support. But what if she agreed to participate in this ridiculous farce and lost? No, it was better for him to find someone else at the outset. Someone who was clever with words as well as gems.

She shoved her chair back abruptly and coffee slopped over into their saucers. "No, Mitch, I can't. The stakes are too high." And she fled the suddenly stifling room for the cool comfort of the deck.

Here and there a cigarette glowed, but for the most part the deck was deserted. A couple passed arm in arm and a drift of expensive perfume reached her, but no one interrupted her solitude. As her panic subsided, a web of anger tightened around her heart and she lashed out at Mitch when he suddenly joined her. "How could you assume I'd take part in this?"

He was plainly taken aback by her feelings. "I never once thought you'd react so strongly. I apologize. Don't worry, I'll find someone else. But at least take a look at the collection with me."

The lure of the legendary Dressler Collection was overpowering. Besides, angry as she was with Mitch, she didn't want him to be entirely disappointed with her. And he quite obviously wanted her to see the display with him.

Only a few people were allowed in at a time and one of their party was dark-haired Randy Fletcher. Mitch nodded politely, but Rena knew he wasn't at all happy when the other man attached himself to them. Fletcher's hands were deep in his pockets, but when he pulled them free to light a slim brown cigarette, Rena noticed the huge diamond ring he was wearing. The stone was oversized for a man's ring, and she wondered if perhaps it had originally come from a different setting. Nevertheless, it was beautifully cut and reflected the light with a thousand prisms. It was hauntingly familiar, and Rena wondered if she had appraised it at some time.

"Well, Mitch, is that your expert?"

Mitch neither denied nor affirmed the question. "Rena Drake, may I introduce Randy Fletcher."

Fletcher recovered well, but a look of surprise touched his features. His earlier desire to be friendly noticeably cooled. Glancing at his watch, he found the perfect excuse.

"It's later than I realized. If I'm going to have a look at these beauties I'd better do it quickly."

Her gaze followed him. "What was that all about?"

"Perhaps the thought of you as competition frightened him."

She shook her head. "He doesn't look like the kind of man who would frighten easily. There was something about my name . . ."

"That tells you I'm right. He's heard of you."

"No, I think it was something else."

"Your sixth sense?"

"You don't need that to realize he was startled when you introduced me." Her puzzlement was replaced with wonder as they toured the room. "Rumor doesn't do justice to this collection." She stopped by an exquisite jade butterfly. The detailing was superb and it looked as if it could be poised for just a moment within the case.

"Could you be changing your mind?"

"Don't spoil it, Mitch." But she couldn't deny the lure of the star sapphire winking back at her. She glanced over at Mitch and battled the temptation to say, *Yes, I'll do it. I'll participate in this ridiculous game. Only please, don't break my heart.* But she didn't.

When their twenty minutes was up, Mitch took her back on deck. The cooling breeze off the bay was a welcome balm to the tension created by the treasures inside.

"You were right. The collection is fabulous. I wonder what Hugh Dressler must have paid for some of those pieces?"

"A lot, but probably not nearly as much as they're worth today. He's had a good many of those pieces for years." Mitch allowed her a moment to rest against the railing of the ship before he again asked, "Have you changed your mind?"

"No, I can't. Please try to understand."

He tucked a strand of hair that had blown loose behind her ear and stirred her senses. "How can you pass up the chance of a lifetime?"

"Mitch, I'm sorry." So sorry that she could have cried, but she couldn't trust herself to once again be in Mitch's employ. Her heart just couldn't stand it.

"Then I guess I have no alternative but to find someone else." She was of course replaceable. Rena knew that and in this instance was glad. It would be awful if Mitch lost all that money because of her. But would things ever have the easy sameness between them again?

Moonlight had transformed the night into something enchanted, and Rena wasn't all that surprised when Mitch kissed her as he held the car door open. It wasn't the first time, they were after all old friends. Forlornness made her cling somewhat desperately to his jacket lapels. His arms stole around her in response, and his warm mouth moved from her lips to brush the sensitive curve of her neck.

The pain of longing filled her soul as she stood in the shadows and watched Mitch drive away. He had thought her safely inside, but she had tricked him so she could watch until his taillights vanished.

Shay was waiting when Rena let herself into the apartment, her lips and throat still feeling the imprint of Mitch's kiss. The soft light of a single lamp cast a hazy halo around her sister's head.

"You didn't have to wait up for me."

"I wanted to. Anyway I had a good book to read."

Shay was reading one of the romance novels she loved and laughed. "I know you don't approve of my reading material."

"It's only that your interest surprises me. Do you still believe in happiness ever after?"

"Perhaps not ever after. But I do believe in love."

"You're an incurable romantic, Shay."

"And you, my dear sister, are more of one than you realize."

"I'm not—I'm very realistic."

"If you believe that, you'll believe anything. A realist wouldn't still be trying to find the person who ruined Dad's reputation."

"You don't forget when you care about someone."

"I'm glad you realize that, at least. That should prepare you for the fact walking away won't get Mitchell Johns out of your system. A realist would know that. Oh, Rena," and her gesture was almost one of pleading, "don't throw away this chance at happiness." Then she saw the look of mulish determination that crossed Rena's face. "Never mind. Let's not quarrel. Instead tell me about tonight." And she tucked her feet up under her housecoat.

"It was certainly an interesting evening." And Rena proceeded to enlighten Shay.

"Half a million just to enter? I'd forgotten what high stakes some people are willing to play with. But then the prizes are rather tantalizing. Are you going to get involved for Mitch's sake?"

"No, I am not!"

"Sounds like he's counting on you."

"He should never have assumed I'd be willing to participate."

"I don't see how you can resist." And Shay's face shone.

Rena closed her eyes and remembered the tantalizing treasures resting in the hushed light of the ballroom. A king's ransom, they were almost impossible to resist, but she would have to. Rena couldn't put her heart through a summer of wanting Mitch and knowing he was out of her reach, now more than ever. "I have no choice."

"You don't think you should be there for him now."

"Shay, it's not like he was in dire trouble and I was the only one who could help him. There are lots of qualified gemologists he could hire. Besides, as I told him, someone who can decipher puzzles might be a better bet."

"Maybe under the circumstances he doesn't want to trust just anyone."

"I cannot become involved with Mitch again."

"Did he kiss you good-night?"

"Of course he did, we're old friends."

A subtle, knowing smile played on Shay's lips. "Oh, yes, all my old friends kiss me good-night."

Rena blushed and ducked her head—too late—to hide it. Then she sought to defend herself. "We might not be seeing each other for some time."

"It's a wonder to me that man doesn't shake you until your teeth rattle. You must drive him crazy with your unreasonableness. I know you darn near do me." Then Shay's expression and voice took on a touch of earnestness. "Don't you think you'll be sorry when he's permanently out of reach?"

"I hate to think of him with any other woman. But I know it's for the best—for both of us."

Shay shook her head despairingly. "I've never seen anyone run away from happiness quite as deliberately as you. But we've argued the point until it's in tatters—so I'm going to leave you to your decision. See you in the morning."

"I'll get the lights. I thought I might make myself a cup of tea."

Rena was glad of the quiet as she sipped her orange spiced tea and looked out at the sleeping city. How she loved Seattle and all its moods. Even the vagaries of its weather were part of the city's charm. Rena had really hoped to stay for a while, but then she had also thought she'd put Mitch in proper perspective in her life. Less than seventy-two hours back in the city and she'd found out how wrong she'd been.

Setting the half-empty mug aside, she returned to the window. It was an hour when very few people were about, although the glowing flare of a match betrayed someone lurking across the street like the hero in an old-fashioned detective thriller. Rena smiled at the thought and wondered who or what the person was waiting for. Probably they couldn't sleep.

Letting the curtain drop into place, she carried her cup back into the kitchen. There was no sense in remaining in Seattle—not now. Checking first of all to make certain Shay's door was closed and that she wouldn't disturb her, Rena then went to the telephone and dialed a number well-known to her. Within ten minutes she had a flight booked to Honolulu. She would run away from Mitch, but she would run to paradise. She had a while before she was due in Scotland.

Her bags piled and waiting by the door, Rena began penning a note to Shay. Before she had a chance to even begin her sister came to sit beside her.

"So you're off?"

"I didn't mean to wake you."

"That's all right. Actually I can't get to sleep either. Where are you going this time?"

"I have a flight booked to Honolulu. I'll be out of here by eight. If Mitch should call, please don't tell him where I've gone."

"Okay, I'll let you fly off into the sunset—sunrise or whatever. But do write. And do think what a mistake you're making." She held up her hand to forestall any comment on Rena's part. "Think about it, that's all I ask. Think about your feelings for Mitch without considering my failed marriage or Mom and Dad's. Because every situation is different. Don't lose the most precious thing in the world because someone else didn't have sense enough to know they'd already found the pot of gold at the end of the rainbow."

"You never got over Bryan, did you?"

"No, and given another chance I'd never let him get away a second time. But I'm not likely to have the chance, so I live with reality and maybe someday I'll fall in love again. Speaking of Bryan, I suppose there's no need for me to ask where you'll be staying."

"His place on Kauai. He did give me carte blanche to stay there when I tried to return the key. Why don't you come with me?"

"No, the chances of running into Bryan would be too great and the memories too good. I don't need to be reminded of everything I've lost. Well, have fun. Are you going to try and get any sleep?"

"No, I'm too keyed up. I'm going to dig out some of my old journals and see if I can place a stone I saw tonight. It was familiar, although the setting wasn't, and I've been trying to remember where I've seen it before. Since I've photographed every piece I've worked on I thought I might be able to jog my memory."

"Well, happy hunting. And have a good flight." Hesitating in the doorway of her bedroom, she added impulsively, "If you see Bryan—give him my love." And the door clicked shut.

Rena spent what remained before flight time poring through her careful records. But not one bit of writing or one photograph was anything like the stone adorning Randy Fletcher's ring. Checking her watch, she frowned and gave up the search. The clue to the diamond's identity was not among her notebooks. But she could have sworn she'd seen it somewhere.

The taxi ride to Sea-Tac International Airport was uneventful. There was the usual last-minute bustle as her luggage was checked and her ticket claimed. Then she was boarding the plane and ready for takeoff. This was the moment when exhilaration usually took over, but her sleepless night was catching up with her and it was an effort to keep her eyes open. Someone settled into the seat beside her and out of politeness she opened her eyes.

Randy Fletcher's smile of greeting was definitely a little forced. "Small world, isn't it?"

"It certainly appears to be. Where are you headed?"

"You should know that as well as I do."

"Oh, of course, the treasure hunt. Well, I'm off to my ex-brother-in-law's place on Kauai."

"That sounds like a nice arrangement." A pleasant enough statement, but it suggested there was far more to her relationship with Bryan than either of them could ever want.

"Just because he's no longer related to me by marriage doesn't mean we have to be enemies."

"No, probably not, but then I don't imagine a woman like you has many enemies—unless they're professional."

"I try not to cultivate any of those. It accomplishes nothing."

Rena was being perfectly friendly and open, adopting the air of a traveler who wants to while away the hours and then good-bye without any regrets. But there was something underlying Randy's surface friendliness. Something was bothering him. Could it possibly be the competition of which she wasn't even a part? Of course he didn't know she wasn't. "Who's sponsoring you in the Dressler competition?"

"No one—I'm working for myself."

Her look of surprise was too quick to hide. "At a half-million entry fee?" She felt his rueful grin was the first honest emotion he'd shown during their conversation. "Makes my stake in the thing rather high. But with more to gain it also means I have more to lose. I have to see to it I don't."

"Then you're feeling confident?"

"Let's say I have a background that will help in ferreting out the treasure. Since it's valued at three and a half million, I think I'll break even."

"I see you're planning on winning."

"I can't afford to lose."

"Do you intend keeping anything you find?"

"I'll take a couple of years off with the profits."

Rena was tempted to say, *My, aren't we cocky!,* but refrained. "I thought you might be a collector."

"What gave you that idea?"

"Your ring."

"Oh, that. I picked it up in a pawnshop in Reno, Nevada."

Now why, she questioned herself, *don't I believe you?* "Someone must have dropped a bundle."

"People don't take care of things the way they should. I know that for a fact. Tell me how you tumbled to a solution of the number-one clue so fast?"

If he could figure the clue out so quickly why couldn't she? But she was too tired to challenge him. "I'm not entered in the competition. So I have no idea what the first clue is. My trip to Hawaii is purely vacation." He visibly relaxed. Rena *knew* she didn't imagine it.

"Why not? I thought you were Mitchell Johns's special protégée. It was my understanding Johns would do anything to get his hands on the Dressler Collection. You were his best bet—how did he ever let you get away?"

"The hunt conflicts with previous plans—even if I were tempted to gamble with someone else's money. Tell me, does the first clue lead to Hawaii?" She doubted he would tell her.

His broad smile was amused. "You don't really expect me to tell you, do you?"

"It was worth a try."

"You might not be in the game, but what's to stop you from wiring the location to your boyfriend with the big bucks."

"My boyfriend?"

"Yes. The wealthy, influential, and not-to-be-crossed Mitchell Johns."

"That certainly doesn't sound like the Mitch I know."

The tone was bitter, the look insinuating. "Oh, I imagine he shows the—ladies in his life a different side than he shows anyone who gets in his way."

"I'm not one of the ladies in anyone's life. I used to work with Mitch and we're old friends."

"Yeah, I'll bet."

"You, Mr. Fletcher, have a dirty mind."

"No, what I have is a tired one. So if you don't mind I think I'll take a nap."

"Just don't snore."

"Not a chance and I don't talk in my sleep either."

"Darn, and I thought I'd learn all your secrets."

"I'd like to see you try."

His tone made her blush and Rena turned away. Randy Fletcher chuckled and closed his eyes. There was no denying he was an attractive man, but his constant wisecracking and use of innuendos spoiled it. Of all possible seatmates, why him?

As they drew near their destination, the pilot dipped the wings and called the attention of the passengers to Pearl Harbor. Rena felt the familiar excitement she always did before a landing.

The moist, warm air of the tropics rushed to meet her as she stepped from the plane. Tour groups were being met with leis and laughter, making Rena wish there was someone meeting her.

"Well, here we are."

Rena turned to find Fletcher standing beside her as they waited to claim their baggage. "I love it here."

"I've worked here and I have to admit it was profitable."

"Oh, where?"

"Various hotels, but that was years ago." He grabbed his suitcase and smiled. "Well, I'm off. Enjoy your vacation."

"I intend to." Her own bag took its time getting off the plane and she was beginning to wonder if it had gone somewhere else when it finally appeared. Most of the other luggage had been claimed so she no longer had a crowd to fight as she carried her one suitcase and tote bag to the nearest telephone booth. Impulsive as her trip had been, she decided she'd best check with Bryan's Honolulu office before trying to book a flight to Kauai—just in case someone else was using the house at the moment. She never expected to connect with Bryan himself.

"Rena!" He sounded genuinely glad to hear from her. "Are you on the island?"

"At the airport. I just arrived."

"Why didn't you let me know you were coming?"

"Because I didn't know myself until the wee, small hours. I was just lucky to call for a reservation directly on the heels of a cancellation."

"Where are you staying?"

"Is the offer to use your beach house still open?"

"Definitely. The place hasn't been used in months. I'd be glad to have you there for a while."

"If I were you and lived this close I'd be over there every weekend." She could have bit her tongue, but the words were out and it was too late. "I'm sorry, Bryan. I forgot." But how could she forget Bryan and Shay had ended their marriage during a hectic week at his Kauai estate.

"Don't apologize. I don't go there any more than I have to because of the unpleasant memories, but I can't bear to part with it because of all the happy ones. How is Shay, by the way?"

"She sends her love."

"You don't make a very good liar, Rena."

"Bryan, I'm not lying. That's the last thing she said to me before I left."

"Tell me, is there anyone new in her life?"

"She's still very much on her own. How about you?"

"Too busy. The reason I lost her in the first place." A heavy sigh punctuated his sentence.

"Why don't you take the time to call her?"

"Shay has no desire to hear from me, Rena. Remember, she's the one who ended the marriage."

Rena decided to take a chance in an effort to get two of her favorite people back together. "Perhaps she just wanted to get your attention."

"If I believed that, I'd fly over to Seattle and wring her lovely neck. But I'm a workaholic and there was the problem. How about you? Still appraising lovely gems?"

"I work at it."

"I thought Mitch might talk you into participating in this crazy treasure hunt set up by Hugh Dressler."

"He tried, but I declined."

"Still running away from the obvious fact you're crazy about Mitch and he's not totally oblivious to you?"

"It would never work, Bryan."

"I think you're wrong, but then who am I to give anyone advice? If you're at the house for any length of time maybe I'll fly over."

"That would be great." And it would be. Rena had a soft spot for her former brother-in-law. "Well, I'd best see about getting a flight to Kauai."

"If you can't make connections give me a call."

"Thanks, I may do that."

Luck was again with her and she found a seat on the next plane to Kauai. Soon she was disembarking on the garden isle of Hawaii. Warm, floral-scented winds brushed against her and she filled her lungs with their sweetness. Was there ever anything so good for the soul as the peacefulness of a

tropical isle? Rena again claimed her luggage and was going in search of a
taxi when a smiling Hawaiian approached her.

"Rena Drake?"

"Yes."

"Mr. Windsor called and asked me to meet you. I'm Carl, the caretaker."

"Fantastic, I was just going in search of a taxi to take me to the house."

It took only a little while to drive to Bryan's place. Secluded among lush
vegetation, it still had a sweeping view of the South Pacific.

Carl held the door for her and effortlessly hoisted her suitcase onto his
shoulder. She was glad to let him do it because her own arm ached from
carrying it around. Orchids were streamers of color among the green fo-
liage. She positively yearned to stretch out in the sun.

The cottage wasn't overly large, but roomy enough for several people to
stay without getting in each other's way. Wicker furniture was filled with
bright floral print cushions and huge vases were filled with flowers.

Carl deposited her bags in one of the bedrooms and again appeared. "Is
there anything I can do for you before I call it a day? I've stocked the
refrigerator with fresh fruit and sweet bread in the cupboard."

"Thank you. I really appreciate that."

"No problem. Mr. Windsor told me what you liked and I was able to get
it at the store not far from here."

"Thanks."

His car drove away and then everything was silent. She hadn't eaten all
day, since airplane food invariably didn't agree with her, and the thought of
fresh fruit was enticing. Intending to indulge in a perfect orgy of mangoes,
guavas, and fresh pineapple, Rena heaped a plate high and then sliced off
two thick wedges of yummy bread. Bless Bryan, he did remember what she
liked. Both he and Mitch had that talent.

An image of Mitch floated to the surface of her mind as she carried her
dinner to the lanai. Seattle seemed far away and she could daydream about
Mitch now that she was a safe distance from his charms.

As she nibbled on a slice of pineapple, Rena thought back to her father
and the original reason she'd studied to be a gemologist. Those damned
LaSalle jewels. Her father had said appraising them would make a difference in his career. How right he'd been. They'd ended it. She'd watched
him as he worked, and he'd pointed out to her how uniquely some of the
stones were cut. There'd been one necklace of pearls and diamonds that was
utterly special. Remembering, she closed her eyes, then sat bolt upright.

That was where she'd seen the stone in Randy Fletcher's ring. It had
once been a part of the LaSalle necklace. She was positive. No wonder she'd

been struck by its haunting familiarity. Where had he come by it? She didn't believe for a minute that he'd picked it up in a pawnshop.

Here was the clue she'd been searching the world for. But where was Randy Fletcher headed? The only way she could track him was to be a part of the treasure hunt. Suddenly her appointment in Scotland was no longer of primary importance. Randy Fletcher had said Mitch would do anything to obtain a share of the Dressler Collection. Well, she would do anything to clear her father's name.

Her meal forgotten, Rena flew inside and placed a call to Seattle, praying that Mitch would answer the phone himself, drumming her fingers against the table until he did. When she heard his voice she knew her luck was holding.

"Mitch, it's Rena. Am I too late to change my mind?"

CHAPTER 3

Rena held the phone to her ear for an eternity of moments after Mitch hung up. Then she let the receiver slide from her hand. She'd flown thousands of miles to escape her love for Mitch, only to call him and cast herself voluntarily back into the sphere of his influence.

Unnerved by what lay ahead, Rena began pacing the floor of the now-shadowed living room. Belatedly agreeing to take part in Dressler's treasure hunt was probably a mistake. How else would she keep tabs on Randy Fletcher?

Identifying the flashy diamond he wore had been almost a fluke. No, she'd identified it because of her fantastic memory when it came to gems and gemstones. Once handled and studied, gems were filed away in her memory. Now, would he lead her to the source, or was he the source himself?

The carpet was velvety as she walked to the picture window that allowed a sweeping view of the horizon. Ribbons of color slashed the clouds banked above the ocean as night hovered and waited to settle in. How long would it take Mitch to arrive? How long before the lion entered her den?

Having never desired great wealth, Rena found the responsibilities accompanying it almost overwhelming. Even if she stood a chance of becoming a part of Mitch's life, she doubted her ability to adjust any better than Shay had adjusted to Bryan's. But that didn't stop her from loving him even though he apparently loved someone else.

Rena's midnight hair fell forward across her face as she bowed her head against the anguish of knowing she'd never have the only man she'd ever wanted.

Once they were together again, she would concentrate on solving the clues to the Dressler treasures. That way she could keep track of Randy Fletcher and at the same time give Mitch his money's worth. She was positive Randy had unwittingly presented her with the first solid lead to the long-missing LaSalle jewels. She didn't believe his story of finding the ring in a Reno pawnshop any more than she believed the role he was playing. Instinct—the sixth sense Mitch was so fond of—warned her the Randy Fletcher persona was at least partly facade. He knew more than he was telling, but the only way she knew to prove it was by getting close to him. And the only way to do that was by accepting the challenge presented by the Dressler treasure hunt.

The sun had relinquished its tenuous hold to the night as Rena turned away from the window. She was conscious of the silence and the aloneness of Bryan's beach house.

But she was used to being alone and on her own. Just as she was used to loving a man who for a variety of reasons could never be hers.

Rena made herself a pot of Kona coffee and carried it over to the television set where she stayed until her eyelids began to droop.

Discarding her clothes, she took a quick shower and slipped into a sheer nightgown. The sheets on the bed smelled faintly of lavender and the muted sound of the not-so-faraway sea lulled her into complete relaxation.

Rena was almost asleep when she heard a sound. She sat up abruptly, sending her senses spinning. There it was again, a noise coming from near the front of the house. Had she remembered to lock all the doors?

There wasn't a phone in her room, so she slipped quietly from the bed and walked into the living room. Moonlight illuminated the house. She was opposite the front door when she decided to turn on the entry light. Her fingers hovered by the switch as the front door swung inward. It was difficult to say who was the more startled, she or Mitch.

"What are you doing here?"

"You invited me, remember?"

Rena pushed back her rain of midnight hair and pulled up the flimsy strap of her nightgown. "I know, but I never ever expected you so soon."

"I thought I'd best get over here before you changed your mind."

She was tempted to say, *How wise.* But being equally wise, she didn't.

"Well, aren't you going to invite me in?"

"Oh, I'm sorry. Of course, come in. But tell me, where did you get the key?"

"I had the foresight to stop by Shay's before leaving Seattle. I was sure I'd arrive while you were asleep and I didn't want to have to wake you."

"You didn't stop to think you might give me heart failure when I awoke to find I wasn't alone?"

"I wasn't planning on being in the same bed."

"Well . . ." and she stumbled over a retort. "I didn't think you would be. You know what I meant."

Mitch tossed his jacket over a nearby chair and Rena switched on the light. Immediately, she noticed the dark circles under his eyes and the wrinkles in his shirt, and she felt guilty that he'd felt so unsure of her he'd flown instantly to her side before she could change her mind. Did this Dressler business mean that much to him? She felt a little twinge of conscience to be using him in this way, and again resolved to keep an eye on Fletcher but not at Mitch's expense. She would claim at least one of the treasures for him as she pursued her own interests.

"It was a long flight, but I must say you are literally a welcome sight for weary eyes."

Glancing down, Rena was jolted into recalling that she wasn't really dressed for company, except of the most intimate kind. Hastily she tried to explain. "I thought you were a burglar. I was on my way to the phone when you walked in."

"Lucky for me I finally got the key to work." His glance traveled lazily over her, making her very aware her nightgown was sheer and more than a little on the skimpy side. Friends had no reason to be self-conscious about their state of dress or undress. Still, she turned away to break the confusing emotionalism of their gaze. "Can I fix you anything to eat?"

"No, just point me in the direction of a comfortable bed."

"That I can do. This place has five bedrooms. You can have your pick."

"Oh, really? Any of the five?"

He had to be teasing her. "Any of the five, minus one."

"Somehow I knew you'd say that. Where's your spirit of adventure?"

"Safely stored with my sense of self-preservation. Anyway, don't be silly."

"Who's being silly?"

I am, she told herself. *For even considering you might be serious.*

She stood aside, suddenly chilled as he brushed past her. What would he do or say if she had the foolish courage to ask him to warm her? "Will this room do?"

"Perfect, although it really wouldn't matter if the room held a bed. I'm beat."

Rena watched him, her arms folded protectively across her breasts.

"Can I get you anything else?"

"Just a good night's sleep."

"Then I'd best leave you alone." She turned toward the doorway and was almost safely through it when he called to her.

"Rena—" There was a definite hesitancy—an unsureness.

"Yes?" Rena knew she did not imagine that his gaze lingered, caressed, and enjoyed the scarcely covered outlines of her body. Her heart and her breath both seemed lodged in her throat, unable to move in either direction or to resume their normal functions. Then he looked away and his shoulders sagged from exhaustion.

"Nothing, I'll see you in the morning."

"Night." Her bed was a secure haven, but she tossed and turned most of the remaining hours before dawn.

Once the amber glow of morning began to feather the sky, Rena forced herself groggily out of bed. Mitch's early arrival had been unexpected and she'd been unable to relax knowing he was just down the hall. As many years as she'd known him, they'd never spent a night under the same roof. Now she had a whole day to get through and her body felt like lead.

Rena wandered into the bathroom and splashed cold water on her face. Its stinging chill was reality, just as much as the fact she was going to have to deal with Mitch several hours sooner than expected.

It had been ages since she'd started her day with a brisk run. Pulling on yellow shorts and matching tank top, securing her long dark hair with a very unglamorous rubber band, she was ready.

As she slipped outside, she closed the door as quietly behind her as possible. The longer Mitch slept, the longer she had for peace of mind. Rena headed for the tortuous path to the beach. Vegetation had almost taken over in places, making the footholds hard to find. She could hear the ocean and pushing aside a tall plant she couldn't identify, Rena jumped down to the sand. She had the beach to herself. Good, that was the way she liked it.

That's why the beach house on Kauai was so perfect for her. It allowed freedom and solitude in one of the most beautiful spots she could imagine. There was little solitude in Mitch's life—little freedom from the crowds.

Balmy breezes released the fragrance of exotic flowers. Waves hissing and exploding against the sand were the shade of aquamarine, so prized in ancient times for having captured the mystical hue of the sea.

Perspiration beaded her skin and her breathing had been reduced to ragged bursts when she finally stopped running. Collapsing to the sand, Rena rested her head on her knees.

Too tired to move, she let a shallow wave wash around her. How surprised she'd been the first time she'd discovered the warmth of the ocean around Hawaii. Having grown up by the chilly waters of Puget Sound, she hadn't realized that tropical waters held the warmth of the sun. Not that she minded the sometimes blue, often gray seas of home, particularly when they were whipped to a pewter frenzy by winter storms. Then she would dress warmly, prowl the shore, and many times wonder what the winter storms were like in Mitch's house on the hill above the city.

Rena pulled the rubber band from her hair, snapping herself in the process. Removing her already wet shoes, she stuffed her soggy socks into the toes and tied the laces together so she could fling them over her shoulder. Then she waded into the inviting curl of the waves and turned back the way she'd come.

The brightness of the morning sun forced her to squint and shade her eyes with her hand, but there was no mistaking she now shared the beach. A faraway figure moved toward her, but even if there'd been a wall between them she would have known Mitch was near. Something she couldn't understand or fight lay deep within her and was attuned to him.

Slowly, she raised the guard she hid behind in his presence. He must never suspect how much she cared for him. Especially not now when she held the first clue to the fate of the LaSalle diamonds in the palm of her hand. Nothing must interfere with solving the mystery of what had happened to them. To clear her father's name, Rena was prepared to risk her own heart.

Sunlight caught in Mitch's hair, bringing out the sherry color that reminded her of topaz mined in Brazil. He wore white casual pants rolled to below the knees and walked barefoot in the surf that lapped around his ankles. How Rena wished she could touch him with the same caressing abandon. His blue chambray shirt was open to reveal a sun-bronzed chest and Rena wondered if anyone seeing this early morning beachcomber would suspect he controlled an empire worth more millions than many people could count.

She stopped, waiting for him to cover the rest of the distance. What would she do with Mitch's love if a miracle happened and it were hers? Weren't their worlds too different?

The distance between them breached, Mitch stood facing her. "I suspected I'd find you on the beach."

Rena smiled and threaded her fingers through the tangles of her windswept hair. "Just working out the early morning kinks."

His gaze swept the length of her, touching her senses with a fire as deep as any burning in the finest opals. She was reminded of his ability to make each individual feel special. She mustn't misinterpret his attentions.

He tucked her arm through his and then laced his fingers with hers. Rena's heart tugged with the sweetness of the gesture.

"Have you ever been to Bryan's beach house before?"

"No, but I take it you have."

"He allows me to use it, yes. For which I'm thankful. Sometimes I need to get away and I can't always afford the price of a hotel."

"You're always welcome to my condo on Maui."

What good would that do her when she was fleeing from an overdose of his company?

"Of course I'm the first to admit it can't compare with this place."

He'd saved her the need for a reply she couldn't summon. "It was Shay's favorite. She felt she could be herself here."

"Why should she have difficulty in being herself? Everyone knew their marriage was a love match. Shay had absolutely nothing to do except love Bryan."

Many times in the past Mitch had made it plain he found Shay's behavior puzzling.

"Sometimes love isn't enough."

"It's a damn good starting point."

"Perhaps if Bryan could have torn himself away from work a little more often their marriage would have worked. Shay was left alone too much."

"Isn't Shay alone now? Only the prospect of Bryan ever coming home is missing."

Rena thought of Shay's small apartment, nine-to-five job, and limited social life. "Yes." She hoped he wouldn't ask if her sister was happy.

"You know, I've often wondered at something."

Brushing aside a strand of wind-whipped hair Rena queried, "What?"

"Why is it some women will do anything to snare a man with money and others will run as fast as they can from the same situation?"

His fingers tightened around hers, jumbling her thoughts and emotions. Otherwise she might not have spoken the truth. "I suppose in some instances they're afraid."

"Afraid? Of what?"

"Of not fitting into a life-style most people only dream about."

"What a waste of good years when two people could be together doing what two people who love one another do best."

There was no mistaking the meaning behind his words. They were said in an offhand manner, but that didn't dim a mental picture of lovers entwined. Rena turned away hoping he wouldn't notice the color staining her cheeks. The image branding itself on her memory was the two of them; his fingers threaded through her hair, his lips bruising hers with desire.

Rena tried being flippant in an effort at clearing her own restless thoughts. "You sound more like a romantic than a hardheaded business-man."

"I know I can succeed as the latter, but I seem constantly frustrated in my attempts to bring a little romance into my life."

"What about your fiancée?"

His hand tightened on hers. "That state is purely a figment of my imagi-nation. I have yet to persuade her."

"Surely there's no problem?"

His sea-colored eyes were enigmatic. "Maybe she doesn't like money."

"Come on, Mitch, be serious. If you've found someone to love," Rena wondered how she kept from choking on the words, "then don't give up trying to persuade her to marry you."

"That's your advice, is it?"

"Yes, don't give up on something—or someone—you want."

Mitch pulled her close against his side in a friendly hug and Rena tried to swallow her thudding heart. How could the woman he loved resist him when his slightest touch sent her senses soaring? She seriously doubted her powers of resistance should he ever turn to her with love. It was easy to hold fast to supposed ideals when those same ideals weren't in jeopardy.

"Rena, what made you change your mind about the hunt? I admit I was surprised, especially when you told me where you were calling from. That's why I didn't waste any time in getting over here. I was afraid you'd recon-sider again."

"No, I'm in this to the end, now."

"But why? You were so against it."

Rena was tempted to confide in him, but then thought better of it. If she was about to embark on another wild-goose chase, then she'd as soon no one else knew about it. "I simply couldn't resist the lure. Did you bring the clues with you?"

"The starting one, I did."

"Why not the others?"

He shrugged. "One clue at a time. That's the rules."

"The whole thing quite literally boggles my mind."

"Don't let it. Simply look on it as the game it's intended to be."

"How can I when the highest stakes I've ever played for were during Monopoly and then the money wasn't real. It doesn't take a deck of for-tune-telling cards to know you've never been broke."

"Maybe I'm just a good poker player."

"Come, Mitch, you don't bluff with half a million."

"You might be surprised at the stakes."

"After seeing the line of people waiting to throw their money away on a chance at this treasure hunt, nothing would surprise me. Now tell me, have you looked at the clue?"

"No, it's in a sealed envelope and I was going to let you have first chance at it."

"I told you I wasn't very good at such things! You're going to be the brains on this job, I'm along as technical adviser."

"I'm not worried. Your knowledge of gems will give us an edge."

Rena hoped he was right, but a knot of panic clutched at her stomach and refused to let go.

They started up the steep, volcanic rock path, with Mitch going first and pulling her up behind him. She hoped he would be as much help with the clue. Rena was very much afraid she was going to regret the awesome responsibility she'd taken on in an effort to pursue her own goals.

Level ground finally reached, Mitch released his hold on her and Rena felt suddenly abandoned. How was she going to handle it when he settled down with the woman he loved?

"Do you want to go out for some breakfast?"

"There's plenty of food here if you don't mind."

"No, whatever you want."

Rena suppressed the urge to say what she wanted would shock him. "I can easily fix something and we can ponder the clue while we eat. I don't suppose we should waste any time."

Rena busied herself with pulling a variety of fresh fruit from the refrigerator and piling it on the counter. "There's some Hawaiian sweet bread on the counter. You can slice it if you want."

"You mean I have to work for my breakfast?"

"Would you rather sing?"

"I think we'd both be in trouble if I did."

Rena began cutting up an assortment of fruit and slicing some cheese. "Tell me, how did you get here as quickly as you did?"

"Have you forgotten, I keep my private jet ready to go anywhere at a moment's notice."

She paused midway in slicing some pineapple. "I had forgotten." Just as she'd forgotten how his shirt pulled across the muscles of his back and how the morning sun spun skeins of gold in his hair. Her thoughts were running away with her common sense when the caretaker appeared in the doorway.

"Good morning, do you want me to pick up anything at the store?"

Rena glanced at Mitch. "I don't think we'll be staying, so what's here is fine—thanks."

"Then I'll make up the bed and be on my way."

Bed? Did Carl assume they'd shared the same room? An immediate look of chagrin crossed her face and Mitch didn't miss it.

"Don't worry, Rena. You've made it very clear how you feel about men in my financial bracket. I would never be fool enough to misinterpret otherwise."

CHAPTER 4

Breakfast was strained and Rena sat there crumbling her bread into bird-size pieces. She had hurt Mitch and that was the last thing she ever wanted to do. Her appetite was spoiled and the only thing at the table besides Mitch that held any appeal for her was the steaming Kona coffee. Somehow she managed to pour herself a fresh cupful without spilling any on the white tablecloth.

Rena ran her finger around the gold rim of the Limoges cup. Fragile as it was, it nevertheless felt heavy in her hands—just as regret lay heavy in her chest. In trying to hide her true feelings, she had hurt the only man she'd ever loved. How, other than bringing home first prize, could she make it up to him?

"Mitch, let's have a look at that first clue. I have a feeling we've already wasted precious hours." He couldn't know appearances suggested Randy Fletcher had over a twenty-four-hour head start.

Mitch pulled the sealed envelope from his pocket, slitting it open with a gold penknife. Then he extracted a heavily embossed card and handed it to her.

"Don't you want to read it first?"

"You're the gemologist."

Again she tried to conrol the panic arising every time she thought of the costly enormity of the task facing them. "But you promised to help with the clues. I'm only along to make certain you aren't fooled by any clever fakes."

"You're along for a lot more reasons than that."

She was relieved to see him scan the raised gold lettering on the card. "Well?"

"See for yourself." And he nonchalantly tossed the card across to her.

Rena grabbed for it and missed. It landed face side down on the fruit platter. Retrieving it, she wiped it off with her napkin and felt her heart thud almost uncomfortably as she read the two scant lines of engraving.

"Afloat in a fragrant sea
Are butterflies here really free?"

The rhyme was harder than she'd even anticipated. Slowly, she raised troubled eyes to query Mitch. "Oh, Mitch, how will we ever figure this out?"

He reached across the table and took the clue from her unresisting fingers. "Difficult, but not impossible. I don't admit to that word."

Rena almost glared at him. "Of course nothing would seem impossible to you. You were born with the world at your doorstep." The words were unfair, but Rena's nerves were too tightly wound for her to care.

"You really believe that, do you?"

His unwavering stare made Rena decidedly uncomfortable and the tone of his voice made her defensive. "It's certainly the impression you give."

"Perhaps I prefer to carry my own burdens—silently."

"Are you implying I don't?"

"Well, what would you call your repeated assertion that you can't even think of settling down until you clear your father's name? Couldn't you have quietly done that while living your own life? You're going to wake up one day and find that the bloom in your cheeks is no longer natural and that firelight picks out the silver in your hair as well as the ebony. Maybe then you'll realize what a lonely quest you've set yourself."

Rena was tempted to say she didn't take time-out to care for anyone because he was the only man she cared for. She could imagine his shocked embarrassment if she did, as well as his mumbled explanation that he was flattered, but his affections were already engaged.

"We do what we feel we have to."

Mitch didn't speak for an uncomfortably long time. When he did, his words were accompanied by an almost amiable grin. "You're right, we do. And at the moment we have to solve the riddle of clue number one. The stakes are enormous, therefore we can't expect things to be easy."

"I'd at least like to feel I stood a chance."

She looked again at the enigmatic words worth so much. Regardless of what Mitch said, it seemed almost hopeless. Then an idea popped into her head. She opened her mouth to speak and then thought better of it. Mitch didn't miss it however.

"You were going to say something?"

"No, it's almost too obvious."

"Maybe that's the whole idea."

"All right. I have no idea what the first line refers to, but I wonder if maybe the butterfly mentioned could be the jade butterfly in the collection."

"Your solution isn't quite as obvious as you seem to think. I had totally forgotten the jade until you mentioned it. I'm afraid it didn't leave much of an impression."

"I know you've never been interested in collecting jade. I think the value of this piece lies chiefly in its antiquity. I'm quite positive it's archaic."

"Does that mean what I think?"

"If you're thinking it's very, very old. There's a legend surrounding the butterfly which has led to its becoming a symbol for lovers. I found it exquisite."

"Then it would please you if we found the butterfly before anyone else?"

"Of course it would please me! Then perhaps I would feel deserving of the faith you have in me." But she wondered if they stood much of a chance being first to the prize.

Mitch dismissed her worries with a decisive gesture. "I wish you'd quit worrying about that. I've needed this change of pace."

"Is something wrong?" Surely he wasn't having some kind of health problem?

He hastened to reassure her. "No, I simply needed some time away from the business. Being self-employed can eat you alive if you let it. It's not the best of all possible worlds some people think."

Rena rested her elbows on the table. "You could always sell out."

"And have my grandfather not only turn over in his grave, but come back to haunt me? No thanks. I imagine I'll die at the helm just as he did."

Rena hoped that wouldn't be for a long time. "If that's what you want."

"Haven't you discovered, Rena, that rarely do any of us get exactly what we want?"

Their glances met, held, and then Rena's backed off. What exactly was he referring to? People didn't always get what they wanted, but Rena was not going to let that stop her. She would find the LaSalle diamonds and the thief who had stolen them, ruining her father's reputation. She wouldn't stop until she had.

"Is there supposed to be a message in there for me?"

His expression was one of surprise. "Most definitely not. It was a reminder to myself."

"What could you possibly want that you don't have?"

The expression in his eyes was one of regret. "It's an old cliché, but money does not buy happiness."

"You seem happy enough. Don't tell me you're haboring some unfulfilled longings and desires?"

"If I had everything, would I be here now?"

"Oh, yes, how could I have forgotten your desire to own part of the Dressler Collection."

Mitch sighed heavily. "Of course, why else would I come all this way? We must concentrate on the jade butterfly and where she's lit."

"She?" Rena deliberately made her tone teasing.

His smile was again the easy one she loved. "Aren't all elusive creatures female?"

"Not necessarily. I've known some men you couldn't pin down or figure out if you worked from a maintenance manual."

"Perhaps that's because you're not reading between the lines."

"Should I have to?"

He concentrated a minute. "No, probably not."

Rena began stacking the dishes and he moved to help her. "That's okay, I can manage. Too bad Dressler didn't come with a maintenance manual. Maybe if we knew a little more about him than the fact he's a recluse, we might know what the clue meant."

"You have a good idea there. Dressler isn't quite the recluse everyone thinks. A very private person, yes, but he does occasionally venture out. He's also very egocentric, and if I remember correctly, he commissioned someone to write his biography a number of years back. If we could find one it might be of help."

Rena brightened. "It's certainly worth a try. Do you suppose the library in Honolulu has a copy?"

"I'll call. Maybe I can find something out."

The kitchen was quickly slicked up and Mitch was still on the telephone. Not wanting to interrupt, Rena decided to change as she still wore her running clothes. Glancing longingly at the bathtub, she settled on a quick shower. Flipping on the faucets, she waited for the water to warm up and stripped out of her clothes.

Stepping into the shower, Rena gasped as the almost too hot water hit her. Quickly, she adjusted the temperature and began lathering with a heavenly-smelling bar of herbal soap. She sniffed it, promptly got some bubbles in her nose, and sneezed.

"Gesundheit!"

Startled, the bar of soap slipped easily from her hand. She glanced quickly at the frosted glass in the shower door and then relaxed. "I didn't realize you were out there." Her tone implied he should have warned her.

"Thought you might like to hear what I found out."

She stood on tiptoe so she could peer over the top of the glass. "Good news?"

"Could be." He lounged against the open doorway and grinned at her.

"Come on, don't tease me. I want to know."

"A Dressler biography exists. I was able to verify it through a book collector friend. Finding a copy might be a little more difficult."

"Did you call the library?"

"Yes, but they'd never heard of it. Which isn't so surprising. Dressler is undoubtedly the most private and least-known billionaire on the block."

"Is he really worth that much?"

"Easily."

"How does he manage to keep it a secret?"

"The only glamorous part of Dresser is his collection. Since he doesn't surround himself with beautiful women anxious for a piece of the pie, he isn't very newsworthy." Then he added, deliberately feigning a leering tone of voice, "Speaking of beautiful women—would you like me to scrub your back?"

Rena was extremely glad there was no way he could detect the heated blush spreading over her entire body. The thought of him in the shower with her was—well, not to be considered. "Aren't we getting off the subject?"

"A little diversion never hurt, did it?"

"I'm going to ignore that. If you won't tend to business I will—and I'm sure the rest of the contestants have their bloodhounds out. There will be time enough for diversion when we're holding the prize."

"Is that a promise?"

It was ridiculous for her foolish heart to leap as it did. Mitch was only kidding—and that's exactly the kind of answer she'd return. "Whatever you want. After all, you're the boss."

"I'm not going to forget you said that."

"Oh, oh!" Would he suspect her dismay was not feigned? Quickly, she returned the conversation to business. "Do you suppose we could find a copy of Dressler's biography in a used-book store?"

"I was going to suggest flying over to Honolulu, although I don't think we should pin any serious hopes on finding a copy."

"Probably not, but I feel helpless to figure out what is meant by 'Afloat in a fragrant sea.' "

"You and me both. I've a few loose ends to tie up so if you don't mind, I'll take care of business while you look for Dressler's biography. Then we'll meet for a late lunch."

"Okay."

"Can you be ready in an hour, or would you like some help?"

"I can manage on my own, thank you. Once you're engaged officially, Mitch, you're going to have to stop flirting with the help."

"I'm only trying to be helpful. Especially since I think we need to be on our way as soon as possible."

"I'm hurrying."

"Then I expect I'll see you ready and waiting before long."

Rena heard the door close behind him. Only then did she turn off the water. Briskly, she toweled dry.

The day was already warm as she slipped on a minimum of underwear and a sundress that left her shoulders bare. The print was a wild profusion of brightly colored flowers that probably didn't exist outside the designer's imagination. But it was colorful and cool.

While she struggled to remove the tangles from her wet hair, Rena glanced over at the shower. The brush slipped from her hand and clattered noisily into the sink. The shower door was not quite as opaque as she'd thought. True, you could only see the dim outline of the faucets, but you *could* see them. Wait until she got ahold of Mitchell Johns!

Rena brushed her hair and then twisted it up in a secure knot atop her head. Next, she deftly applied the light touches of makeup she was accustomed to, concentrating most of her efforts on her eyes. Hopefully, people would notice them and not the fact her face was a little rounder than she would have liked.

Now to find Mitch and give him a piece of her mind. He wasn't hard to track down.

The lanai was surrounded by flowers. Notably the royal poinciana trees which were at their flaming best. Much of the plumeria too was in bloom, filling the air with the sweetest of scents. Mitch waited comfortably and sipped a delicious-looking drink.

"That's not one of those rum concoctions guaranteed to knock you for a loop when you least expect it, is it?"

He glanced in her direction and his glance lingered. "Guilty to a degree, except I left out the rum. You know that bit about waiting until the sun is over the yardarm."

"Can I have a sip?"

"Be my guest."

She took a long drink, closed her eyes in appreciation, and ran her tongue over her lips. "Umm!"

"If that's what you call a sip I'd hate to see you take a drink."

"I was thirsty and it tasted good."

"I would never have guessed."

Rena noticed rather than turning the glass back around to the side he'd been drinking from that he resumed drinking from the side she'd used. Was it deliberate, or didn't he think? It was an intimate gesture that sent chills of delight down her back.

Surely it wasn't deliberate! She mustn't even think like that. But she was shocked at how the idea excited her. How many times would she have to remind herself they were together for business and not pleasure? Which reminded her there was a score to settle. "By the way, when did you develop a yen to be a Peeping Tom?"

He choked and looked up. "What the hell are you talking about?"

"I don't recall inviting you into my shower."

"No, I don't either. Did I miss something?"

"On the contrary, you must have gotten an eyeful."

There wasn't one ounce of shame in the grin he flashed her. "You didn't complain at the time."

"I wasn't aware of the view offered."

"Well, don't let it bother you. Any secrets you might have are still safe—with you."

"What do you mean?"

"All I could see, except for the very top of your head, was the vaguest of outlines. Not even the most easily pleased of Peeping Toms would have been satisfied. So erase those frown lines."

"Then you do the same thing with that look of seedy speculation!"

Mitch shook with honest laughter. "Seedy speculation? That's a new one. Actually, I thought my lurid imaginings were rather high-class."

Rena grabbed a pillow from a nearby lounge and threw it at him.

She purposely used clipped tones for her next statement. "Shouldn't we be leaving?"

"Probably, although I think I could stay here forever." He raked her with a glance that left her toes tingling and forced her to remind herself it was only part of the game they played. "Do you intend to go barefoot?"

Rena glanced down. "I guess I'd better get some sandals on. It seems so natural to go sans shoes when I'm at the beach. I'll only be another minute."

Rena was as good as her word, digging flimsy sandals from her suitcase and slipping them on. Then she took a minute longer to stuff her over-sized purse with everything she thought she might need for the day.

Mitch waited by the open door and they walked together to a small car. He held the door for her and then climbed in and started the engine. "Not very roomy, but certainly maneuverable."

"It's fine. I like being able to rest my chin on my knees without having to move."

"It has its advantages—doesn't it?"

"I'll try to think of one." The miles sped by and they practically had the road to themselves. "You know, I sometimes wonder where all the people go who pile off the airplanes. Except for Oahu there's very little traffic."

"I know what you mean. I imagine they're all where I'd like to be."

"Which is?"

"Stretched out somewhere in the sun."

"Well, promise yourself a trip to an island paradise once we've cornered all of Dressler's little hidden baubles."

"You're certainly confident now. What happened?"

"What do you mean—what happened?"

"You weren't feeling very positive at breakfast."

"No, I wasn't, but I'm practicing positive thinking—visualizing that gorgeous butterfly resting on the palm of my hand."

"You really like it, don't you?"

"Yes, it was exquisite."

"A romantic taking to a symbol of romance. Perhaps in another lifetime you were the butterfly you told me about."

"If that's the case, do you think my present form shows much progress?" Her tone was teasing.

Treating her to a glance capable of scorching the upholstery, he retorted, "Most definitely."

His response left her speechless—or almost. "Watch the road, please."

Reluctantly he turned his gaze back to the highway. "If you insist."

"How long do you anticipate your business will take?"

"A couple of hours."

"If I run out of used-book stores I can always go shopping."

"You'd be deliriously happy in Hong Kong."

"Good shopping, huh?"

"And duty-free."

They reached the airport at Lihue and parked the car. Mitch glanced her way as he turned off the ignition. "I imagine we'll be back tonight, don't you?"

"Even if we find some marvelous lead I don't think we'd be ready to go immediately."

"Then I won't turn the car in."

Mitch took her arm as they entered the airport. Rena looked casually around and smiled. "I love this airport."

"Why?"

"Because when I land and discover I'm surrounded by sugarcane fields I really get the feeling I'm someplace exotic. You experience that sense of excitement leading to adventure."

"I don't think there's any doubt we're embarking on one."

They boarded the plane and Mitch gestured, "There's a couple of seats together near the back."

"Fine." She settled by the window, fastened her seat belt, and looked out at the cane fields.

Once the plane was in the air Rena turned to him. "Why aren't we taking your plane?"

"I sent it back to Seattle."

"You did?"

"I thought it would be easier to take commercial flights as well as being a little less obvious."

"You're probably right. Even at the busiest airport a private jet is a little difficult to overlook."

Twenty-seven minutes later they landed at Honolulu International.

Rena hurried along behind Mitch, thoroughly enjoying the heady atmosphere of an international airport. Fragments of different languages drifted above the noise and general hubbub. She relished speculating where they might come from and whether or not the riddle weighing so heavily on her shoulders might not be quite simple to them.

Mitch found an unoccupied corner where they would be out of the way. "We can take a taxi into town and I'll drop you off. Maybe the driver will know of a secondhand bookstore to get you started."

"Where and when should we meet later?"

He named a well-known restaurant offering a terrific view of the city and harbor. "I think I can have everything wrapped up by five-thirty. Sound good?"

Rena nodded. "I'll see if I can find anything to help us."

"Then let's find a taxi and be on our way."

Traffic was heavy as their driver threaded his way a little too daringly for Rena through a steady stream of cars. But he did know of a used-book store where he and Mitch dropped Rena. She waited on the sidewalk until they drove out of sight, then turned to enter a shop that was like looking into a dark tunnel. Once her eyes had adjusted to the dimness she saw it was well stocked and organized by category.

The smell of old books hung cloyingly in the air and Rena wrinkled her nose as she stepped down into the shop which was below sidewalk level. She appeared to be the only customer. In fact, for a while, she seemed to be the only person in the shop. Then a shuffling sounded from the back.

A bearded young man in sandals and an overly vivid Hawaiian shirt greeted her with a smile. "What can I do for you?"

"I'm looking for a specific book. I suspect it might be like locating a needle in a haystack."

"Maybe I can help. As you see, we've a good-sized stock." And with an expansive gesture he indicated the room which was filled with thousands of books.

"I'm looking for a volume that might even have been self-published."

"You'd be surprised how many of those find their way here." He smiled at her helpfully. "Why don't you just tell me what it is?"

Rena took a deep breath and then wished she hadn't as the dust of old books tickled her nose and made her sneeze. "I'm looking for a biography of Hugh Dressler. He's . . ."

"I know who he was—is, I should say. You must be involved in that crazy treasure hunt he's put together. You're the second person in here today looking for that book."

Her heart literally sank. Even if they'd had a copy the chances of them having two were very slim. But who was here before her?

The attendant of the shop was more than happy to fill her in without even being asked. "A man—tall, rather devil-may-care-looking—wondered if I had such a volume."

"Did you?" The description fit Randy Fletcher too well to mean anyone else.

"No, it was the first I'd heard of it. But I sent him on to another store that specializes in biographies and autobiographies. I can give you the name and address if you like."

"All right, but I don't suppose there's much chance of my finding anything. Locating one copy would be a miracle, finding two would be almost impossible."

"You never know. This woman buys stock from all over."

Rena took the address, but without much optimism. "Thanks, I appreciate your efforts."

"Glad to be of help. Good luck."

Rena muttered to herself once she was out in the sunshine. "I'm going to need it."

The next shop was six blocks away and she decided to walk, wondering all the while if she would run into Randy. But she didn't, and the biography shop was as empty as the first store. The proprietress was sitting up front on a high stool. She reminded Rena of a contented spider as she surveyed her domain.

"Can I help you?"

"I hope so. I'm looking for a biography of Hugh Dressler."

The woman shook her head. "You and the man that left not ten minutes ago. 'Fraid I can't help you."

"Well, I thought it worth a try. There might not even be any of those books around."

"There are—I had one until about three weeks ago. Somebody working for Dressler paid me a lot more than it would ever be worth."

"They did?" Now why, she wondered, would they ever do that unless the book really did contain something useful?

The owner of the shop gave Rena a couple more addresses, but they were some distance away. She decided to find a telephone and call them. It would save time and maybe beat Randy.

Rena headed back toward Waikiki and the big hotels that sprawled along the beachfront. Entering one that was spacious and airy, she located the phone booths and selected one on the end. Then she looked up the numbers of the shops and called inquiring about the biography. Both of them were sorry, but they couldn't help her, though each of them volunteered the information that someone else had also been looking for the same book.

Satisfied Honolulu was a dead end as far as finding a copy of Hugh Dressler's life story, Rena dialed the operator and placed a collect call to Shay. She would settle up with her sister later.

Several times the phone rang across the distance and Rena was about to hang up when her sister answered.

"Where were you?"

"Just coming in the door. How are you?"

"Fine. Probably the most foolish woman you know, but fine."

"Why foolish?"

"Oh, I had a change of heart and Mitch and I are now hot on the trail of Dressler's treasure."

"I assumed that might be the case when he picked up the key to Bryan's place." Shay's pleasure was evident across the miles. "Any luck yet?"

"No. I've been trying to track down a biography Dressler had done aeons ago, but no luck. Seems he made an attempt to get them off the market recently."

"Sounds like they might have been helpful."

"I thought the same thing, but that doesn't do Mitch or me any good. So we're left trying to figure out a cryptic little clue."

"Tell me—maybe I could help."

"If I remember correctly, you always came in first on those dreadful treasure hunts which were all the rage when we were growing up. I'd be forever grateful if this meant anything to you."

"Well, I'm waiting. Try me."

"Afloat in a fragrant sea; Are butterflies here really free?"

Shay's tickled laughter reached across the distance.

"What's so funny?"

"Nothing, really. Have you figured any of it out?"

"I think the butterfly part refers to a jade butterfly in Dressler's collection. But that's as far as we've gotten."

"You know, Rena, perhaps if you shared my taste in reading material you might be a bit more informed."

Rena pictured the stacks of romance novels her sister devoured and wondered how they could possibly be of help in this situation.

"Your silence is very loud, Rena."

"That's because I'm wondering how *Lover's Promise* could help me now."

"It isn't *Lover's Promise*, but *Tomorrow's Promise*. It took place in Hong Kong and the author begins by enlightening the reader that Hong Kong means Fragrant Harbor. I realize harbor and sea aren't quite the same thing, but it might be worth a try."

Like pieces in a puzzle, the clue began to fit together. "Bless you, Shay! Bless the author of *Lover's Promise*. I'll be in touch. Bye."

She barely heard her sister who corrected her for once again mistaking the title. A smile on her face, Rena literally ran to meet Mitch.

CHAPTER 5

The shadows cast by the sun had reshaped themselves several times and still Rena waited for Mitch.

Wondering where he was had taken the edge off her good news and Rena was beginning to feel a bit uncomfortable holding down a table and ordering nothing but soft drinks. She kept assuring the waiter her friend would be arriving any minute and then they would order. But with every passing quarter hour Mitch was making a liar out of her.

It was not characteristic of him to be late, and decidedly uncharacteristic of him not to leave a message for her. Her nerves dangled on finely strung wires when the waiter returned yet again. This time she didn't order a soft drink.

Rena was halfway through her Blue Hawaii when Mitch spoke behind her. "How can you drink anything that color?"

"It matches my mood. Where have you been?"

Mitch eased into the chair opposite her. "There were even more loose ends to tie up than I'd thought. I phoned and left a message. Didn't you get it?"

"No, all I've gotten have been inviting looks from that red-haired man at the bar."

"I think my arrival has discouraged him. He's definitely not smiling now. If you'll excuse me, I'm going to complain about your not receiving the message. There's no excuse for that."

She reached out and caught his arm. "Never mind. It doesn't matter now that you're here."

"Of course it matters. You were undoubtedly uncomfortable and I thought I'd taken care of things so you would at least know why I was late."

"Please, Mitch. It doesn't matter."

He eyed her with a hint of dissatisfaction, but he remained in his chair, although he did glower in the direction of the bar. Rena would have laughed if she hadn't been so keyed up. As it was she almost felt sorry for her flaming-haired admirer.

The waiter approached their table, quite obviously hopeful they intended to order.

"Do you want another of those noxious-looking drinks, or would you rather have dinner?"

"I'd rather have dinner."

"Something exotic or would you prefer a steak?"

"A steak sounds fine."

Mitch ordered the same thing and at last the waiter left them alone. "Well, did your foraging among Honolulu's used-book stores bear any fruit?"

"We did get lucky today."

"You found the book?" His tone more than gave away his surprise.

"You knew as well as I did how slim that chance was. It might interest you to know someone else had the same idea and was a book store ahead of me all the way."

"Who?"

"Who do you think?" As soon as the words were out of her mouth she realized they might not have been wise. After all, Mitch was unlikely to be devoting as much thought to Fletcher as she was.

"I haven't the faintest idea."

"Randy Fletcher." Then she hastily added on, "He's the only contestant besides me that I know. We didn't really circulate that much at the party."

"Because I hadn't seen you in a long time and I didn't want to share you. I wonder how he came up with the idea? I wouldn't have thought Dressler's biography was common knowledge. Do you know if he found a copy?"

"No, Dressler called in all the volumes he could find."

Mitch shifted in his chair. "That suggests the book might have been helpful."

"It more than suggests it, for all the good knowing that does us."

"If you didn't find the book, how did we get lucky?"

"After exhausting the book stores I called Shay. I wanted her to know I would be leaving Kauai and happened to mention what I'd been doing."

"Was she able to help in some way?"

"Definitely, yes! And I couldn't believe the source of her knowledge." With great delight, Rena enlightened him.

His laughter was totally spontaneous and several fellow diners turned in their direction. "It's beautifully simple once you know the answer."

"You don't think it's too simple?"

"No, I think we're on the right trail."

"Will getting into Hong Kong pose much of a problem?"

"Just getting seats on a plane. Our passports will let us stay a month."

Their salads arrived and Rena began savoring the combination of tiny orange slices, almonds, lettuce, and piquant dressing. Then a shadow of doubt obscured her pleasure. "I was so pleased to actually be looking at a solution to the puzzle I completely overlooked something as important."

"What?"

"Where do we go and what do we do once we're in Hong Kong?"

"Perhaps we'll receive another clue once we're there. I don't know if you're aware of it or not, but we're to keep the game masters informed of our whereabouts. So I imagine more information will be forthcoming once we've arrived and checked into a hotel."

"I certainly hope so."

Their steaks arrived cooked perfectly, and for a few minutes they did nothing but enjoy their meal. The hum of surrounding conversation and the clink of crystal were enough background for the moment.

"Can you be ready to leave immediately if I'm able to book us seats on a plane?"

"Sure. I didn't bring much with me and it won't take me long to pack."

"Then if you'll excuse me I'm going to phone the airport and see if I can get us on our way."

Contentedly Rena continued with her meal. She sensed the man standing behind her chair before she actually saw him, and she was prepared for either Mitch or the waiter, but never for Randy Fletcher.

He sat down, uninvited, in a vacant chair. "I've been watching and decided I'd make use of the boyfriend's absence to come over and say hello."

"I don't know why you persistently misunderstand our relationship." His insinuations made her angry.

"No man looks at a friend the way he looks at you."

His persistence goaded her. "Anyway, why should you care, *Mr.* Fletcher?"

"Touché."

"Well, you haven't answered me." She was a little more than curious to find out why Randy Fletcher persistently insisted on a nonexistent relationship between her and Mitch. They were friends—special friends, but Rena knew anything more existed only in her dreams.

"Because," and he curved his hand familiarly over her bare shoulder. "I would like to know you better myself."

Rena resisted the urge to flinch away—barely. Somehow she managed to smile rather than grit her teeth. "Even though I'm the competition?"

"But you spent quite a bit of time aboard the flight to Hawaii convincing me differently."

Rena shrugged. "You know that old saying about it being a woman's prerogative to change her mind."

"I take it you've changed yours."

"Yes, the incentive was suddenly upped." The chance to once and for all clear her father's name and free herself of an old obligation was more incentive than all the gold in the world.

"Well, I welcome the competition and the chance to meet with you once again."

"I would say you had plenty of competition without my entering the race."

"Except none of the other competitors have hair the color of a raven's wing or skin with the translucence of the finest pearls."

Rena could think of absolutely nothing to say. Randy Fletcher spoke in a low, intimate tone while the clamor of a busy restaurant during the dinner hour rang around them.

"You have quite an imagination as well as a silver tongue."

"I never speak anything but the truth."

Rena doubted it and glancing down at his elaborate ring, decided to test his claim. "I'm fascinated by your ring. Aren't you afraid someone will try to take it?"

"They'd have to get it off of me first, and I'm well able to take care of myself."

She didn't doubt that for a minute. "My father would like something like that. Would it be possible, do you think?"

"I doubt it. A friend made it for me especially."

Rena was tempted to contradict him with his own lie, but knew she'd never win his confidence that way, only his animosity. So she didn't remind him of the Reno pawnshop. Yet it did surprise her to have so easily tripped him up. Like a fleeting shadow, the thought crossed her mind that the mistake might have been deliberate.

"Too bad. Well, have you located the first treasure?"

"Now I think you already know the answer to that. You weren't very far behind me all day." His smile was knowing.

"If you knew, why didn't you stop and let me catch up with you?"

"Because as yet I hadn't proved what we sought couldn't be found."

"Oh."

"Makes you curious, doesn't it, as to what that drab little book contains."

"Tell me, how are you doing?"

"Well enough. And you?"

"The same." She wanted to arrive in Hong Kong first for Mitch's sake, but she didn't want to lose track of Randy Fletcher and his diamond either.

Fletcher removed a cigarette from a gold case, started to light it, and then hesitated. "Do you mind?"

She did, but decided not to say so.

"Have you talked with anyone else involved?"

Here at least she could be honest. "No, I haven't. For all I know, we could be the only ones."

"No way. There are at least twenty other people trying to beat us to the treasure."

"Perhaps they decided not to stop over in Hawaii." The words were out before she could halt them. If Randy was still looking for the prize in Hawaii, he'd definitely have second thoughts now.

He didn't miss the significance of the slip. "What do you mean, stop over here?" His eyes narrowed and his tone was almost accusing.

Rena tried desperately to improvise. "I mean here in Honolulu."

"You don't think this Pacific crossroads is a treasure site?"

Rena knew for certain now that Randy had no idea what the first clue meant. At least not as far as the location went. But now how was she ever going to convince him she didn't either?

"I said here in Honolulu. You surely don't think Dressler would hide something in a teeming city?"

"I think that's the most likely." He hesitated and Rena could almost hear the wheels turning in his head, but his next suggestion was totally unexpected. "Why don't you and I join forces? You know the old saying, two heads are better than one."

"You surprise me, Randy, wanting to share the wealth."

"There's enough for both of us."

"True, but you forget I already have a partner and I'm afraid Mitch would definitely consider three a crowd."

"He wouldn't have to know."

To agree with Randy would definitely keep him in touch, but she could never betray Mitch. So she tried to diplomatically extricate herself. "I appreciate the offer, and if it had come a little sooner then I would certainly have considered it. But I've already agreed to help Mitch. And when I give my word I always keep it."

"An admirable trait, but in this case not one I can admire. Well," and he stood up, obviously reluctant to leave, "I imagine I'll be seeing you around."

He practically swaggered as he walked away, which Rena was beginning to learn was characteristic of him. Several women followed him with their stares and Rena suspected he knew it. He was a man obviously used to and expectant of female attention. Yet something about him made Rena feel cold all over.

Rena took a gulp of coffee, found it cold, and grimaced. The remains of her dinner looked totally uninviting and she pushed the plate away.

"Hello, Rena."

For the second time in Mitch's absence a tall, good-looking man stopped by her table. But there was nothing feigned in her enthusiasm this time. "Bryan!" She reached out to hug him and he lowered his head to kiss her soundly. Distinguished was a word that could have been coined to describe Bryan—from the steel gray of his hair to his carefully clipped mustache.

"Do you mind if I sit down?"

"No, please do. I'm so glad to see you." Divorced from her sister or not,

Bryan Windsor was one of the nicest people she'd ever met and one of her favorites. "How did you know I was here?"

"I met Mitch in the lobby. He told me. I'm due to meet some friends for dinner, so this is a lucky coincidence."

"And one I'm totally thankful for. I had hoped we'd get together while I was here, but now it looks like Mitch and I will be leaving soon."

"Hot on the trail, are you?"

"Did Mitch tell you?"

"He mentioned you'd agreed to help him." Bryan signaled a waiter and ordered a cocktail, then he turned his full, penetrating gaze on Rena. "When are you two going to admit how much you care about each other?"

Rena looked away, suspicious her eyes would betray her. "We're just friends, Bryan, nothing more."

"Oh, yes, I forgot. How careless of me."

"You're making fun of me."

"Rena, I'm only humoring you, because I know someday you'll come to your senses and admit you can't live without each other. Just as I hope someday Shay will arrive at the same realization and come back to me."

"Have you given her any indication of how you feel?"

"She's always known."

"I don't think so, Bryan. If you want Shay back, you're going to have to do something about it. She's embedded in a little rut that may be boring but it's comfortable. Instead of filling her life with love she's filled it with romance novels. She doesn't date or even look at another man."

"Is that so?" He was definitely thoughtful.

Rena plunged on, "She keeps your picture beside her bed. I'm surprised the torch she's carrying isn't visible all the way over here."

"Then why did she leave me?"

"I don't know. Maybe she just wanted to get your attention. You never contested the divorce, Bryan, or fought her in any way."

"Because I thought leaving me would make her happy and that was all I ever wanted to do—make Shay happy."

Rena shook her head despairingly. "Bryan, as a businessman you're tops. How can you be so naive when it comes to love?"

"Probably because I never loved anyone before Shay or after."

"Your problem is you always gave her exactly what she wanted—including that mistake of a divorce. I'm convinced all she ever wanted was more of your time."

"I'm afraid it's too late now."

"It's never too late for love, Bryan."

"Perhaps not, but how do you expect me to heed your advice when you won't heed mine?"

"Because the situations are different."

"Now that has got to be the lamest excuse I've ever heard. But enough of this. We're both obviously convinced we're right. Tell me instead who that man was leaving the table as I approached."

Rena drew in a deep breath and wondered how much she could and should tell Bryan. He was, as she knew, trustworthy. Knowing Mitch could return at any moment, she launched quickly into an explanation of why she'd changed her mind about the treasure hunt.

"And Mitch doesn't know any of this about Fletcher?"

"No."

"Well, as long as you give your all to Mitch I don't see any problem. Maybe this is your chance to clear your father's name. If so, you should grab it, not so much for your father's sake, but for yours. You've your own life to live and I know you won't start doing that until this other business is cleared up."

"You don't think I'm being unfair to Mitch by not telling him?"

"A little; after all, he might be able to help. But I can see why you want to keep things to yourself."

"So you won't tell him?"

"No, your secret is safe with me." And he gave her an indulgent smile.

"I'm glad I told you. It makes it easier."

Bryan stood up, a tall, impeccably dressed, very imposing man. One glance would tell you he was successful. "My friends have arrived, so I'll say good-bye for now. Be careful, Rena. Just be damned certain Fletcher doesn't raise the stakes of this thing too high." With that somewhat disturbing remark, he left her.

It was at least another ten minutes before Mitch returned. Time enough for the waiter to clear the table and bring fresh coffee.

"I was about to send out a search party."

"I'm glad to discover you missed me. From where I was you seemed to be kept pretty busy. What did Fletcher want?"

"Any information I was willing to give him." That at least was the truth.

"You certainly seem to fascinate him."

Rena flashed Mitch a startled look. "Don't be ridiculous! He was probably just being friendly."

"Don't kid yourself, Rena. I doubt Randy Fletcher ever did anything without a motive. I'm not even convinced he operates totally within the law."

Rena didn't want to say any more about him for fear she'd give herself away. "Did you accomplish everything you wanted? I didn't think making plane reservations took so long."

"We want a place to stay when we get there, don't we?"

"True."

"Besides, I had some more business to tie up. If you've had enough coffee let's leave."

Once at the airport they had a delay. They could either sit and wait or browse the shops. Rena stopped by a store specializing in oysters and pearls. You selected your own oyster for the pearl it contained. Then you could have the jewel mounted.

"Look!"

Mitch smiled indulgently. "Want to try your luck? I'll treat if you do."

"That isn't necessary."

"Sure it is, call it a celebration present. After all, you did break the first clue."

"Only with considerable help."

"So what? The credit is still yours. Come on, it would be fun."

Rena decided it would be silly to argue, especially since the cost for the oyster was nominal. She could always decline a piece of jewelry. "Okay, why not."

The oyster she selected didn't stand a chance in the deft hands of the merchant and soon a creamy, gold-toned pearl lay in her hand. Rena turned surprised to Mitch.

"It's beautiful."

The clerk smiled at her pleasure. "You were very lucky. We don't always find one this nice. Would you like it in a setting of some kind?"

"Oh, no, I'll just take it as it is."

"Don't be silly, Rena. It's a lovely pearl and deserves a proper setting. What do you think, a ring?"

A ring? Rena's nerves tingled. She was old-fashioned enough to consider a ring—especially from a man—to be a very personal gift. "Really, the pearl by itself is plenty."

"If we don't have it set in a piece of jewelry you'll only end up losing it. If a ring doesn't strike your fancy then how about a necklace?"

For the sake of ending an awkward moment, Rena agreed. There was nothing overly personal about a necklace. "All right, since you insist."

"At least you can be sensible about some things."

"I'm always sensible. How do you think I keep from doing foolish things?" And she added to herself, *Like declaring my love for you.*

"So you're doing nothing foolish? Well, that's debatable."

"What are you talking about?"

He was slow to reply and it had nothing to do with her question. "Never mind. Here, let me fasten your new necklace."

Rena turned and waited while he fumbled with the clasp. The warm brush of his fingers on her bare neck sent electric shocks throughout her system. Would she ever get over loving him?

It was dark by the time they arrived back on Kauai. Mitch preceded her into the living room and switched on a light. "Would you mind making us some coffee?"

"No, not at all." She was almost to the door when his voice stopped her.

"What did you and Bryan find to talk about?"

"Shay mostly."

"Why Shay?"

"Because I think she's lonely. She loves Bryan and I think he still loves her. I was in hopes I might be able to convince him to get in touch with her."

"Why, when you're so convinced that kind of relationship won't work?"

"I think perhaps they could settle their differences now."

"How is that possible? I wasn't aware Bryan had lost his fortune."

The thrust of his words was well understood and she could think of nothing to say in rebuttal.

"Well, I'm waiting. Are you possibly changing your mind about men with money?"

"This is different. Shay needs Bryan. I can hardly bear the thought of her going through life alone."

"Do you think Shay is the only person who needs someone?"

"Of course not. But Shay's the one I'm concerned with."

"Rena, I'll be so glad when you get your family taken care of and can lead your own life."

"When you care about people you want them to be happy."

"Yes, I know." He studied her with an expression she couldn't begin to comprehend and she escaped gratefully to the kitchen and the coffeepot.

Standing by the sink, Rena looked out into the darkness while waiting for the coffee to perk. Soon the aroma of freshly brewed coffee filled the kitchen.

Filling a heavy mug, she carried it into the living room. However, Mitch wasn't there. A laugh coming from the den alerted her to his whereabouts. She should have realized he'd be using the telephone.

She hoped to set the coffee down without disturbing him if possible. But his next words literally stopped her in her tracks.

"Carmen, of course I miss you. I can't get along without you at home, so how could I not regret your absence when I'm away?"

There was laughter in his voice and an instant ache in Rena's heart. A twinge of jealousy followed the pain. Was Carmen the unidentified object of his affections?

Rena willed herself to deliver his coffee—to act normal. It shouldn't matter that Mitch had filled the special place in his heart where she would never dare to venture.

"Keep the home fires burning and I'll be back in Seattle before you know it."

His carelessly spoken words conjured up an image of a blazing fire, an empty bottle of champagne, and a soft, soft rug. Violently, Rena clamped down on her runaway imagination before it got away from her. She set his coffee down with a thump and barely acknowledged his thanks as she fled from the room and the house. A moon, luminous as the pearl she wore around her neck, hung suspended against the black satin night. A perfect lover's moon, except she had no lover. Moonlight lit the path to the beach and Rena didn't hesitate as she ran toward the bluff.

The way was no less treacherous in the dark. Yet without much thought she scrambled downward, clutching at firmly rooted plants as she descended. All the while her way was illuminated by the gleaming pearl—Queen of Gems—that reigned in the night sky.

Once or twice she thought she heard footsteps following, but when she stopped to listen she put it down to her imagination. Probably all she heard was her own thudding heart. Why should Mitch pursue her, when she had made it clear innumerable times that she preferred her own company? Besides, he was no doubt preoccupied with Carmen. Whoever she was!

Rena combed her memory for some hint to this woman's identity, but she knew no one named Carmen. Were her looks as exotic as her name?

Finally, Rena reached the beach and sank down on the sand to catch her breath. She knew Mitch was in love, but now the woman had a name it was much worse.

Tears—hot, salty, and unwanted—ran down her cheeks and into the corners of her mouth. Over and over she told herself she didn't care Mitch had someone to keep the home fires burning. She was where she wanted to be—hot on the trail of the LaSalle diamonds. She didn't need or want a man to keep her warm on cold nights. That's what electric blankets were for . . . Why then did she give in so easily to the strong arms that suddenly enfolded her? And why couldn't she resist the hard, demanding lips that drove all thoughts of Carmen or loyalty to a cause from her mind?

CHAPTER 6

So caught up was Rena in the all-encompassing sensation of the embrace that she didn't immediately realize something was wrong. The strong scent of men's after-shave filling her senses did *not* belong to Mitch. His was so understated as to be barely noticeable. Someone else had followed her to the beach. The ardency meant for Mitch was a welcome for a stranger.

Belatedly, Rena began to struggle, pushing with all the force she possessed against the man's chest. After her warm welcome, he was caught off guard and she was able to break the hold that was no longer welcome. It was mitigated only a little by the sudden realization it was Randy Fletcher, not a stranger, who embraced her. Anger replaced fear at his audacity.

"Hey! Why the change of heart?"

"I thought you were someone else." The words were out before she had time to even think how they would be interpreted.

"Were you expecting maybe your 'good friend'?" The sneer in his voice matched the one on his face.

"I—I wasn't expecting anyone. Least of all a trespasser. What are you doing here anyway?"

"I was coming to see you, and when I saw you run for the beach I followed."

"So, it was you I heard." In the future, she would give more credit to what she thought was her imagination.

He shrugged. "I didn't see anyone else."

"Why didn't you call out?"

"I didn't want to startle you."

"Creeping up behind me wasn't meant to startle me?"

"I'm sorry." But he didn't sound it.

Rena scrambled up from the sand and only by great effort kept from slapping him. She reminded herself that she needed to stay on Randy's good side if she was going to find out anything about the ring he wore. Only why did he have to make it so difficult? Why couldn't he be charming and nice and therefore make it easy for her to like him?

Rena pushed back her rumpled hair and gathered what little calm remained to her. "Why did you kiss me?"

"Isn't that what moonlight is for?"

Exactly the thought she'd been trying to suppress when he'd startled her. Except he was the wrong man. "How did you know where I was staying?"

"You more or less told me."

"When?" She could remember no such thing.

"When you mentioned you were staying at your brother-in-law's place on Kauai. So you weren't hard to locate. I just asked at the airport."

"But how did you know his name?"

"You mentioned it."

Had she? Rena really couldn't confirm or deny his statement. But she did know that Randy Fletcher was following her. Why? Was it personal or simply because he thought she was on to a solution of the first clue?

She had to discover the real reason behind his pursuit of her. "Be honest, Randy. Why are you after me?"

"Because I couldn't get you off my mind after our meeting this afternoon. We might be competitors now, but that won't last forever."

The surf hissed behind her and she had to lean forward to catch his words. She supposed if she were susceptible she would find his voice seductive.

"It's been a long time since I've been so—attracted." His knuckles brushed along her jawline and his hand definitely lingered as he brushed her hair away from her temple. Rena braced herself for the kiss she knew was coming. It was purposely gentle and very expert. Almost expert enough to make her forget she really didn't like him.

His breath was warm against her cheek, his hand gentle beneath her chin. Where the sudden softening of his approach would have led them Rena would always guiltily wonder, but at that moment the murmuring surf foamed around them, catching them both off guard.

Rena started to laugh. Randy swore and then, thinking better of it, joined her in laughter. But Rena suspected he was more than a little perturbed that his shoes and slacks had received a good dousing with seawater.

The spell he'd almost succeeded in casting was broken and Rena wondered at Randy's sincerity. When they'd first met he'd exhibited a notable lack of enthusiasm once introduced to her. Why had he changed his mind if it wasn't because of the treasure hunt?

Together they ran away from the encroaching sea. Rena's laughter was genuine, but it died abruptly when she looked up at the bluff. Someone watched them as they stood together; someone who would no doubt misunderstand the reason why she clung to Randy; someone who would not realize it was for support and not out of passion. She was helpless to do anything as she watched the man she knew was Mitch turn and start back up the path to the house.

A wintery feeling settled in the region of her heart as she wondered how much he'd witnessed. She wanted to run and catch up with him and explain what he'd seen. But she couldn't. After all, it couldn't possibly matter to him on a personal level, for he had Carmen. She could only hope he wouldn't mistrust her loyalty.

It was only for the sake of any future relationship that she asked Randy in once they'd reached the cottage.

"No, I think I'd best get back to my hotel and dry off."

Rena waited until she heard him drive away and then went inside. The house was dark except for a single light in the living room. Rena was surprised to find Mitch waiting for her, because it was obvious that was exactly what he was doing. She steeled herself for an encounter that threatened to be unpleasant.

"Did you invite Fletcher here?"

"Certainly not!"

"Then how did he know where to find you?"

"I guess I must have told him on the flight to Hawaii." Too late she realized that wasn't the thing to say.

"He was on the same flight as you?" Mitch's voice sounded like iced steel.

"Yes, fate seated us side by side."

"Is that why you changed your mind about the treasure hunt?"

She supposed this was the moment to tell Mitch the truth, but if she did she was afraid he would think she was using him. Which in a way she supposed she was. He wasn't likely to believe that she would give him his money's worth at the same time she trailed Randy Fletcher and the LaSalle diamond. So she lied. "No, it isn't why I changed my mind. Unless you were to say some of his enthusiasm rubbed off on me."

"Then why is he here?"

"I don't know." And she moved restlessly around the room while Mitch sat as still as if he were carved from stone. "He says it's because he's personally interested in me."

"But you don't believe him?"

"I don't think any man is going to take time-out to pursue a woman when he's paid half a million to be involved in a treasure hunt. You might get her name and address to look up later, but you'd tend to business."

"So why do you think he's here?"

"I suspect he's trying to find out if we've solved clue number one."

"Then you don't think he knows?"

She came to rest on the arm of the sofa. "No, I believe he thinks it's somewhere here in Hawaii."

"But he'll no doubt be watching us?"

"I imagine so." The unwavering steadiness of his gaze unnerved her.

"Then it's up to us to try and get the jump on him. Can you be ready to leave almost immediately?"

"I suppose so." Then she amended her answer. "Yes, of course I can."

"Then I'll see if I can arrange a flight to Honolulu tonight. I doubt he'd suspect us of leaving before morning."

Rena didn't even wait for the call to the Lihue Airport. She knew Mitch's influence too well to doubt he'd make the necessary arrangements. When he knocked on her bedroom door she was already packed.

"We're leaving in twenty minutes." He was unsmiling.

"I'm ready."

He had turned away when she reached out verbally to stop him. "Mitch, please believe me. I didn't invite him here or tell him anything."

"I want to believe you, Rena, but I'm having difficulty with what I saw on the beach. The moon made things almost as bright as day."

Damn, he'd seen everything. And the only way to prove his assumption wrong was to explain she'd thought—even hoped—it was him. To confess that would only embarrass them both. So she settled for what sounded like a rather lame explanation of what must have seemed almost traitorous behavior, but was in actuality the truth. "Sometimes things aren't what they seem."

"I'd like to believe that, but I'm afraid seeing is believing."

Like a receding tide, a simple misunderstanding carried the dearest person in the world away from her and Rena was helpless to do anything for fear she would risk everything. It was almost unbearable knowing Mitch thought she was becoming romantically involved with Randy Fletcher. Almost as unbearable as thinking of Mitch with Carmen.

As they boarded a private plane for Honolulu, Rena and Mitch carried two extra passengers—the unknown Carmen and the specter of Randy Fletcher. Rena tried several times to start a conversation and somehow bridge the chasm growing between them, but Mitch wouldn't cooperate. It was obvious he was hurting. There seemed no way to assure him of her loyalty outside of finding the Dressler treasure they believed to be in Hong Kong. But could she do it? Even thinking about it filled her stomach with knots.

The Honolulu airport was virtually empty when they arrived. "When does our flight leave for Hong Kong?"

"In the morning."

"Are we going to a hotel?"

"No, we'll wait here. This way we'll know who arrives and who doesn't."

"You don't really think Randy will follow us?"

He fixed her with a hard glare. "I'm not quite sure what to expect."

"You were with me all the time so you surely don't think I called him?"

"At this point, Rena, I really don't know what to think." And he ran his hand through mussed blond hair.

Rena wanted to smooth away the worry lines etching his face. It was hurtful to know she'd put them there. At this point, it was far more important to locate the jade butterfly for Mitch than to find out where Fletcher had found the diamond in his ring.

Be careful, she warned herself, *or you'll let your caring show.*

Rena could think of nothing more to say, so she found herself an empty chair next to a wall. It gave her weary body something to lean against. The next thing she knew, Mitch was shaking her awake.

She blinked and looked around frantically for her bags. Mitch interpreted the direction of her thoughts. "I've already checked them on the plane. It's time for us to board."

"Already?"

A slight smile touched his lips. "You've been out for quite some time. I felt guilty when I saw how tired you were, but the lack of a bed didn't seem to stop you from catching forty winks."

"I didn't mean to fall asleep."

"Don't apologize, there certainly wasn't a need for both of us to keep watch."

He seemed a little more friendlier and relaxed. Was it possible her impromptu nap encouraged Mitch to believe she wasn't on the lookout for Randy? If so, then it made all the subsequent aches and kinks worthwhile.

Rena loved the excitement of boarding a plane and the anticipation before takeoff, but today her enjoyment was tempered by what lay ahead. If she could accomplish all of her goals without turning Mitch against her then she would ask for nothing more—or so she would try convincing herself.

Today, as the huge silver plane rolled down the runway and took off with its nose pointed into a cloudless blue sky, they were very much employee and employer. There was no other way to describe his remoteness.

This no doubt was the austere, unbending side of him Randy had referred to. Damn Fletcher anyway! If he had left her alone none of this would have happened. Hopefully, he was still asleep or lingering over morning coffee, secure in the thought they hadn't left. She couldn't hide a smile of satisfaction at the thought of his surprise.

Mitch had insisted she take the window seat and now that they were airborne she had a beautiful view of the morning sky. It was streaked with a gold almost the same shade as the sun streaks in Mitch's hair. She turned her head, which rested against the back of the seat, to find him watching her. The icy speculation in his eyes froze her just as the warmth in them had once warmed her.

Surely, he wasn't again having second thoughts. "What's wrong, Mitch?"

"I've been trying to figure out how a woman as fastidious in all things as you could possibly be attracted to Randy Fletcher. Rena, the guy's a sleaze!"

"I keep telling you, I'm not attracted to him."

"Come on, are you forgetting the little scene I witnessed on the beach? That certainly wasn't mouth-to-mouth resuscitation he was giving you."

She turned away so he wouldn't notice the tears misting her eyes as she repeated, "Things aren't what they seem." Which was true. However, she wasn't sure she would have believed him if he'd tried to persuade her the telephone call she'd overheard meant nothing beyond friendly conversation.

He reached over and gripped her arm. "Are you forgetting a full moon made the beach almost as bright as day? He held you like a lover, Rena!"

"If you had such a ringside seat then you must have seen me push him away." *Once,* she added to herself, *I realized he wasn't you.*

"Push him away? Wasn't it more a case of coming up for air? You were obviously enjoying yourself and I felt like a damned Peeping Tom."

There was no way she could tell Mitch it was him she loved. "Why don't you like him?"

"Because, for starters, he doesn't care how he gets what he wants."

"A lot of people are that way."

"Fletcher is just plain unscrupulous! He has an unfortunate habit of being around when jewels turn up missing."

"Are you suggesting he's a thief?"

"No one's ever been able to prove it, but the suspicion has crossed more than one mind. He's to be watched, because he'll lay his hands on the Dressler Collection by fair means or foul."

"I never heard of him before, but there's something familiar about his face."

"Five years ago Randy Fletcher suddenly began showing up at art exhibits, gem shows, and all the better parties. Apparently he has the kind of charm some women find irresistible and so he gains entrée to all the best places."

"He is good-looking."

"He looks like a damned gigolo. All that slick black hair doesn't even look real."

"Have you some personal reason for feeling so strongly?"

"I've seen him operate. Add that I don't like the way he's moved in on you and you have enough reason for me not to like him." He folded his arms and closed his eyes. Still the lines of strain showed in his face. "If he didn't feel up to the challenge of the hunt then he should never have entered. Let him sponge off someone else if he doesn't know what he's doing."

Rena voiced a nagging thought. "Do you suppose he intended to even try and find the jewels himself?"

"Meaning?"

"Well, perhaps he meant to follow whoever seemed on the right track and to steal the prize from them. Maybe that was his intention all along."

"I wouldn't put it past him!"

"Maybe it's his *modus operandi.*"

Mitch barely opened his eyes, but Rena could tell he was looking sideways at her. "Does any of this change your feelings for him?"

"I keep trying to tell you, I don't have any feelings for him. You have totally misunderstood the situation."

"I'd like to believe you, Rena, I really would, but I can't get last night out of my mind. Like a bad taste, it won't go away."

Rena swallowed hard. There was nothing for it but to tell Mitch at least part of the truth or he was going to drive them both crazy with his suspicions. Unfortunately, the stewardess chose then to arrive with breakfast and Rena's resolve had almost fled before she had the opportunity to again speak.

Toying with unappealing-looking eggs, she broke the silence between them. "Mitch, I've a confession to make. And please hear me out before you hit the roof. Okay?"

"I was wondering when we were going to get around to the truth."

"We've already gotten around to it—if you would just accept the fact."

"Okay, then I can only assume you intend to do something I'm not going to like."

"Possibly."

"Then there's still time not to."

Rena shook her head. "I'm afraid not."

"Why?"

"Because I intend going ahead as I've planned whether you like it or not."

"Then why tell me?"

"Because of the totally wrong impression you've gotten about my feelings for Randy Fletcher."

"Don't tell me you're going to once again try and convince me I didn't see what I know I did?"

"No, you saw what you think. But it really didn't mean anything."

"That doesn't sound like you, Rena. I've never known you to give a man false hope."

Did she imagine the hint of regret in his voice? No, of course not. "Like you, I think Randy is using me for what he hopes to find out. Since that plays into my hands I don't mind."

"What are you getting at?"

"Have you by any chance noticed the diamond Randy wears?"

"Who could miss it? I'd hardly call it in good taste."

"Do you recognize it?" Then she answered her own question. "No, why should you. I sat next to him all the way to Hawaii and even then it was some time before I placed it. The reason I changed my mind about being involved with you in the Dressler hunt was because I wanted to keep an eye on Randy Fletcher. Which will be easier if he doesn't let me out of his sight."

"You've lost me."

"That ostentatious diamond was once part of the LaSalle jewels."

"Are you positive?"

"Absolutely! Once I recognized it, there were no doubts. I don't see what took me so long, considering I've been tracking them for years."

"So you think he can lead you to the rest of them?"

"I don't know. I've asked him twice where he got the ring and I've gotten two different answers. I'm in hopes I can get close enough to him that I'll find out where he really got it."

"What if you get close enough to find out he's the thief?"

"Then that's even better. Although I seriously doubt he's the one who originally took them. I think I'd remember him if he'd been around at the time."

"You mentioned there was something familiar about him."

"There is, but I don't think it has to do with the time of the LaSalle theft. I think I've probably just seen him somewhere."

"What if he suspects what you're doing?"

"Then he suspects. I can't let that deter me."

"Do you really think he'd let you walk away knowing you could possibly send him to jail? If what you suspect is true then he's very likely an international jewel thief and I would suspect dangerous. He won't let you find out anything, and if you do, he won't let you implicate him. Only a fool would think to get away with this."

"Thanks for the compliment and the vote of confidence. See if I ever confide in you again."

He encircled her shoulders with one arm and took her left hand in his. "Look, I'm glad you did. You don't know how I hated the thought of your being attracted to Fletcher. But this is a dangerous game you propose playing."

"I agree, but after long years of searching, one of the LaSalle diamonds has surfaced. I have no choice but to follow this lead."

"No matter how dangerous it might turn out to be?"

"That's right."

"What if it turns out Fletcher merely bought the diamond?"

"If it turns out he did, then I'm right back where I started. At least I won't have any regrets that I didn't follow up every lead."

He released her to push away his own barely eaten breakfast. "Your abrupt change of heart on the subject of the treasure hunt has puzzled me all along. Now at least I know why you changed your mind."

"But be assured, Mitch, I fully intend to find those pieces for you. You'll get your money's worth, don't ever think you won't."

"Don't worry about it, Rena. I won't hold you to our deal."

"What are you talking about? I want to be a part of the hunt. I'm caught up in the excitement now."

"Not if it means you're going to continue tailing Fletcher. I won't be a party to putting you in any possible danger."

"Don't be ridiculous. I'm not in any danger."

"You can't know that."

"And you can't know I am. I don't intend following Randy into a dark alley and then accusing him of grand theft."

"No, you intend to let him romance you instead."

He was still bothered by the scene on the beach. "Is there any harm in that?"

"Some men don't take kindly to deceptions of that kind."

"True, but aren't we mutually agreed Randy is only using me as a means to the Dressler treasure? I doubt he's any more personally involved than I am. Really, I suppose we should be flattered he thinks us clever."

"There's the very real possibility he's attracted to you, Rena. You're a very beautiful and desirable woman. Fletcher might easily be mixing business and pleasure." His gaze didn't waver from hers as he continued. "A good many men do that."

Was he remembering a time when business had been seasoned with pleasure? Was that how he'd met Carmen?

"Mitch, you can't expect me to walk away from this opportunity."

He hesitated and she suspected he was weighing what he wanted to say against the obvious truth of the situation. "No, I have to admit you're right."

"And you're not mad at me for sort of using you to pursue him?"

"You mean agreeing to take part in the hunt?"

"Yes, I promise to give you your money's worth."

"I don't doubt that. Your integrity has never been in question. I'm crazy to let you go on with this, but I really don't know how I can stop you."

"No, I don't either. Even if you cast me adrift, I'll still go after Fletcher on my own. He asked me to join forces with him and I guess I could if I had to."

"Don't you dare!"

"I won't unless you throw me out."

"That's blackmail, Rena."

"No, it's a simple statement of truth."

"Then promise me one thing."

"I'll try."

"Don't attempt this on your own. Let me help you."

"Do you think Randy will waste time pursuing me if you're always around?" She was flattered Mitch wanted to help, but she had to be realistic.

He studied her almost harshly before responding. "You're really willing to risk possible danger in order to write *finis* to this business of the LaSalle jewels?"

"It's been a driving force for so long, I don't see how I can turn around and walk away when I have—quite honestly—the first solid lead I've come across." Everything about her pleaded for him to understand and when she saw some of the iciness leave his eyes she knew he had.

"All right, but I want you to promise me two things." And there was a no-argument tone to his voice.

"I'll try."

"When all this is over, I want you—regardless of the outcome—to pursue happiness for Rena Drake."

"Who said I'm not happy?" There was no hiding her surprise.

"I'm not saying you're unhappy, and perhaps I'm about to sound chauvinistic with my next statement. But Rena, you need to love and be loved.

To have some man gather you in his arms and make love to you and care about you. You're too beautiful, too loving, to be so alone."

She couldn't help a nervous laugh. "What you're asking is a little easier said than done."

"I know a lot of eligible bachelors." Then he hastily added before she could say anything, "And not all of them have too much money."

There was no way Rena could resist reaching out to touch him. "You are very, very sweet." She wanted desperately to add, *And I love you so very, very much.*

He caught her hand and held it against his cheek. "You might find I'm a lot of things—if you could ever get past counting my bank balances."

This was ground they'd covered so many times, and it was no less dangerous than before. Mitch's wealth and the unknown Carmen stood in the way of anything more than friendship.

The silence between them quivered with unspoken feelings. "What else do you want me to promise?"

"The last is easy. You have to let me help you on this."

She opened her mouth to protest but he would have none of it. "I insist, Rena. I already know all of your objections. I promise to give Randy plenty of room. But I'll be there in the background just in case I'm needed. Okay?" Then he tacked on with a grin, "Just in case you need to borrow a dime. Money can come in handy—when you run out of shells and beads to bargain with."

Rena sniffed with mock disdain. "I'm going to ignore that." Then she continued seriously. He had to understand how important this was to her. "You have to promise to be discreet."

He nodded. "I will be."

"And you're not mad at me?"

"No, I actually understand."

She was glad he did. It made everything easier. She also hoped he would understand when she gave him the slip. Rena knew there was no way in the world she could trap Fletcher with Mitch doing guard duty. Mitch could think as ill of Randy as he wanted. But the latter was clever, perhaps more so than either of them thought. How else had he avoided exposure all of these years, if what they suspected was true?

The airplane seat was a lot more comfortable than the one in the airport terminal had been, and so Rena settled herself in hopes of grabbing a nap. Mitch had pulled his briefcase out from under the seat and seemed deeply engrossed in a jumble of papers. Did he ever go anywhere just for fun? But then she guessed fortunes weren't made with idle hands. Maybe the mysterious Carmen would be able to force him into taking a vacation once in a while. Rena couldn't help wondering what she'd be doing once Mitch was married.

If this LaSalle business was cleared up then she really would have to look for a new direction. Maybe Mitch was right and she should begin looking around for someone special. But it wasn't quite as simple as ordering from a catalog. Especially when she'd already found whom she wanted. Too bad the price was so high. The sleep settling around her was more than welcome.

A glance at her watch when she awoke proved she hadn't been asleep all that long, just long enough for her dreams to be a jumble and for Mitch to take his turn napping. Rena smiled as she watched him. Asleep he hardly looked like the international businessman he was—or the many times a millionaire she knew him to be. How easy it was to recall the first time they'd met. She'd been fresh out of school, her degree in gemology crisp and new. Pacific Imports were hiring and so she took a chance. She'd been so scared before the interview. Mitchell Johns had a reputation as being a tough boss.

She'd been terrified, hardly the picture of the young sophisticate she'd hoped to project. Her knees had been about to give out when he'd invited her to sit down. He'd been businesslike but kind, very much aware she was a novice. But also very much aware she'd earned an impressive degree. Her interview had run into the lunch hour and she had thought it only courtesy that had prompted his invitation for lunch.

Later there had been plenty of people to tell her differently and to make her aware she'd been singled out for a special favor. Over dessert he'd told her to report for work the following Monday. Their friendship had begun that day, and quite frankly she couldn't imagine her world without Mitchell Johns. The last year away from him had been long and lonely and so very empty. How she wished she had the courage to let herself love him—to see if maybe he might love her in return. If only he didn't have so darned much money.

He opened his eyes and stretched. "Sleep must be catching."

"There's certainly little else to do on a flight like this."

"There's always paperwork." He indicated the pile on his briefcase.

"Why don't you pretend you're on vacation and forget about all that?"

"When something the size of Pacific Imports rests on your shoulders there's no such thing as time off."

"You have to get far enough away from the telephone and not take any paperwork with you." On impulse she added, "I know a couple of out-of-the-way places where you could be sure of getting a rest."

He studied her seriously. "When we're done here why don't you show me?"

Her heartbeat quickened. "Won't you be busy?"

"I thought the whole idea was to see I got away from business?"

"I mean," and she floundered for words. "Won't you be getting married?"

"You really want to put me out of circulation, don't you?"

"You were the one who brought the subject up."

"A fact you've never let me forget." His tone left no doubt he regretted ever having mentioned it.

Rena was very careful to keep the hope from her voice. "Have you changed your mind?"

"Do you think I should?"

"What you do in that respect is entirely up to you."

"One always hopes one's friends will approve."

"I want you to be happy, but when you marry it's bound to change our relationship."

"Yes, I'd have to agree with you."

He was smiling and Rena wondered if he was contemplating a life spent with the unknown Carmen. She longed to ask. Like most of his female employees, Rena had fallen for his blond good looks. As their friendship deepened, she'd become increasingly wary of the role his money played.

It opened doors that would otherwise have stayed shut. It smoothed a lot of rough paths. He'd paid her twice the salary she would have earned anywhere else, and argued that he paid the best salaries because otherwise he couldn't expect to hire the best. She doubted Mitch had ever had to pinch a penny.

Their relationship eventually reached the stage where it was poised on the point of possibly turning into something more. Then Shay and Bryan's marriage fell apart. As with her parents' failed marriage, the problem seemed to be money. Rena became suddenly leery of any situation where one person was worth a lot more financially than the other. It created an inequality difficult to bridge.

Her mother had been a society belle fascinated by the young gemologist hired to appraise the family collection. Theirs had been a whirlwind courtship, and a classic example of the old saying—marry in haste, repent at leisure. Rena had been crushed when her mother had walked out—permanently. Their father had easily won custody, although there had been weekends and vacations with their extravagant and generous mother. But the financial inequality of her parents' marriage had left its mark.

Her mother had long been remarried and perfectly at home in European café society. This time she'd chosen a man of similar financial and social background and it was working.

She loved Mitch too much to risk the consequence of a marital disaster.

"Why are you shaking your head so vehemently?"

"I didn't realize I was. I was just thinking."

"It must have been pretty heavy to cause such a dour expression."

She refused to look at him. "It was."

"Are you having some second thoughts about our venture?"

"Never that, although I have given some thought to what my life will be like once this LaSalle business is cleared up. I'll have to find a new direction."

"I could suggest one or two."

"Nothing quite so harrowing as this Dressler business, I hope. The half million you've laid out is never far from my mind."

"No, it would be far more relaxing."

"Are you going to tell me what it is?"

"When the time comes—and don't try to convince me otherwise."

Rena knew Mitch well enough to know he meant what he said. Still, she couldn't help being curious.

The FASTEN YOUR SEAT BELT sign flashed on, and a pleasant voice informed them they were at last approaching Kai Tak Airport after multiple hours in the air.

The landing was smooth and so was customs. "They're terribly efficient, aren't they?"

"With all the people passing through, how could they be otherwise?"

Traveling with Mitch was an experience in how well everything could run. Was it his money or the fact he expected and knew how to obtain the best service? It was marvelous not to have to struggle with luggage, customs, taxis, or anything. She could just relax and enjoy the global mixture of people surging around her.

As she scanned the crowds, her breath caught and held once or twice when she saw someone resembling Randy Fletcher. Each time it was only a resemblance, but she was reminded she really did expect him not to be far behind. They might have lost him for the moment, but he'd soon pick up their trail.

They were safely in a taxi and on the way to their hotel room when Rena inquired, "Do you think someone will be getting in touch with us regarding additional clues for locating the butterfly?"

"I hope so. What we have isn't enough to go on."

"That's an understatement." Still, she couldn't shake the nagging suspicion they'd been told all they were going to be.

Rena watched as they passed through both old and new sections of Hong Kong. Flashing neon signs were unreadable. She'd taken French in high school and college, but it was unlikely to be helpful in locating the jade butterfly, although she was reminded that in French she would be looking for *le papillon*. The weight of the task facing them couldn't be dismissed even in all the excitement.

"Why the heavy sigh?"

"I didn't realize I'd verbalized my feelings. I was thinking I might have benefited from a crash course in Chinese rather than all the years I spent conjugating French verbs."

"Just not any Chinese, but Cantonese."

"There's a difference?"

"Definitely. The written language is the same everywhere, but the dialect understood here would be unintelligible in Peking or Shanghai."

"How encouraging. You don't happen to know the Cantonese for butterfly, do you?"

"No, do you think it's necessary?"

"I wish I knew. I also wish I knew why I keep feeling like we've gotten all the help we're going to get in leading us to *le papillon*."

"The butterfly; I too had four years of high school French."

"Yes, well, too bad we're not in Paris."

"I'd like that, you know." And he reached over to brush aside a wayward strand of her hair. "It's a city I know well, and I'd like the opportunity to show it to you."

Rena tried not to be electrified by his touch, but it was impossible and she wondered how he could not suspect her breathy voice. "Well, who knows, we may get there yet." If only she felt as breezy as her words suggested. Years of close contact with him should have inured her to his touch, but she doubted if she'd ever be old enough or jaded enough not to be affected by him. "Where will we be staying?"

"I debated about that. I have no desire to rough it and didn't imagine you did either. At the same time I thought you might want to stay somewhere with atmosphere. I think you'll approve my choice."

"You sound very pleased with it."

"I am, and we were probably lucky to get a room on such short notice."

Rena suspected his wealth had something to do with that. "I assume a room is just a figure of speech?"

"Not exactly. We have a suite, so you'll have all the privacy you could want."

So, they were traveling first class all the way. "Do you ever have the desire to get out and rough it?"

"I go hunting in Canada every fall, you surely remember that."

"But I bet you stay in a nice, cushy lodge somewhere."

"Does the meat somehow taste better if you freeze your fanny off in the snow?"

"It's more in the spirit of the great hunter."

"And when was the last time you camped out in a blizzard?"

"Well, never, but I think it might be fun—adventuresome."

"Would you go along with it if I arranged something of that nature?"

She was surprised that he'd suddenly decided to take seriously her good-natured baiting. "You and me?"

"Naturally. I could be the big-game hunter and you could be the camp cook. Someplace in the wilds of Canada, perhaps."

She was saved from having to answer by the taxi's screeching to a sudden halt before a hotel that was visually everything she could have wished. Once inside Rena expressed her satisfaction. "This is perfect. I'm almost reminded of the way it might have been fifty years ago." Then she leaned closer to Mitch and whispered, "Do you think that man over there might be an international spy?"

"He looks more like a bit player from an old Fu Manchu movie, but I do admit he has style."

"I like his white tropical suit—why don't you get yourself one?"

"Because I have no desire to be mistaken for a spy. Come on, they're holding the elevator for us."

The elevator ran smoothly but had the look, if not the workings, of an antique. Plush carpeting cushioned their footsteps as they walked to their room. Once inside, Rena gave herself up to the enthusiasm inspired by the other-era opulence of their accommodations.

"This is fantastic—I won't even ask how much it costs."

"Good. You always want to spoil things by fretting about money."

Was that really how he saw her? "If you'd ever had to pinch pennies, you might understand."

He caught her arm and swung her around to face him. "How do you know I haven't had to?"

His anger surprised her. "Mitch, everyone knows how much you have."

"Then everyone doesn't know as much as they think." He released her and snapped open his suitcase. "How would you like to pinch pennies, as you put it, while trying to keep not only a life-style but a large corporation afloat?"

"Mitch, I'm sorry if I hit a nerve. I assumed, I mean people don't usually plunk down a cool half-million dollars to take part in a treasure hunt if they're hurting financially. Unless . . ." And the horrible thought crossed her mind that maybe this was all a gamble to save his business.

"Look," and his arm circled her shoulders. "The money I'm spending today I can afford to spend. So don't think you have to order the cheapest thing on the menu or find a freighter on which to work your way home. Okay?"

"Okay." But was it really? She'd always taken Mitch's wealth so much for granted. Had she perhaps been wrong? His next words did nothing to put her at ease.

Busily unpacking his suitcase, he didn't see the horrified look that crossed her face as he spoke. "Anyway, I look at the money spent on the Dressler hunt as an investment. Sure the clues are hard, but with you along how can I miss finding at least one of the treasures?"

"Don't have too much faith in me."

He glanced up. "I won't. Don't worry."

She had to make him see the reality of their situation. "I may know gems, but I don't think that's necessarily the big plus you seem to think."

He gave her his full attention. "You're a skilled professional with an exceptionally well-trained eye. Not everyone would have made the connection between Fletcher's ring and the LaSalle diamond. And not everyone would have remembered that scarcely memorable jade butterfly. I didn't. Your skills, your training, and the background that goes with them make you invaluable in this situation. I'm depending on you, Rena, and I have complete faith in that dependence."

Rena could almost hear the trapdoor clang shut. Perspiration broke out all over her body and she fought a rising tide of panic. It was wonderful he had such faith in her, but not to this blown-out-of-proportion extent.

"Mitch, I appreciate your confidence in me, but the sense of responsibility you're laying on my shoulders is frightening."

"Don't let it overwhelm you. All I ask is that you do your best. If it works out—that we go home with a share of the booty—then great. If not, well, then we will at least have had a good time."

The overwhelming sense of responsibility remained, along with the knowledge she deserved every bit of guilt she was feeling. Her own selfish pursuits had gotten her into this. Did she really stand any chance of keeping Mitch from being the loser?

CHAPTER 7

Rena stood for a moment in the well-lighted entrance of their hotel. The night side of Hong Kong awaited her and she was only a little apprehensive about venturing out on her own. She had to get some fresh air; to get out from under, at least for a while, the sense of responsibility Mitch had inadvertently heaped on her shoulders. It had seemed so easy and perfectly all right to use the treasure hunt as a means to keep tabs on Randy Fletcher. She hadn't bargained on the guilt or the feeling of indebtedness that hung around her neck like an albatross.

Over and over in her mind the same refrain kept playing. What if Mitch lost money because of her? What if she failed to retrieve even one of the treasures?

Rena shook her head in an effort to banish the persistently negative thoughts that were hounding her. She would follow Fletcher to the source of the LaSalle jewels and she would be the first one to the jade butterfly.

Colored neon lights flashed garishly, looking from a distance like colored jewels in the light tiara that was the skyline of Hong Kong. They enticed her to explore on her own. Mitch was busy with phone calls and hadn't even heard the door close behind her. Chances were she'd be back in the room before he even knew she was gone.

Rena hurried along the sidewalk, passing people from all over the world. How easy it would be to disappear in this cosmopolitan throng. Perhaps she would do exactly that when both the LaSalle and Dressler business were finished.

After several blocks, she located an appealing restaurant. Here was some place to quiet her noisy stomach. She selected a booth to the back, ordered something she couldn't pronounce, and tea.

Before long a plate of steaming food and a pot of tea were set down before her. The food smelled good and tasted even better. What was really refreshing was the almost scalding beverage. It seemed to warm every part of her down to her toes, and she poured herself cup after cup as she tried—unsuccessfully—not to think. She actually hoped Randy did manage to follow them, then perhaps she could finish the LaSalle business once and for all. At least that would eliminate the sense of obligation she carried around with her.

Mitch scolded her for assuming the burden of clearing her father's name. But did he ever guess how many times she'd actually been tempted to abandon it? Then a rumor would come her way or she'd overhear someone rehash the whole business and she'd determine once again to clear the family name. Randy Fletcher was her one big chance to be free. Then she'd smile, allow Mitch a farewell kiss, and take her breaking heart off and build a new life.

No matter how hard she tried, Rena could think of no solution but to run —away from Mitch, but mostly from the consequences of her own traitorous feelings and desires. She could almost see Mitch's look of embarrassment and pity when he realized how she felt about him.

She drained the last of her tea and ended up with a mouthful of grounds. If she kept her mind off Mitch maybe things like that wouldn't happen. If only she had the courage to try for some kind of life with him.

Often he'd look at her endearingly, but that was only because he was fond of her. They were dear friends; why shouldn't he look at her with affection?

Now it really wouldn't work. The waiter approached with more tea and she kept her fingers crossed that his command of English was better than hers of Cantonese. "Could you tell me where I might find some really fine jade?"

"The logical place to look would be the Jade Market."

It was a long shot, but so far Dressler had counted on the inobviousness of the obvious. "Can you tell me how to get there?"

"Sure—no problem." His English was no problem.

"Wait—let me get something to write on."

"It's north on Nathan Road, just off Kansu Street. Near the Yau Ma Tei Typhoon Shelter. If jade is what you want, you'll find it there."

"I hope so."

She easily found her way back to the hotel, in fact was almost a little disappointed to find she really hadn't wandered all that far. But while the distance wasn't great, the passage of time was and she almost collided with Mitch as he came out of their hotel.

He seized her shoulders none too gently and shook her soundly. "Where have you been?"

Rena was aware people were staring. "I went for a walk and when I got hungry I stopped to eat. You were so busy I decided to go off on my own. I felt I needed a little breathing space and thought maybe you could use some also."

His hands dropped away and she almost teetered as she felt the sudden loss of support. "I'm sorry if you feel stifled by my company."

"It's not your company, but the situation."

"Look, if it will make you feel any better, I don't care if I get anything out of this venture or not. I'm enjoying the vacation away from the phone." Then he grinned as he realized how contradictory that sounded compared to the facts. "Appearances to the contrary, that is. Because I'm the one doing the calling so there are no unwanted interruptions. Most of all I'm enjoying being with you. I missed you during the last year, Rena, more than you suspect."

"I don't see how you had time to miss me, all things considered."

"Like what?" He slipped his arm about her waist and nudged her toward the doors of the hotel.

"Well, you've been busy getting yourself engaged."

"How many times must I repeat that I've been thinking about it—not exactly doing it. I'm tired of rattling around in that huge old house by myself. But most of all I'm tired of worrying and wondering if the woman I love has found someone else."

"I doubt it. I'm sure she returns your affections."

"Are you?"

"There isn't any reason why she shouldn't. I believe you're a very eligible bachelor." The last was lightly said.

"Ah-h, yes, but eligible in one person's book is not necessarily eligible in another."

His words threw her off guard. "Mitch, she'd have to be crazy not to be crazy about you!"

"Perhaps. But she's not the easiest person to understand. She has some funny ideas about what it takes to make a romance work."

Rena's nerves tightened. If she foolishly gave her imagination free rein then she could almost believe they were discussing her. But of course they weren't. "I'm sure you'll overcome her objections."

"You can damn well bet I'm going to try."

Would any woman Mitchell Johns set his sights on stand a chance? Rena doubted it.

Evidently determined not to let her out of sight again, Mitch escorted Rena to their suite. He locked the door firmly behind them. "I trust you won't be wandering off again tonight?"

"No, I think I'll retire. The night air makes me sleepy." And she added to herself, *I want to be up and away from here before you wake up in the morning.* Not that she didn't want Mitch's help or his company, but Randy wasn't likely to appear if Mitch was along.

When Rena at last crawled from bed in the morning it was hardly to feel rested. Her night's sleep had consisted of a series of catnaps. Worried she might oversleep, she had jerked awake every few minutes the entire night. But at least it had paid off. It was early morning and she could be away before Mitch awoke.

Quickly she showered, glad her bathroom was away from Mitch's room. Just as quickly, she dressed in slacks and a sleeveless blouse. Already the heavy humidity had crept inside and she didn't feel fresh for long. Unbuttoning the bottom of her shirt, she tied it in a knot around her waist.

Next she wound her hair into a knot atop her head. She scarcely needed a curtain of hair in the way today.

She'd been told the market didn't open until around ten, so she walked away from the hotel until she found a place to have breakfast. After satisfying her hunger, she checked her slim gold watch, hailed a taxi, and directed the driver to take her to the Jade Market.

At first all she could do was stand and stare. It seemed disorganized bedlam, but then she realized it wasn't. Only the crowds and bargaining made it seem that way. As she browsed among the merchants and their displayed wares, Rena realized she had her fingers crossed for good luck. Truthfully, she had no idea where to look and realized there must be some specific plan she was overlooking.

Then in the throng of people she saw a tall, dark-haired figure she recognized. It wasn't hard to do for he towered over most everyone. There was no way Randy Fletcher could have followed her. Therefore she must be on the right path. Surely two people couldn't be wrong. Again she walked the length of the street, carefully scrutinizing every vendor she passed. All the while her heart thudded against her chest as she realized anew the importance of being first.

On the fringe of the market were several kite vendors. Dozens of brilliant shapes bobbed in the sky as fierce dragons pursued exotic birds. So intent was she in watching the wind-tossed antics of a dancing dragon that she collided with a sight-seeing couple.

Her attention was brought back to earth with a thump and she resumed the seemingly hopeless task of locating the jade butterfly. But even with her attention earthbound, she still bumped into a distinguished-looking gentleman.

He smiled, touched his hat, and begged her pardon in French. She watched as he continued on his way while trying to control a kite and wend his way through the throng of shoppers. She stopped, shaded her eyes, and scanned the blue sky for the one belonging to him. Staring wide-eyed, she identified a superbly crafted, butterfly-shaped kite.

Then it dawned on Rena. He had deliberately run into her. Was it an unlikely coincidence or was this the further clue she had been expecting, but hadn't recognized? Either she was more desperate than she thought or Dressler was being terribly clever, as well as obvious. On a whim fueled by her desperation, Rena pursued the man by following his bobbing butterfly. If it hadn't been fluttering against the azure sky she undoubtedly would have lost him. Then she saw him stop, reel in his kite, and wait for her against a building. She knew then her wild hunch was right. With a smile of greeting, she approached him.

"Good morning, Monsieur—would it be Papillon?"

"Oui, it would." Then he continued in heavily accented English. "I have deliberately bumped into three of your fellow contestants, but none of them have made the connection between a Frenchman flying a butterfly kite and a jade butterfly they seek. And we thought the kite vendors at the end of the street made it doubly obvious. I congratulate you and advise you to take care of your little treasure. It is perhaps more valuable than even you guessed."

Rena couldn't help the slight trembling of her hands as she accepted the well-wrapped package. But she wasn't too awestruck not to think ahead. "What about the next clue?"

"Being the first to receive it is also part of the prize." And he handed her a sealed envelope identical to the first one.

"What about the others? Must they find you to receive the second clue?"

"Mr. Dressler knows where all of you are staying. They will be summoned to a gathering in forty-eight hours. Part of your prize is that much head start. A reward for ingenuity—and observation." He touched his hat again, smiled, and melted into the crowds surging around them.

Rena's exhilaration was quickly replaced with the awesome responsibility of the treasure now in her possession. She hugged the package close to her and then decided such a gesture was too conspicuous. Hesitating a moment in indecision, she decided to stuff the package into her tote bag. It would not look totally out of character for her to be guarded about her bag.

Then she nonchalantly walked away from Hong Kong's famous Jade Market. Once she was safely inside a taxi she unwrapped her treasure. It was just as beautiful, just as worthy of possession, as she remembered. Mitch would have his prize.

The taxi deposited her outside the hotel and clutching her tote bag she entered, approached the desk, and asked for the manager. He arrived quickly. While traveling back to the hotel a plan had formed in her head.

She would see the butterfly into safekeeping, return to the market, and if Randy Fletcher were still there she would follow him. Once she accomplished that she wasn't certain what her next step would be. She would worry about that when the time came and improvise if necessary.

As she waited for the manager, she realized how much she would like to see the look on Mitch's face when he opened the package. But to do that would keep her from trailing Randy—the matter of first importance now that she had the jade.

The manager arrived wearing a large smile. "Can I be of assistance?"

"Yes, I wish to leave a package in your safe. Also, I wish to leave a message for Mitchell Johns; he's staying here in the hotel."

"Oh, yes, Mr. Johns has stayed here often. But I understood you were staying with him."

"I am, but I still want you to give him a message which will direct him to the safe. However, don't under any circumstances give the note or package to anyone else. I want it personally placed in his hands."

"I understand. Could you perhaps place some value on the package?"

"It's quite literally priceless."

The manager blanched somewhat, but didn't argue. After all, that was not what he was being paid for.

The butterfly taken care of, Rena hailed a taxi and returned to the Jade Market. It was a long shot that Randy would still be there, but she had to give it a try. Two hours later her eyes ached from scanning the crowds and she still hadn't located him. The day was humid and hot and her slacks and shirt clung uncomfortably.

Her stomach had been rumbling for hours and she decided to go in search of food. After she'd eaten, there would be time enough to pursue an alternate plan of action.

Rena began walking, not really paying attention to the direction she went. People's faces were beginning to blend together and one street looked much like another. Giving up on finding an appealing-looking restaurant, she decided to settle for a container of noodles from a smiling street vendor.

Walking as she ate, she wondered if Mitch had gotten the jade butterfly yet. And if he had, what he was thinking. She wished now that she'd given it to him herself—to have witnessed firsthand his hoped-for look of delight. Well, it was a little late for regrets.

The thing to do now was begin phoning the various hotels in search of Fletcher. A telephone wasn't hard to find, but he was. Rena almost wondered if he was sleeping in the streets. She knew he spent a good deal of his time watching her. There was no other explanation for how or why he kept turning up. Was there the possibility if she made herself visible he might save her some time by appearing?

The best place to start would undoubtedly be her hotel. That way if Fletcher had lost track of her and was watching the entrance he would be able to pick up her trail again. Then if she could work it right, she could follow him. No doubt he would be flattered and hopefully lower his defenses. Rena realized it might not be the best plan around, but at the moment it was the only one she could think of.

A taxi took her back to the hotel. After paying the driver, she stood for a moment and surveyed the crowd, hoping to catch a glimpse of a familiar face. But it wasn't to be. However, she wanted everything to appear natural if he were watching and so she decided to go inside and sit in the lobby for a few minutes. Hopefully, she could spot Randy and avoid Mitch.

For the briefest of moments, she let her eyes close and her thoughts wander. How she would love to be back on Kauai. The Dressler treasure hunt was proving to be exhausting, both mentally and physically.

It was an effort to force her eyelids open, and when she did, the first thing she saw was Mitch talking to the manager of the hotel. She was thankful for the potted palm that provided some cover.

Her heart thudded as she watched. Here was her chance to judge Mitch's reaction without being seen. If he spotted her then she would make up some excuse for not coming forward. The package was placed safely in his hands. Rena realized how nervous she'd been when an audible sigh stirred the palm fronds. The treasure was Mitch's responsibility now.

She watched him hesitate, open the package, and then look around the lobby. Evidently he didn't see her, because he quickly rewrapped the package and was obviously grilling the manager. The latter could only shake his head, shrug, and point to the entrance. She could sense Mitch's anger from the set of his shoulders.

He handed the package back to the manager, obviously to be redeposited in the safe, and then strode toward the entrance. Rena dropped her head and scooted down in her chair. When she dared to glance up she could see him questioning the doorman. It seemed none of them had noticed her leave or reappear.

Her chance for escape came when Mitch hailed a taxi and drove away. As soon as he was out of sight, she fled the hotel without bothering to look around for Fletcher. If he were there he could follow. If not she had plenty of time to walk off her confusion over what to do next.

Diverse sights paraded past, but Rena knew she wasn't appreciating them as she should, even though it didn't take much imagination to know she was wandering into areas of the city not on the usual tour. There were shops specializing in fortune-telling—and it was a temptation to see what her future might hold, but she told herself she didn't believe in such things and only read her horoscope in the daily paper out of curiosity. But it was more than curiosity that made her yearn to discover how her present situation would turn out.

Then there were the shops devoted to herbalists. The display of dried sea horses was fascinating and Rena wondered if they did have any healing powers. The shopkeeper saw her hesitate and approached her in broken English with a recommendation she try tail of deer. Everyone knew it was a highly recommended aphrodisiac.

Rena shook her head and walked away. An aphrodisiac definitely was not what she needed. As yet there was no sign of Randy as she strolled narrow back streets that entered onto wider thoroughfares.

Rena was becoming increasingly aware of her aching feet. Spying a small cafe, she entered and chose a seat at a tiny table near a window. She ordered tea and with it arrived some delicious almond-flavored cookies. No one else in the minuscule restaurant seemed to be paying her any attention so she slipped out of her shoes and wiggled her toes. They felt so good to be released from cramped quarters that Rena prolonged her tea and cookies as long as she could.

Finally, it came time to move on. Deciding she might later need the remaining cookies, she tucked them in her bag. She hoisted it onto her shoulder and discovered it had gained several pounds since entering the shop—or so it felt. It was a very real indication she was tired out and probably should be returning to her hotel. But to do that was to admit momentary defeat in her pursuit of Randy Fletcher. And once she returned, Mitch wasn't likely to let her out of his sight again so easily. She would give her search another hour at least.

So she continued to walk, prowling the sometimes modern, sometimes narrow, reminiscent-of-the-past streets, keeping herself alert for signs of Fletcher. Perhaps this preoccupation was what kept her from noticing it had clouded over, grown unusually still, and that people were going inside and taking their wares with them. Awnings were rolled up, and everything that could be was carried inside.

Several drops of rain slapped against her, then it began to fall harder, ricocheting off the street, stirring up dust until the dust was mud. Within seconds, Rena was drenched, her clothes plastered to her body and her hair dripping wet. The wind had risen and she seemed to be walking directly into it. All the shops were closed up tightly and she was reluctant to beat on any door and demand to be let in.

Finally, the wind and rain became so forceful that she ducked into an alley protected by a corrugated metal overhang. A scroungy dog had done the same thing and they eyed each other nervously before deciding the alley was big enough for both of them. Rena had never had any doubts, but it was obvious that at first the dog had. He was as drenched and bedraggled as Rena, but unlike her he hadn't filled up on tea, cookies, or anything much for some time. The pitiful sight of him tugged at her heart even when he growled halfheartedly.

Rena glanced around and wondered if she could stay there until the rain passed. It fell literally in sheets that were fascinating even to someone raised in the moist environs of the Pacific Northwest.

The street outside was a mess and a mini-river washed down the opposite side. It certainly wasn't encouraging for a foray back into the storm. As she stepped back a little farther into the alley her shoes squished uncomfortably.

Rena glanced once more into the depths of the alley. Was it her imagination or had the mangy dog moved closer? There was nothing menacing about him now as he shivered and looked up at her with soulful eyes. Rena remembered sticking two of the seemingly endless supply of almond cookies into her bag. They still lay on top, wrapped securely in a Kleenex.

Breaking off a small piece, she offered it to the dog. He cautiously sniffed her hand and then the cookie and then daintily helped himself. Before long, both of the cookies rested in his not-so-hollow stomach. He'd definitely decided Rena was a friend and now rested his wet head against her leg. She was so wet and muddy that the essence of the woebegone dog didn't really matter and she patted him on the head. She just hoped he didn't have any wild ideas about adoption.

The sky was darkening and the rain continued. Rena was cold, still very wet, and knew she couldn't hang around her dry alley much longer unless she planned to spend the night there—which she didn't.

Looking down at the dog, she gave him an apologetic look. "Well, pooch, this is where we part company. This alley might make a good place for you to spend the night, but I've got to be moving on before it gets too dark."

He wagged his stub of a tail and looked hopefully up at her.

Rena tried to still the tug on her heartstrings, slung her tote bag onto her aching shoulder, and stepped out once more into the rain. It hit her with such force it almost knocked her off her feet. She stepped back quickly into the dubious comfort of the alley.

Rena wouldn't pretend she wasn't a little uneasy, but she wasn't exactly alone and glanced down at her new friend who had now decided to sit on her foot. Perhaps to keep her from wandering off?

"If we're going to spend the night together I guess we should introduce ourselves. I'm Rena and I think I'll call you Cookie."

The dog again wagged his tail, whether in approval of his new name or in hopes Rena had some more food.

Rena leaned against the rough side of the building and closed her eyes. She was so tired!

She actually dozed off as she leaned wearily against the building and awoke with a start when she heard the dog growl low in his throat and saw him move to take a stance between her and the opening to the alley. A large figure blocked the entrance, making it darker than it really was. Rena's heartbeat accelerated and she clutched her bag wondering if she could use it as a weapon. It was heavy, but was it heavy enough?

"Rena, is that you?" He ducked into the alley, flicked his lighter, and she saw it was Randy Fletcher. His sudden appearance might be welcome but it was also highly suspicious.

How could he have found her if he hadn't been looking? In order to find her he would have to have a pretty good idea where she was. Why then would he ignore her until now?

"What are you doing here?"

"Never mind, let's get you somewhere warm and dry."

"I'd follow anyone who promised me that."

"How did you get this far off the beaten track?"

Her lie was glibly easy. "I was sight-seeing."

"You'll have something to talk about when you get home."

"It's an experience I could have done without. Not only am I wet, but lost."

"There's a hotel not far away; take my arm and we'll be off."

Rena hesitated. "You mean you're not going to take me back to my hotel?"

"Too far, and I haven't seen a taxi in hours. I'm afraid the old adage any port in a storm is going to have to do for tonight."

Randy hardly gave her a chance to refuse as he practically dragged her down the muddy street. Once her shoe stuck in some mud and she walked out of it, but when she hollered at Randy to wait he only shook his head. A hotel wasn't far away and she was grateful when they turned into its un-locked door. Perhaps it had stayed open with the hope of luring rain-soaked tourists into its doubtful interior. Rena knew she would have passed it by if she'd been alone. But then a more reputable place would no doubt have chased away the adoring dog that had followed her and even stopped to retrieve her shoe.

Rena accepted it, slipped it on, and followed Randy to the desk. He asked for one room and she didn't protest since it looked like the kind of place where even a chair under the doorknob might not suffice. "Do you think Cookie can come up with us?"

Randy looked in disgust at the soaked animal sitting adoringly at her side. "Why don't we just kick him back outside? He reeks!"

Rena blinked in surprise and stepped protectively closer to her furry friend. "How can you even suggest that?"

"Easy, take a good look at him. Where did you pick him up anyway?"

Rena bristled. After all the dog had rushed to her defense when he hadn't known Randy was a friend—of sorts. And Rena admitted to herself that she used the word friend loosely. She deliberately gave a haughty lift to her chin when she responded. "We shared an alley."

"He can go back there as far as I'm concerned."

"I can't turn him out in this weather. He thinks he's found a friend."

"So, people lose faith in their friends all the time. It's hardly been a long-standing acquaintance, Rena."

She was very tempted to book her own room and take the poor mongrel with her. But she was still dubious about staying alone in a place where the only other two people in the lobby were men who eyed her as if she might be a commodity for sale. "Randy, please, he can't take up much room."

"He'll take up a lot of air space and who knows what 'friends' he's harboring. The answer is no—unless you care to book your own room."

He knew she didn't. With a heavy heart, she looked down at the little dog waiting so patiently beside her and hated herself for what she had to say. "Sorry."

She saw his ears droop and made up her mind to hit the streets with him again when the desk clerk—a classy name for the rheumy-eyed individual waiting on them—spoke. "He can sleep down here and I'll give him some scraps from my dinner."

Suddenly, the place was a four-star hostelry as far as Rena was concerned. "Thanks, I'll pay for his food."

"Don't bother. He might as well have them in here as dig them out of the garbage cans out back."

But Rena was nonetheless grateful.

The elevator wore a faded OUT OF ORDER sign, so they took the ominously creaking stairs. Randy led the way and Rena clutched her bag, careful not to bump the grimy walls.

"Randy, don't you think we could do a little better than this place?"

"You're welcome to try if you want. Frankly, all I care about is staying dry."

Rena did not want to return to the torrential rains that pounded the streets and filled the gutters to overflowing. Even if she managed to find someplace better, there was the very real possibility they wouldn't accept Cookie. Rena had discovered her distrust of Randy and her aversion to their temporary quarters was nowhere as great as her aversion to abandoning the dog who thought he'd found a friend. However she almost changed her mind when Randy unlocked the door and it swung wide.

Cracked and water-stained shades were pulled down over the windows, and only a dim bulb hung from the ceiling. There was a battered bureau against one wall, a sagging bed against another. The mattress was stained, but surprisingly clean-looking bedding was neatly folded and waiting.

"Some place, huh?"

Rena stifled a laugh as she realized that no matter how ludicrous it might seem, she was spending the night in a place that could have starred in the old movies she loved to watch. It managed to take the edge off her mood, although it didn't help her to ignore the obvious fact there was only one bed in the room.

She scanned the room and saw an overstuffed chair. "I'll take the chair if you'd like."

"I think you know what I'd like, Rena."

Her hackles rose. "And I think you know your chances of getting it. This sleazy excuse for a room doesn't entitle you to any privileges. Not even those of suggestion."

He approached and she stepped back until she was against the wall. "But I think the advantages are all with me. I don't believe anyone around here is likely to care what you want."

"Somehow I didn't think you were the kind of man who needed an edge —at least not that kind." She would not let him see how uneasy she'd become. And she hoped he'd see her statement for the backhanded compliment it was, without seeing it as an invitation for anything more.

"No, you're right." And he turned away. Ignoring her for a moment, he sauntered over to one of the windows and lifted the shade. "It's still raining."

Rena went over to the other window and looked out. The neon sign across the way illuminated the rain that still fell. It seemed to have let up a little, but she couldn't be sure. Regardless of the weather, she was marooned until daylight. She was not going to wander the streets after dark.

Randy turned away from the window and Rena was surprised to read exhaustion in his features. Perhaps she wasn't the only one events were taking a toll on.

"Take the bed, I don't care. Just spare me a blanket for that chair. It's probably got more varmints than that dog you've picked up."

Grateful he wasn't going to push the advantage they both knew he had, Rena spared a sheet and a pillow. Those available allowed them one of each and the room was warm enough. However, there was no bathroom and she had to wash the mud off. She was not going to bed in this grimy condition if she could help it.

"Where do you suppose the facilities are?"

"Probably down at the end of the hall. Aren't they always?" He was already lounging in the chair, his feet up on the edge of the bed.

"Do you suppose it's safe?"

"I suppose that depends on how badly you want to use it."

She deliberately chose to ignore his surliness and gathered up her tote bag, grateful she always carried some toiletries and a change of clothes in it. "If I don't return, send out a search party."

"Sorry, but I limit myself to one rescue per evening." And he closed his eyes.

Rena narrowed hers, clenched her fist, and stomped out of the room. Why had he bothered to rescue her if he was only going to be rude?

The bathroom was better than she'd expected. Deciding to brave a quick shower, she turned the water on and watched it trickle out. It wasn't much, but it would at least get rid of the mud. Quickly, she lathered herself and then waited for the halfhearted stream of water to rinse her off.

It was only as she stepped from the shower that she remembered she didn't have a towel. And the bathroom certainly didn't have any. She kept an extremely old pair of jeans and a top in her bag for emergencies or for when her luggage went astray. She'd wear them and towel off with her others. A container of talc had spilled on them, so she smelled mightily of honeysuckle.

The hall was still empty as she hurried back to their room, and then she had a few anxious moments when the door stuck. For a moment she thought Randy had locked her out, but finally the knob turned. He appeared to be asleep.

The mattress springs creaked as Rena reached over to switch out the light and then tried to get comfortable around all the lumps that poked up in the most uncomfortable places. It was impossible. Her last thought before an abrupt rattling of their doorknob was for the dog she'd left below.

Rena lay absolutely still and held her breath, all the while willing whoever was on the other side of the door to go away. She certainly wasn't going to respond and Randy showed no signs of stirring. Or did he? She felt the weight of his feet shift where they were propped on her bed. Then she heard them hit the floor and him mutter unpleasantly. Well, she didn't blame him. She certainly wasn't overjoyed about being disturbed at this hour. Not to mention being decidedly uneasy.

But she became a lot more uneasy when she recognized the voice at the door. Mitch! How had he located her?

Randy got up and opened the door.

"Johns, what the hell are you doing here?" Randy had been asleep and his voice showed it, slurred with the first moments of wakefulness, but nonetheless angry.

"Looking for someone who belongs to me." Mitch's voice was in control and silky smooth with authority.

Rena's senses stirred at Mitch's words. How would it really feel to belong to him?

"Then you've come to the wrong place." And Randy yawned audibly.

"I don't think so." Mitch hit the light switch, flooding all but the corners of the room with dim light. "You're not alone."

Rena blanched at the taut anger in his voice and hoped he wouldn't direct it at her.

"Do the rules of the game say I have to be?" Randy's insolent tone was not calculated to make Mitch back off.

"Pick up anybody you want, as long as it's not my girl."

Rena was filled with an apprehensive thrill she could barely suppress at the proprietary note in Mitch's voice.

"If she's your girl, then why is she spending the night with me?"

Rena could almost see Randy as he spoke, insolently leaning in the doorway and only letting Mitch so far into the room. She wondered if Mitch would ignore the tone of suggestion in Randy's voice. It would have been impossible to miss.

Then she heard someone hit the floor and could be still no longer. She jumped from the bed and saw Randy sprawled on the worn linoleum. Mitch's unsmiling gaze met hers. "Rena, I would never have guessed you capable of such thoughtless behavior. Do you realize the hell you've put me through?"

"Mitch, I can explain—truly."

"Save it, Rena. I'm afraid I'm not in a very understanding mood." Randy groaned from the floor. "Come on, before I'm tempted to hit him again."

Rena decided not to argue, grabbed her bag, and edged past Mitch into the hallway.

Mitch followed, clamping a tight hold on her upper arm. "How could you spend the night with him? And in a place like this?"

Rena knew she had to defend herself. "Mitch, it was only a place to stay out of the rain. Nothing more. Please believe me."

"I want to, Rena. I really do. But the evidence to the contrary is rather damning."

"Things *aren't* always what they seem."

"So you're always telling me."

"Mitch, please don't be like this."

He stopped then, rounding on her with blazing anger. "Why shouldn't I be? I raised no objections to your using my money to pursue Fletcher. But I did ask you to let me in on things—and not to try and deal with him on your own."

Rena had no defense. "I know I shouldn't have, but I didn't think we'd get anything out of him if we pursued him as a team."

"How much did you get out of him in that room?"

He was desperately hurt and making no attempt to hide it. Rena would not lie or pretend imaginary success. "Nothing; I was too busy keeping him on his side of the room."

"I want to believe that, Rena. You don't know how much."

The lobby was empty except for the desk clerk, and sleeping under a chair, her friend the dog. He perked up as soon as she descended the stairs and came wagging his tail toward her.

Mitch stopped and looked down. "Don't tell me you've acquired that animal?"

"We got acquainted today—when we ducked into the same alley to get out of the rain."

"You're damned lucky that's all you found in the alley."

"Well, I didn't look for anything else."

"Why did you bring him along?"

"I didn't, you just followed—didn't you, Cookie?" Her answer was a thorough licking.

"Cookie?"

"He likes almond cookies, don't you?"

"Obviously he's a stray."

She looked up at Mitch. "But still in need of love."

Mitch regarded the two of them and Rena imagined she saw a slight thawing of his mood.

"I suppose you want to bring him back with us?"

"Yes." Not a *do you mind* or *is it all right?* She was not about to leave her pet.

"Okay, but if he's going to share our hotel room he's going to have a bath. Come on, I've a taxi waiting."

"You mean a meter's been ticking the whole while you've been in here?"

"And during the five minutes it took me to convince the manager to tell me where you were."

"You could take it out of my wages."

"You're damned lucky I don't take it out of your hide!"

"You wouldn't do that—would you?"

"As much as I would like to, no. Decking Fletcher satisfied my baser instincts."

He hustled her into a comfortable taxi and even helped Cookie when he was unsure if he was meant to follow. The taxi sped off through the rainy night and Rena clutched the door handle as they rounded corners.

It wasn't long before they were driving through a familiar section of the city. "I wasn't all that far away from the hotel after all. If I had known that I would have braved the weather a bit longer. Randy led me to believe I wasn't close."

"And what else would you have expected, Rena? He couldn't very well influence you if you were snug and safe where you belonged. He took you to that dump because he knew your defenses would be down there."

"You may be right. But he didn't even try anything." She could gloss over his threats now that she was away from him.

"He would have."

Now that Rena thought about it, it seemed very strange Randy hadn't even asked about the butterfly. Maybe he'd thought she had it with her. Maybe he would have searched her bag when he knew she was asleep.

"How did you end up where you were?"

"I told you in my note I was going in search of Randy."

"Yes, but I expected you to return by nightfall. Do you have any idea how worried I've been? I've been to the police, the consulate, and I've bribed more hotel clerks than I care to even think about. Only to find out they could tell me nothing." He looked away to stare out the window into the rain-slick night. "Then when I do find you and discover you're with Fletcher . . ."

He left his sentence unfinished, but Rena had no trouble understanding what he couldn't say. "I don't think Cookie likes him either."

Mitch looked down and flicked the mongrel's ear. A gesture that won him an adoring glance. "Why?"

"Well, when he and I were sharing the alley, he growled at Randy when he showed up."

"Oh, he did, did he?" Mitch took a long hard look at the animal. "Nothing wrong with you that a bath and a few regular meals won't cure."

Rena had to turn away to keep her smile from being seen. Then a thought disturbed her. "Do you think I'm taking him away from his home?"

Mitch ran a knowing hand over the dog's sides. "I don't think so. Anyway, if you have, they deserve it. This fella hasn't been eating on a regular basis."

"And yet he's a well-mannered diner, aren't you? Mitch, I want to keep him."

"I think you'll have to settle for finding him a good home."

"Why?"

"Because we're going to be in and out of too many countries with too many different animal quarantine laws."

"But I don't know anyone."

"I do, so I'm sure I can find him a good home." Then he added in a gentler tone, "It just isn't feasible for you to keep him."

They stopped outside the hotel and Mitch turned the dog over to a bellhop, asking that he be cleaned, groomed, and seen by a veterinarian. Rena bid Cookie farewell and followed hurriedly in Mitch's wake.

"Little nicer than what you left, isn't it?" The door clicked decisively behind him.

"I'd be a fool to deny it."

Tension and intimacy charged the atmosphere. Rena felt it swirl around her, taking command, shattering her defenses. She was helpless to define how she knew and just as helpless to stop it. Yet she tried.

"I appreciate your rescuing me, Mitch. But I haven't had any sleep, I've walked miles today, and I'd love a hot shower."

"Am I stopping you?"

She blushed. "No, I—I didn't mean to imply you were." Quickly, she grabbed up a gown and ran for the bathroom. There she took another shower, scrubbing her skin almost ruthlessly with the rose-scented soap provided by the hotel. If she took long enough, surely Mitch would have retired, postponing the inevitable confrontation until morning.

Rena smoothed body lotion over her skin and then slipped the lace and satin nightgown over her head. It slithered the length of her, coming to rest just above her toes.

Her tired eyes looked back at her from the mirror as she brushed the sleek length of her ebony hair. It was in stark contrast to her snowy gown as it tumbled over her shoulders and down her back. Rena switched off the light and stepped back into her room. She hoped Cookie was feeling as scrubbed and sleepy.

The darkness was broken only by the bedside lamp so at first Rena thought she was alone. Then a sound from the corner of the room alerted her. She spun around, sending her long hair swinging away from her like a fan. Her hand went to her throat as she realized Mitch occupied one of the wingback chairs in the corner. "You startled me."

"I thought you knew I'd be waiting."

"Mitch, I'm so tired."

"So am I, Rena. Tired of wondering where you are and if you're safe."

Rena moved away from the light. "I'm truly sorry . . ."

"Are you sorry enough to drop the facade you're hiding behind?" His gaze feasted on the curves accentuated by clinging satin and lace.

He rose from his chair and now stood much closer. Lamplight darkened the gold of his hair and cast shadows along the angles of his face. His blue eyes were navy pools of desire as he bent his head to brush her lips with fire.

Rena tried to resist molding herself against him just as she tried to resist arching her neck so it would be easier for him to kiss.

"The thought of Fletcher touching you has been eating away at me ever since I found you. You are not available to him, Rena, or to any other man. It's time you realized that."

A kiss placed near the hollow of her throat stopped any protest. She had always known she wanted him—desired him. But the abandon of that need now shocked her with its intensity. She had no will to resist even as she fought for control of the moment.

"How did you find me, Mitch?"

"That doesn't matter—now."

Rena featherd her fingers against his ear. "Yes, it does."

Mitch groaned into the cloud of her hair. "I don't see what difference it makes. But I have someone following Fletcher."

"You have, why?"

"You believe he's linked to the LaSalle jewels so I ordered someone on him all the time. They report in every evening and tonight when they finally got ahold of me they told me Fletcher wasn't alone."

"I'm sorry." Her breathy apology stirred the hair at his temples just as his kiss on her shoulder stirred her senses. "But I didn't want to spend the night in an alley."

"But why a dive like that, Rena?"

"Randy said there was no place else around. And I certainly hadn't seen any."

"There was quite a reputable hotel around the corner and up the street."

"Well, maybe Randy didn't know that." But Rena wondered if perhaps Fletcher had deliberately picked the place he had because he knew she was unlikely to insist on her own room in a seedy hotel. Had he known someone was following him? Had he deliberately set up the situation he had in order to discredit her with Mitch?

Mitch dipped his head to place a lingering kiss against the fullness of her breast. Rena gasped and barely heard his next question.

"Did you tell him about the butterfly?"

"No, and he didn't ask."

"Don't you find that a bit strange?" Rena's defenses were down. She could no more lie than she could resist.

"He didn't even mention the treasure hunt or how he found me in the alley."

"It takes very little imagination to suspect he's following you. Leave him to me, Rena. I'm a little more able to play in his league."

Rena bristled. "I can take care of myself."

"Not nearly as well as I can." And his seeking lips sought to prove his point.

Rena's fingers entwined behind his neck. How could either of them turn back from the sweet expectancy of the moment? After years of rigid self-control, she was giving in to her fantasies.

Mitch buried his face in her long hair while cupping her chin in his hands.

"You smell of flowers and sweetness and desire. I will not spend another nightmarish night like this last one worrying and wondering." Drawing away he looked down at her, a fire burning in the depths of his sapphire eyes. He memorized her with his gaze and tasted all there was to see with his lips. "You will be mine, Rena. One way or another, you will be mine."

The sheets felt like cool silk against her skin and Mitch lay on the tangled length of her hair. Their bodies touched each other with fire. Somewhere in the shadows her common sense lingered, but it was far more elusive than the truth that she had waited all her life for this one man. Tonight he would possess a part of her and she a part of him that no one else would ever touch. At the moment they met on the equal ground of their mutual desire. Not even his money could affect that. Not even her doubts could stop it.

Mitch murmured lovingly against the sensitive curve of her neck.

"I will not have Fletcher looking like he owns the woman always meant to be mine!"

CHAPTER 8

Rena snuggled down inside Mitch's blue-and-white-striped bathrobe and leaned her elbows on the parapet of their hotel room balcony. A playful breeze blew her hair across her face and she impatiently tucked it inside the collar of the robe.

She sensed Mitch's presence even before he draped his arm around her shoulders. His touch still felt good, still excited her—if anything the early morning hours had only intensified that. Memories of their time together were swift and all-consuming and Rena had only to shut her eyes to be enveloped in the passion that had broken down the restraint of years. She'd been helpless, absolutely helpless to do anything but respond.

"Any regrets?" His breath was warm against her ear.

"What a foolish question."

"Meaning?"

"Meaning that of course I have regrets."

His arm slipped from around her shoulders and she turned, one elbow still on the parapet, to find him frowning. "Do you wish it had never happened?"

Her voice was small, yet echoed her inner turmoil. "I'd be a liar if I said that."

"Then what's the problem?"

"How are we ever going to reconcile last night with our business relationship?"

"Do we have to?"

"It can't help but change things."

"Why? Doesn't it simply bring into the open feelings we've both had for a very long time?"

"It complicates things."

"I disagree and I won't apologize, Rena."

"I don't expect or want you to."

He reached out to her. "I couldn't stand the thought of Fletcher touching you—and more."

"You don't have to worry about that."

"I know that—now."

"Well," and her breath scraped the ragged edge of her emotions. "What do we do now?"

"Continue with our greatly enriched lives. I want to thank you for the butterfly. It's exquisite."

How could he behave so normally when she knew she'd never feel the same? "And the clue? Have you figured it out?"

"I haven't even bothered to open it. It's in the safe with the butterfly."

"How could you not look at it?"

"Rena, your note left me far more worried about you than what Dressler's second clue might say."

"I can take care of myself."

"I wish I could believe that. You don't know the hell I went through when you walked away from Pacific Imports and into the unknown."

Rena managed a laugh. "You make it sound like I booked passage on a UFO or set off for the North Pole."

"How did I know you hadn't? Would a postcard now and then have been too much trouble?"

"The break was hard for me to make, Mitch. It just seemed easier to make it complete. I'm sorry if you worried."

"That's a very mild word to describe how I felt."

"I'm sorry, but you survived and so did I."

"I'm not so sure I would have if I hadn't done something about it."

"What do you mean?"

"After six months of worrying and wondering, I had your whereabouts traced by a detective agency I employ. Then I had them keep track of you for me."

"You had me followed? How third-rate and despicable! I can't believe you did that." She clenched her fists in anger. "You had no right!"

"Rena, no one ever seemed to know your whereabouts. I couldn't live with not knowing where you were or if you were all right."

Rena glared at him, fighting to bring her temper under control. "You keep telling me your money makes no difference in our relationship, that it's not a basis for inequality. But I couldn't afford to have *you* followed. Your money makes all the difference in the world, Mitch. We don't even think alike because of it."

"I think you're misinterpreting my actions."

"*I'm* misinterpreting them? Is that just an excuse because you can't defend them?"

"I don't feel I should have to. I did what I did because I care."

"All the times I was feeling wonderfully free, someone was watching me."

"It's not like he hid in your closet or under your bed."

"I don't care. It's downright creepy to know that when I thought I was alone I wasn't. I'll never understand what made you think you had the right to do such a thing."

"How many times do I have to repeat it's because I care about you?" I'd asked you to write and you didn't. I'd asked you to call and you didn't. Neither Shay nor your father ever seemed to know where you were."

"I didn't get in touch with you, Mitch, because I was trying to break away, to be my own person. I had to see if I could manage on my own or if I was merely an extension of Pacific Imports. And I had asked my family not to tell anyone where I was."

"But you were always going into dangerous parts of the world—alone."

"Women do travel by themselves. It is the nineteen-eighties."

"I know they do, but that was no consolation when I lay awake at night wondering where you were and if you were all right. Rena, don't you know what a prize you'd make?"

"Good grief, I think you highly overestimate my value and certainly misjudge me if you think I could live knowing I was under constant surveillance."

"But you didn't know, not until I told you." Real regret edged his voice. "Confession is supposed to be good for the soul, but I can see in this case it has only made things worse. A gesture that indicated to me how much I care was interpreted by you as interference and invasion of your privacy."

"I want to be my own person, Mitch. To rise and fall on my own merits."

"I certainly wouldn't interfere with that."

"Yes, you would. By simply becoming involved with you I would forfeit the right to be me. I would be simply an extension of a very wealthy man. Oh, yes, Rena Drake—she's Mitchell Johns' latest interest."

"Not just latest interest, Rena, but one of very long standing." His heart was in his words and his eyes.

"I've been on my own too long. I can't have someone tell me what to do and where to go."

"Even when it's for your own good?"

His voice was softly teasing. Rena wasn't when she answered. "Yes."

There was an alarming stillness surrounding them. If Rena had wanted distance between them, she had it. The rapturous night just finished might not have happened. Victory was hers, but it was not sweet.

If asked, Rena could not have said what she did with her day.

She mourned the night that shouldn't have been and yet was the most perfectly beautiful moment she'd ever experienced. How she loved Mitch. But she was afraid what that love might do to them. Giving in to it had destroyed their friendship, and now things would never be the same.

She wandered the whole day, pausing only for tea when her aching feet demanded a little consideration. Every place she stopped served almond cookies which constantly reminded her of Cookie. She felt guilty for not having checked on him before fleeing the hotel. But she knew Mitch would take care of the dog no matter how angry or disappointed he was with her.

And so she prowled the streets until after dark. Not a sound came from Mitch's room as she let herself into her half of the suite. Rena discarded her clothes, climbed into the big bed, hugged the pillow he had used, and silently cried herself to sleep.

Deep into the night she awoke. Something had broken her slumber.

The window onto the balcony was open and the curtain fluttered inward. Perhaps some sound from the street below had disturbed her. It was hard to say why, but instinct made her hold her breath. Accustomed to the darkness, Rena probed the room with her gaze. Only when her gaze flew back to the window did she notice anything out of the ordinary. A shadow moved on the balcony.

She lay as quietly as she could and watched the dark figure prowl around the room. The safest thing seemed to be to let him think she was asleep. Or so she'd once read.

He was definitely looking for something. Could whoever it was know about the butterfly and be searching for it? Well, he'd be disappointed, for it was in the hotel safe. Then her heart seemed to skip a beat. Was it in the safe, or had Mitch removed it?

The intruder continued searching, apparently oblivious to the fact Rena was watching. He was thorough, careful, and very, very quiet.

Mitch's briefcase was on the table and the burglar was going through it. Then he pocketed something and turned in her direction. Quickly, she closed her eyes and held her breath.

Seconds seemed hours before she dared open her eyes and expel her breath. The room was empty.

Reaching over, she switched on the bedside lamp and scooted from bed. Quickly, she closed the doors to the balcony and fastened the flimsy lock. If he was still out there he wasn't going to get back in without a little trouble. Then she went to the connecting doors and turned the knob.

The light from her room spilled over into Mitch's. He slept as if he had no cares. Rena ached to caress him.

"Mitch! Mitch, wake up!"

He mumbled and turned over, taking the sheet with him. Rena looked away out of self-preservation. Why did he have to be so physically magnificent?

"Mitch, wake up."

"What's wrong?" He looked at her somewhat foggily and ran a hand through tousled blond hair Rena longed to smooth.

"There's been a prowler in my room."

Instantly, the fog of sleep was gone and he swung his legs over the side of the bed. "Are you sure?"

Rena nodded.

"Why didn't you call out?"

"I didn't know if you were here or not. And I was afraid of what he would do if he knew I was awake."

"You're probably right. Damn, I don't see how he could have gotten up here."

"Down from the roof maybe. They seem to do that a lot in mysteries."

"It's eight stories either way. Did he take anything?"

"He removed something from your briefcase."

"What?" It was an abrupt question.

"I don't know. As soon as he left I came to get you."

"Hand me those pants, will you?"

Rena gathered up a pair of worn jeans and then turned around as he slipped into them. When she did look, it was only to discover they hugged him as tightly as she had only the night before. "I haven't seen those before."

"I spent some time with your four-legged friend today."

"How is he?"

"A little classier-looking than he was. I'm surprised you didn't stop in to see him."

"I had other things on my mind and I knew you'd take care of him."

"It's nice to be able to count on me when it's convenient—isn't it?"

"I've always counted on you."

"To keep my distance, but every time I get a little close you run away."

"I just wanted some time to think."

"If you want my opinion, Rena, you spend entirely too much time thinking."

Mitch hurried into her room, dumped the contents of his briefcase onto the table, and sorted through them. When he returned his attention to her it was with an expression of bleak anger in his blue eyes.

Apprehension gnawed at Rena. "What did he take?"

"The clue."

"Oh, no!"

"Oh, yes. I'd taken it from the safe earlier today."

"Can you remember what it said?"

"Can I remember it? No, because I hadn't even read it."

"You mean you have no idea what was on it?" Rena couldn't believe what she was hearing.

"That's right. It was still sealed. I was waiting for you to return."

Rena sank down on the nearest chair. "Oh, Mitch, this is terrible."

"You're telling me."

"Can you call Dressler or whoever's in charge?"

"I can try, but I doubt it will change anything."

"Who could have done this? Who could possibly know we had the clue?"

"A lot of people. I imagine word's leaked out by now. But I've a mind to suspect Fletcher. He's the only one I know of who might have the expertise for the job."

"Do you think it could have been a random burglary?"

"When the only thing they happened to take was the clue to the second treasure? Come on, Rena, you surely don't think that?"

Rena hugged herself, suddenly chilled. "Well, I guess it doesn't matter who has it. Not only have we lost our edge, we don't even have any idea where to go. This is all my fault."

"Don't be absurd. You're no more to blame than I am. Let me see what I can accomplish via the telephone, although people probably aren't going to like being disturbed at this hour."

Rena paced the floor while he made several calls, waiting each time what seemed an eternity for someone to answer.

"Would you go in and use your phone to call room service? I could use some coffee. I'm not about to go back to sleep now."

Rena did as bidden, glad to be of some use. Then she perched on the edge of a chair and waited for Mitch. "Well?"

"No luck. We'll have to attend the gathering tonight when everyone receives the second clue."

Rena turned away, unable to hide her disappointment. "I wanted to find the second treasure."

"There are only three prizes, Rena, and only three possible winners. I feel fortunate to have won one of the treasures."

"I'm sorry that the prize I found wasn't one of the more spectacular ones."

"All right, I admit the jade butterfly was not one of my favorites, but you liked it—and it's valuable. So we're ahead in the game."

A discreet knock at the door interrupted.

"That must be the coffee."

"I'll get it."

He caught her wrist. "Not dressed or undressed like that, you won't."

Rena glanced down at the filmy nightgown that was all she wore. "I forgot I wasn't dressed."

The coffee was hot, rich, and plentiful. As she sipped the strong brew Rena felt her courage returning.

After they finished their coffee, Mitch left to check on the jade and Rena began sorting through her clothes. She was weary of wearing the same things. Maybe today would be a good time to go shopping since they could do nothing more about searching for the treasure until after the dinner party that evening.

After showering Rena discovered she'd forgotten her body lotion and without thinking walked into the bedroom in search of it. The air in there was cool after the steamy warmth of the bathroom.

Taking her time, Rena smoothed luxuriously scented body satin over her legs and arms. Tucking the lotion neatly back into its allotted place in her bag, she yawned, stretched, and reached for her clothes, but she wasn't quite quick enough.

The door between their rooms swung open and Mitch came in, only to stop in mid-sentence and mid-stride. Quite naturally, she had turned at the noise he'd made and now flushed at the stare of frank appreciation.

He fumbled with an apology. "I should have knocked, I'm sorry."

Rena dressed quickly. "That's okay. I should have taken what I needed with me into the bathroom. I didn't expect you back so soon."

He watched her as she buttoned a floral-patterned blouse. "You'll be happy to know the butterfly is still safe in the safe."

"What about Randy? I assume you're still having him followed."

"The man detailed to watch him reports he left the hotel where I found the two of you this morning and returned to more elaborate quarters."

"Did he see Randy go out last night?"

"No, but you must remember he watched the front entrance. When I queried him about any other possible exits, he said there was over the rooftops and out the back. He naturally hadn't thought to keep an eye on that and I hadn't thought to suggest it."

"But Randy is still in town?"

"Up until a few minutes ago he was."

"Why do you suppose he hasn't left?"

"Maybe he isn't the one who took the clue, or maybe he feels it will look less obvious if he hangs around for tonight. You must remember he doesn't want to draw attention to himself."

"Then why go to the trouble to steal our clue?"

"Not leaving doesn't mean he can't solve it. He could have a flight booked, be packed, and out of here after a token appearance at tonight's gathering."

Rena began to apply her makeup as he watched. His constant scrutiny made her nervous. "I'm not likely to vanish into thin air if you look the other way."

"Does that promise come with a guarantee—even if Fletcher takes off in a different direction?"

"I agreed to stick this out to the end, even if I lose the chance to clear my father's name. I just wish you understood."

"Who says I don't?"

"You couldn't possibly. The fiasco of the LaSalle diamonds ruined my father's career! We were left with virtually nothing. If you'd ever been poor you'd know why I want to get back at the person responsible. My father was forced to accept handouts from my mother's estate in order to keep Shay and me in school."

"I can understand why you don't relish an inequality in wealth between two people. But why shouldn't your mother have helped financially? She had it and you were her kids as much as his. What was she doing to raise you? Very little from what you've told me. I'm sure the money she sent your father salved her conscience quite nicely."

"You have no idea what it's like to be hard up financially."

"And you have no idea what I know about and what I don't. You give far more virtue to the condition of being poor than it warrants. It's a state very few people strive for. Besides, Rena, it isn't like you to judge a person on what they have or don't have." Neither his words nor his glare would let her escape.

"I don't care what a person has or doesn't have."

"You seem to care very much as far as I'm concerned."

"Mitch, you're making my head ache. Besides, as far as money goes, you would have had to be in need of money to understand. It's that simple. Being able to empathize is not enough."

"Then consider my grasp of the subject that of an expert."

"What do you mean?"

"Because I live well now, because I have money to indulge most of my whims, and because you and everyone else assume I inherited this vast fortune and thriving company, you think I have no comprehension of the other side of the coin. Well, rest assured, I damned near lost more than you ever thought of having. And if I'd gone down so would a lot of other people. So, not only do I know what it's like to be close to bankruptcy, but I also know what it's like to be in danger of sending a lot of other people in the same direction."

"I don't know what you mean."

"When I took a chance on you, Rena, Pacific Imports had been solvent for just two years. I saw something in you that I thought was in tune with something in me. I admired your dedication, your desire to clear your father's name. It reminded me of my desire to clear the name of the company my grandfather had founded and my father had damned near lost."

"I never knew Pacific Imports was in trouble financially."

"Few people did. I was able to keep it quiet, to borrow money, and to get it back on its feet. But only by sitting up nights, pacing the floor, keeping my finger on the pulse of everything happening, and doing a good deal of the work myself."

"What had happened?"

"A classic enough tale. My father liked fast cars and women, and ponies that weren't quite as fast as the cars and women. He left the business to others. His contribution to Pacific Imports was to withdraw huge sums of capital on a regular basis."

"Is this why you've always been somewhat of a man of mystery—keeping your net worth and your women to yourself?" She meant it somewhat jokingly, but Mitch led a pretty circumspect life.

"Maybe I kept my women to myself because once I met an inexperienced, yet bold young gemologist with flashing, dark eyes and a mane of seemingly untamable hair, I never wanted anyone else. I'm not in the least ashamed to admit I've wanted you since we met."

"I can't believe that."

"Why not?"

"Because if you loved me you wouldn't consider marriage to anyone else."

"Talk about words coming back to haunt me! I was only hoping to jar you into realizing we couldn't go on ignoring how we felt about each other."

"Then who is Carmen?"

"Carmen?"

"I heard you talking to her on the telephone when we were on Kauai."

"You heard a phone call to my private secretary."

"But her name is Terri."

"Terri left to get married about six months after you resigned."

"Oh." Then she sought to defend herself. "You certainly sounded—close."

"Because we're good friends. Carmen is very practical, efficient, and also forty-five and happily married." He grinned at her, knowing he'd scored a point. "Now how about easing my curiosity a bit."

"I'll try."

"What did I really see on the beach that night?"

"I had no idea Randy was even around. He came up behind me and I thought he was you."

"You mean all I ever had to do was take you in my arms and all the barriers would have been down? Rena, why in the world did you keep your feelings from me? It doesn't make sense and think of the time we've wasted."

"Because I really don't think it could work."

"What happens if I try to prove you wrong?"

"Mitch, don't—"

"Don't what? Love you as we both want and need?" And he slipped a row of buttons free.

"Don't . . ." and her breath caught on a gasp as he cupped the fullness of her breast. "Don't do that." But her actions belied her words as she leaned against him. She'd always known that once they crossed the boundary of friendship she'd never be able to turn back. She'd loved him too long, too hard, and too completely.

Like her parents, like Shay and Bryan, she could not withstand the irresistible force pulling her toward Mitch. Once having fled, resistance no longer had any place between them.

"Mitch, why are you doing this to me?"

"Because, my dear, I want to make certain you never forget me."

Mitch slept through the warm afternoon. Rena pulled a light blanket around her and walked to the window. The hot air coming in from outside was burdened with the incense of sweet flowers—orange jessamine and frangipani. Rena filled her lungs with its floral sweetness, just as she'd filled her heart with the sweetness of loving Mitch. Ill-fated it might be, but it could not be denied. She would seize the moment as her parents had, as Shay and Bryan had. Like them, she would pay the consequences later.

CHAPTER 9

Rena dressed quickly, left Mitch a note telling him she'd gone shopping, and barely caught the elevator before the door closed. A young woman at the desk informed her to try The Landmark for shopping. She was halfway to the entrance of the hotel before she decided to check on Cookie. The small dog was ecstatic to see her. Each wag of his tail and lick of his tongue more firmly entrenched him in her heart. Yet she knew she couldn't keep him.

A taxi deposited Rena at the five-story mall she'd been directed to and she had to admit it was something with its dramatic fountains and glittering array of designer shops.

As she browsed, Rena thought about what Mitch had told her. She would never have guessed that Pacific Imports once faced bankruptcy. Mitch had covered up well and gone on to create an empire he could be proud of. No wonder he'd always gotten a somewhat sardonic expression on his face whenever people mentioned his inherited wealth.

Rena still couldn't quite believe that all the years she was loving him, he was loving her. It was almost like a fairy tale, except fairy tales had happy endings. Rena wondered if she dared hope.

Rena picked up and discarded a green and gold silk scarf. She'd been in a dozen shops and as yet hadn't seen anything she wanted to buy for that evening. Probably not the fault of the stores, but her wandering thoughts. She decided she'd better begin looking in earnest. As winners of the first prize they'd be the center of attention. So she wanted to look her best.

Finally, in a little shop tucked around a corner, she found what she wanted. The dress was scarlet, slit up the thigh, and covered with gold beads. To go with it she purchased a pair of gold strappy sandals. The dress was simple, but it did great things for her figure and was perfect with her raven hair.

She glanced at her watch and decided she could spare another forty-five minutes for additional shopping. She settled on jeans, a pair of khaki pants, and two cool-looking pastel blouses. Then she caught a taxi and headed back to the hotel, dozing in the backseat while the driver terrorized pedestrians.

When she unlocked the door to their suite, Rena discovered company. "Cookie!" And she knelt to hug him and let him lick her face in warm welcome.

"He's glad to see you—and so am I."

She buried her face in the now sweet-smelling fur of her friend. She hoped her emotions were under control when she released the dog. "You found my note?"

"I did. What did you buy?"

"A few essentials, and then an outfit for tonight. I assumed it was dressy."

"Oh, yes. Dressler is one of those for whom appearances are everything."

"It doesn't hurt to put a good face on things. Besides I like to look nice, and a little elegance never tarnished anyone's life."

"You'll come around yet."

She paused in the middle of unpacking her purchases. "Coming around and fitting in are not quite the same thing. All this glitz and glamour are your world, Mitch, not mine."

He took her by the arms and turned her to face him. His hands were warm against her skin when he brushed her hair back. His words were softly teasing, but his voice was loving. "Then which bright star do you hail from, lovely lady? I could make a fortune importing the likes of you." Warm lips brushed her eyelid.

"Mitch, don't be silly."

"Who's being silly? I'm deadly serious. And I'm not going to let you get away with this different worlds bit."

"It's true. Financially, I'm out of my league with this crowd."

"Well, you have to give them some kind of an edge. After all, you have far more class, style, and beauty than all of them rolled together." This time his lips brushed the tip of her nose.

Rena refused to look deep into his blue eyes. She'd be lost then—hopelessly.

"Just be yourself, Rena. There's no way you can lose then. Just, my dear, like there's no way you can convince me we don't belong together." His lips, warm and insistent, won the battle and she melted against him.

Rena leaned against him for a moment, her defenses down, her objections stilled. This moment of weakness was all she'd permit herself. It was time to gather the forces of self-preservation around her.

"We don't have much time before the party and I want to look my best."

"You always look your best, but never more so than when I'm loving you."

"Don't you think we should tend to business?"

"Is that what you want to do?"

"That's what you hired me for."

He didn't respond and when she looked over at him it was to find him speculatively studying her. "I wonder if I'll ever completely understand you, Rena. I just think I have you figured out and you change on me."

"I thought most men liked a woman to be mysterious."

"Isn't it a little late for that?"

"You don't know everything there is to know about me—yet."

"Perhaps not, but I think I've discovered the key to unlocking most of your secrets."

"I still control the key to my own destiny, Mitch. I am still my own person."

"Are you, Rena? And here I thought you were my woman—my love."

Her heartbeat quickened, her pulse raced. "At the moment I work for you."

"You surely don't think what happened between us was part of your job?"

"What I think is that we'd best get ready."

He came between her and the dress she'd spread out on the bed. "Mitch, please, I want to get ready. The party tonight is reality. What you and I have shared is only part of a beautiful dream."

"Dreams can come true."

"It would never work between us, Mitch. Never! I will not end up with you hating me."

"I could never do that."

"This adventure will end someday, and then we'll be forced to return to the real world."

"What happened between us was real enough. And if it takes me all my life I'll convince you." He strode to the door connecting their rooms and snapped his fingers for Cookie to follow, then tossed casually in her direction, "And remember, I always win."

Rena sank onto the bed and wilted. She cared for him, was committed to him, and yet knew the sensible thing was to pack her suitcase and walk away while they were still friends.

An hour later Rena stood before a full-length mirror. The red dress was striking against her creamy skin and raven-black hair. It sparkled in the light, and she wished she could sparkle in return. She was anxious to be off in pursuit of the second treasure. It would give them both less time to think about being alone together.

She heard Mitch's outside door open and close; an echo of earlier when she'd heard him leave. She waited a moment to see if he would knock on their connecting door and when he didn't she decided to take the initiative. While dressing she'd come up with an idea.

He was standing on the balcony when he answered her knock.

"Mitch, I've been doing some thinking while you were gone."

His gaze traveled the length of her. "I hope those results are as spectacular as the obvious ones."

"Mitch, be serious."

"I am, but before you start let me say I found your friend a home."

"Cookie?"

"How many homeless friends do you have?"

"I was just surprised that it didn't take you long."

"It was expedient, since I expect we'll be out of here sometime tomorrow."

She laughed nervously. "You're certainly confident."

"Don't ever fault the power of positive thinking. Now what is this plan you're so anxious about?"

"You have to promise to hear me out before objecting."

"I'm the epitome of politeness."

"You also like to do things your way."

"I've never been unreasonable. Look how patient I've been with you all these years."

"I think, Mitch, you're dramatizing the situation."

"With you as my leading lady."

He leaned against the frame of the French doors and waited for her to speak. The light of the setting sun set fire to his golden hair while the shadows played games with the light in his eyes, making them twinkle and throwing her off guard. "Well, Rena, I'm waiting. I don't know why you should be so hesitant."

"Because I don't think you're going to like what I'm about to suggest. But I know of no other way to write finish to this business with Fletcher. And as you've told me so many times, I need to get on with my own life."

"Somehow I have the feeling if I agree to that I forfeit my right to object to this plan I'm not going to like."

"Perhaps it would be a good idea to capitalize on Randy's show of interest in me."

"What are you getting at?"

"Well," and she twisted her hands nervously. "We know he's interested in me for one reason or another. If I cultivate this interest, we can not only keep an eye on him, but maybe get a lead on the LaSalle diamonds."

"And how do you propose convincing him of that when you were only too glad to see me the other night?"

"I could tell him you have a terrible temper and I went along with you to avoid a scene."

His eyes snapped blue fire. "You could also tell him you think he's a thief. How often do I have to tell you that I want you to stay clear of him? If he's guilty we'll prove it. But not with you as the bait."

"I think I can handle him."

"If you think that then you're as sheltered as a hothouse plant."

"I can handle myself around Randy, or anyone, quite well, thank you."

"If you believe that then you'll believe anything."

"Do you have any better suggestions? He's certainly not going to take advantage of me."

"How do you know?"

"Because I'm not about to let that happen again."

"What do you mean—again?"

"Can you deny you made very good use of our proximity in this hotel?"

He reacted as if she'd slapped him and Rena knew too late that she'd gone too far.

His eyes flared with anger while the tone of his voice froze her own response. "You could have told me no at any time. Did you really think after all the years we've been together and all we've meant to one another that we could ignore the situation growing between us? A situation that I believe has always existed."

"I thought we were friends—that I could trust you."

"Rena, will you get off that! I haven't wanted to be friends with you in a long time." She started to interrupt and he raised his voice to stop her. "Spare me the boredom of listening to you once again tell me how we can never be anything but friends."

She dropped her gaze in order to give herself strength. "I have to believe it, Mitch. Because I know it would never work between us in the long run." The differences in their lives were simply too great. She recalled without difficulty Shay's tears and pleadings when their father had thought Bryan too old and worldly for her, and the fact their parents had eloped in the face of opposition. They had been carried away by passion and failed. She would not let the same thing happen in her life.

His body seemed to sag and he turned away. "I'm tired of arguing with you. But you're right about one thing. It can never be if you don't want it as I do. Which apparently you don't."

Rena felt hollow inside. "The last thing I've ever wanted was to hurt you."

"Really? I would have thought it was your primary objective. You're wearing a perfume that suggests nights of lingering passion, and a dress that does more than suggest you're the woman every man dreams of but never hopes to possess. And yet you tell me I have to forget you. I'm not a man who can survive on memories."

"Aren't they better than nothing?"

"They don't keep you warm on a cold night. They don't fill you with loving or make you complete. A man needs a real woman, Rena. One he can touch and hold and care for—not a memory that fades like a snapshot."

"Mitch, please, let's not fight. It gets us nowhere and we'll never agree. We shared a beautiful moment and it will become an even more beautiful memory. But there are too many differences we can never bridge." Keep talking, she told herself. Even if you don't convince him, you might convince yourself.

"We could if you weren't afraid to take a chance."

"And risk everything?"

"Why not think of it in terms of gaining everything? I believe we could make it work, Rena."

"I've seen too many people who gambled on love shattered when they lost."

"People get divorced every day, Rena. Too much money isn't always the culprit. Your sister was a spoiled brat who wasn't content with a part of her man's attention. She wanted it all. What was stopping her from building a life of her own that would have enriched their life together? No one, rich or poor, has the right to demand all of someone else's attention. Your sister's immaturity ruined her marriage. Not Bryan Windsor's money."

"That's not fair, Mitch."

He deliberately misunderstood her. "I agree, she was very unfair. And yet Bryan still loves her."

"And she loves him."

"Then why they obstinately stay on opposite sides of the ocean is beyond me. If I loved a woman I would do anything to convince her she belonged in my bed and by my side. So be warned, Rena."

"Of what?"

"That I will convince you we belong together. And I won't stop until I do. You'll be mine, Rena, before this is finished. Just as the jade butterfly is mine. Now, I believe we have a party to attend."

Their taxi took more than one sharp corner, throwing her against Mitch no matter how hard she tried to keep a physical distance between them.

Each time they made contact it was like receiving a shock and Rena felt her inner turmoil mount.

"I don't bite, you know." His tone suggested otherwise.

"Since when?"

"I'll try to remember you don't like it."

Rena blushed in the darkness of the cab, knowing he was remembering as well as she the tender, passionate moments they had shared. He seemed determined to fuel the fire of sensual tension vibrating constantly between them. Mitch had always been one to take advantage of the moment and he hadn't changed. He would find that two people could play that game.

As soon as they arrived at the party she would locate Randy and attach herself to him in accordance with her plan. Mitch was not going to like it. But it would show him she was in charge of her own affairs.

The gathering was as gala and glamorous as the first one, but the atmosphere was a good deal more tense. Except for her and Mitch, everyone present had lost the first round. Rena knew she didn't imagine the somewhat envious and often downright covetous glances cast in their direction.

Randy Fletcher walked through the door, swiftly scanned the crowd, and, spotting them, fastened his gaze on her. Its intensity was startling. As was the purpose with which he parted the crowd and made directly for them.

What, she wondered, did he want?

Fletcher extended his hand to Mitch and then brushed Rena's cheek with a fleeting kiss. "I understand congratulations are in order. How inconsiderate of you not to tell me you'd walked away with the first prize, Rena. Especially when I was nice enough to rescue you from the storm."

"Somehow I thought you'd guessed I had the butterfly." Boldness was the only way to deal with him.

"I've learned to rely on more than guesswork. Not being sure of the facts can get you into trouble. I'm surprised you're here. In your place I'd be off and running." He'd thrown them a verbal challenge Rena had trouble resisting.

Mitch was a study in nonchalant calm. "Then why are *you* still here?"

It was definitely surprise that crossed Fletcher's face and Rena was positive he hadn't known they suspected him. Had Mitch ruined any chance she might have of getting close to Randy by voicing their suspicions?

"I'm still here because I didn't have the good fortune to employ a beautiful sidekick with equal measures of luck and skill. Your foresight is better than mine, Mitch."

"If I can believe everything I've heard about you, Fletcher, your regular line of work employs both."

"I'm an expert in gems—much as Ms. Drake."

Mitch was not so easily convinced. "And where did you receive your training?"

"On the job, so to speak." And he turned away to fill his plate. It was all Rena could do to keep from screaming accusations at him. But what good would that do? It was a relief when Judson Kingsley approached the microphone and asked for quiet. The tension riddling the room was almost unbearable.

"Ladies and gentlemen, welcome to the second phase of our game. As you know, the first prize has already been claimed by Mitchell Johns and his lovely assistant, Rena Drake." A gesture in their direction was followed by a turning of heads and a polite smattering of applause.

Rena was surprised when Mitch called out before Judson had a chance to continue. "In this case I'm the assistant. Rena's expertise located the butterfly—not mine."

"Don't we all wish we had such an assistant? I have to admit, I'm a trifle surprised to find you here. As everyone probably knows, Mitch and Rena already received the next clue. I wonder if they've figured it out or are here hoping to overhear something helpful." He laughed and so did some of the others.

Rena leaned over and whispered to Mitch. "I'm surprised he doesn't tell everyone what really happened."

"Don't hold your breath, the evening isn't over yet." It was plain Mitch was none too pleased by Kingsley's remarks. Rena knew Mitch had trusted the man's discretion, which was proving a bit thin.

"Well, whatever their reason for being here, after tonight the odds will once again be equal. The second clues are available at the door and there is still plenty to eat and drink. So enjoy yourselves. And I hope to see most of you again soon."

Randy had drifted away as soon as Kingsley began speaking. Now Rena saw him slip outside. She touched Mitch's arm. "Excuse me a moment." She had to see where Randy was headed.

The evening air was warm after the air-conditioned atmosphere of the party. But still it was fresher, carrying only the muted scents of fresh flowers as opposed to the cloying mixture of perfumes and cigarette smoke that seemed a part of any large gathering. Rena pulled quantities of clean air into her lungs and looked around. She saw no one, but it would have been easy enough for Randy to leave unnoticed, for the balcony led into a formal garden dimly illuminated by the moon. He had betrayed himself by leaving before Kingsley spoke.

Rena wandered among the shrubs and carefully manicured trees that made up the classic garden. Footsteps sounded on the gravel behind her and she whirled to confront Randy Fletcher.

"Looking for someone, Rena?"

"Perhaps I just decided I needed some fresh air. I might ask what you're doing out here—especially as the clues are being distributed. I should think you'd be first in line."

"They'll save one for me I'm certain. No sense in fighting the crush. What about you?"

"We already have ours—remember?"

"So you do. I'd forgotten for a moment. Being with you has a tendency to drive thoughts of anything else from my head—except for the pleasure of your company. I wish you and I could spend some time together free and clear from this damned treasure hunt."

His comment surprised Rena, especially since it sounded sincere. If he truly wanted to get to know her better then perhaps she could play on that.

"You don't sound like you're enjoying yourself all that much."

"I haven't come off with a prize—yet."

"I'm certain you're doing everything in your power to rectify that situation."

"I have a feeling there are some treasures worth far more than all of Dressler's baubles."

His words reached out through the warm evening to caress her and even though she wasn't attracted to Randy, she suspected the man would be quite dangerous and hard to resist if he were bent on seduction. He was leaving her no doubt as to his interest in her—regardless of what motivated it. She was bound to act on it, as it was perhaps her last chance to clear her father's name.

"And what might those treasures be?" Was that flirtatious voice really hers? Mitch would wring her neck if he could hear her.

"Is there any jewel so rare as a beautiful woman?" This time it wasn't only his words that caressed her. He rubbed the back of his hand along her cheek. But there was no answering spark of pleasure.

"But a woman's beauty fades, Randy. Gems remain forever brilliant."

"True, but a man can't warm himself in the arms of a sparkling gem like he can the arms of a woman."

"Can many of us hope for both love and riches?"

"I'm a firm believer, Rena, that a man—or a woman—can have anything and everything they want if only they'll go after it." Then his tone changed. "Just be sure you can handle the consequences." His last words were harshly spoken and Rena wondered if they were in the nature of a warning.

"I agree a person has to go after what they want. How else would any of us have anything?"

"Exactly." He took a moment to light one of the long, slim cigarettes he seemed fond of, then continued. "Tell me, where are you off to next?"

The directness of his question startled her. "Now that would be telling. You'll have to read your clue and decide for yourself."

"I'm not referring to that, but to after this treasure hunt is finished."

Did she want to tell him, or did she want to throw him off guard? It seemed prudent to settle for a convenient half-truth. "I'll have to find gainful employment elsewhere." He needn't know she'd already done that. Rena didn't think she wanted to make it easy for Randy to find her—if he should decide to come looking.

Randy took a thoughtful pull on his cigarette. "Tell me, Rena, why the sudden show of friendliness?"

"Have I ever been anything but friendly?"

"The only time I think you were genuinely glad to see me was during that rainstorm. Otherwise you've been every inch the cool brunette."

"Well, I'm very appreciative that you were around when I needed you. And I'm sorry Mitch felt it necessary to come on like a caveman. But you seem to have recovered. So I guess it wasn't as bad as it looked."

"Mitch needn't worry. I'll return the favor sometime."

Rena could definitely tell his threat was not an idle one and she shivered at the ominous promise it carried.

"Cold?" A solicitous question, but his tone implied he knew his own words were responsible for the sudden lowering of her body temperature.

"No, I'll be all right, but I do think I'll go back inside. I imagine we'll be seeing each other."

"You can count on that."

Then a hand clamped down on her shoulder and a voice came out of the darkness, startling them both. "It would be a mistake for you to count on anything, Fletcher. In case you haven't gotten the message, get it now. Rena is spoken for."

CHAPTER 10

It must have been a slow night in the district because taxis waited and Mitch quickly bundled her into one. Even after the doors were shut and they were on their way he didn't release his firm hold on her arm.

"Mitch . . ."

"Save it, Rena, for when we get back to the privacy of our rooms. I don't feel like starting a discussion now."

That was definitely not a request to be argued with.

Rena wasn't certain how glad she was to reach the hotel and almost welcomed the delay while waiting for an elevator.

The door of their suite clicked shut and Mitch's hold on his fury released. "I told you to stay away from Fletcher!"

"Mitch, please don't tell me what to do."

"I wouldn't have to if you'd listen to reason! What does it take to convince you he's dangerous?"

"Mitch, I explained earlier I thought it might be to our advantage to be civil to him."

"It looked to me like you were leading him on."

"Don't be ridiculous!" Rena knew she had deliberately avoided doing just that.

"I will tolerate a lot, Rena, but I will not lose you. I waited patiently for you to realize we belong together. I will let no one and nothing come between us now."

"Mitch, I was only taking advantage of an opportunity that seemed too good to miss. He was in the garden. I was in the garden."

"We've been suspicious of Fletcher for some time. And I'd bet money he was our burglar of the other night. He's a professional criminal and therefore dangerous."

"Just because he's a cat burglar doesn't make him lethal."

"You really think a man who's made his living from crime for who knows how long isn't liable to be dangerous if he's crossed or threatened with exposure?"

"I wasn't doing either of those tonight."

"But that's your ultimate goal. He knows who you are; what makes you think he might not be luring *you* into a trap?"

"What do you mean?"

"Perhaps he wants to find out exactly what you do know about him and who you've told. Then he can spring his trap and dispose of someone who might be getting a little too close to the truth. Being beautiful won't save you then." He tipped her chin up and gave her a loving look. "Special as you are, lady, I think he would find you expendable. No. I want you to promise to stay away from him at all times."

"Mitch, you're making me feel miserable. You know I can't do any such thing. Besides, as long as I earn what you're paying me then you have no right to tell me what I can and cannot do—who I can and cannot see."

"You might as well tell me not to care, and it's not like I'm trying to infringe on your life-style. I'm only asking you to stay away from Fletcher for reasons of your own safety."

"Believe me, I'll be all right. I'm not particularly anxious to walk into trouble."

"You won't give an inch, will you?"

"I don't see any other choice."

"Then meet me halfway. I know you didn't like it when you discovered I'd had you followed. But would you have any objections to my having him investigated?"

"I could never agree to that." And she sadly shook her head. "All those years ago when the insurance company was trying to get to the bottom of the missing LaSalle diamonds, Shay and I were constantly being investigated. They showed up at school, they even questioned our school friends. It was unfair and not right and I hated every minute of it. Maybe it would be different if we knew for certain Randy was guilty of all the crimes we suspected. But we don't, and I won't pry into his life because we've made an assumption."

"I think we have more than that to go on. From where I stand the man looks guilty."

"Are you forgetting that people thought the same about my father?"

"This is a little different, Rena."

"Not really. We've taken a couple of suspicious circumstances and woven them into a crime. But we have no proof."

"You want to catch the thief, but you won't use every means at your disposal."

"I'm sorry, but I can't forget how awful it was for us. We were literally hounded! You have to promise me you won't do anything like that. I couldn't bear doing that to another human being. Besides, you've told me you've heard suspicious stories about Randy in the past. Don't you think if there was anything to learn from an investigation of him it would have been done? I'm sure his tracks are carefully covered."

"All right, I'll leave things as they are—for now. I just hope neither one of us lives to regret it. Now if you'll excuse me, I'm tired." He loosened his tie and pulled it free as he walked to his room.

"Mitch, wait."

He turned to face her and Rena saw indeed how tired he was. "Aren't you forgetting the clue? We haven't even opened it, let alone discussed it."

He reached into his jacket pocket and tossed her a somewhat bent envelope. "I'd certainly like to forget it. I had somehow imagined this whole thing as a relaxing, rather amusing vacation. Talk about being wrong." And he started for his room.

"Aren't you going to open it with me?"

"I'm quite confident you can manage that all by yourself."

She couldn't believe his sudden disinterest. "Surely you want to know what it says."

"Not as much as I want a trouble-free night's sleep. Besides, I'm certain I can rely on you to keep me informed. We can plot our next move over breakfast. If anyone wants the jump on us so badly they're willing to sit up all night, then let them. I intend to sleep until I feel like getting up, then after a good breakfast I'll be willing to plan our next move. Not before."

If his words didn't convince her, the decisive closing of the door between their two rooms definitely did.

Rena stood and stared at the closed door for several seconds, then shrugged and walked over to the vast bed. Kicking off her shoes, she assumed a comfortable cross-legged position and carefully opened the envelope.

The clue was printed on the same heavy stock as before and Rena knew she'd never be able to see paper of such quality without thinking of the Dressler jewels. The lamp on the other side of the room didn't cast enough light so, leaning over, she switched on one of the fringed bedside lamps.

Quickly, Rena scanned the clue, then, scarcely able to believe her eyes, read it through again. Was it deliberately easy, or did it just ring a note of familiarity with her?

Eagerly, she slipped her feet to the floor and hurried across to Mitch's room. So eager was she that she didn't bother to knock but walked right in, which was a mistake.

Golden lamplight played along the rippling muscles of his body as he stretched and flexed, no doubt as part of the regime that kept him so superbly fit. But it also highlighted far more intimate memories than Rena needed at the moment.

Blue fire danced in Mitch's eyes and he seemed to know what she was remembering. Yet, when he spoke, his voice carried no hint of invitation. "Did you forget something—or did I?"

"I know it sounds improbable, but I think I've solved the clue."

Picking up a towel, he wiped his face. "Impossible! No, I amend that, with you nothing seems impossible."

Rena chose to ignore the fact his words weren't exactly meant as a compliment. "Either it isn't very hard or it simply rings a familiar bell with me. Here," and she handed him the card.

She knew he'd read it several times before shaking his head in defeat. "Maybe I've too many things on my mind, but I can't figure it out—not immediately at any rate. You'll have to enlighten me."

As if to refresh her own memory, she read the clue out loud. "All that glitters isn't gold, sometimes even glass can be very, very precious, especially if it's extremely old. A symbol of power from an ancient land, I've now been returned to singing sands."

"I'm familiar with the words, but they're still unfathomable."

In hopes of easing the stilted atmosphere, Rena teased. "Honestly, I wonder what you were looking at when we were supposed to be viewing the Dressler Collection. This could fit only one piece."

"Why should I want to look at a bunch of cold gems when I could look at you?"

His answer caught her so off guard that she was speechless.

"Our luncheon that afternoon hadn't been nearly long enough to satisfy my craving for you. Besides, you're the gem expert. So while you studied the collection, I studied you."

"Mitch, how could you, with half a million riding on this? It doesn't even make sense."

"Men in love seldom do."

"I don't know what to say."

"Why not explain that little bit of doggerel."

"I should think it would be readily apparent to anyone having studied geology and having even a brief glimpse at Dressler's treasures." She was deliberately sounding a bit pompous.

"I skipped anything to do with rocks. Besides, I hired you to look after the details."

"That argument won't work, Mitch. I'd already told you no when we went in to see the collection."

"I was confident you'd change your mind. But tell me how geology helped you solve this."

"It would have been impossible to bypass when I loved gemstones as much as I did—still do. It was all part of learning everything I could about them."

Mitch was watching her intently—to the point of causing her discomfort. "You know, I think I might owe you an apology."

"Whatever for?"

"I had always assumed you became a gemologist simply to clear your father's name."

"That was a motivation, but I could never have stuck it out if I hadn't truly been interested in the field."

"So I'm discovering. You really do love everything about gemstones."

"They're fascinating and they carry around the very secret of creation. People love antiques, but how often do they stop to consider the diamond or emerald they wear as a ring is aeons old?"

"It's true, good jewelry is very enduring. Almost as much so as time."

She smiled at him while pleasure welled up inside of her. "There, you've solved part of the puzzle yourself."

"What are you referring to?"

"Jewelry—that's the second treasure."

"I don't remember anything that fits."

"I wonder how many people do, for if I'm right, and I'm almost positive I am, the second treasure hardly looks that at first glance. Yet it could be one of the single most valuable pieces in the collection, not so much for what it's made of, but simply because of its age."

"How long are you going to keep me in suspense?"

Rena felt happy inside. At last he was again showing some enthusiasm. "I still find it hard to believe that you don't recall it."

"Rena, if you don't quit saying that and tell me what we're looking for, then so help me I'll wring your neck."

"Sorry! I'm quite positive we're looking for an Egyptian necklace, probably Eighteenth Dynasty. It was hardly given a place of honor the night we were allowed to view the treasures. But then neither was the jade butterfly, which makes me wonder if the arrangement of items was deliberate."

"I wouldn't put it past Dressler. But enlighten me, how old is Eighteenth Dynasty?"

"The part that concerns us would be in the neighborhood of 1350 B.C."

"How in the world do you know so much about a piece I can't even recall?"

"Because I thought at the time I recognized it."

"Have you seen it before?"

She nodded. "A picture in a book—once, a long time ago. It was unique, or almost so, because of the huge chunk of turquoise somewhat crudely shaped into a falcon pendant. The beads were of glass, carnelian, garnet, lapis lazuli, and amethyst."

"What was so special about this necklace?"

"Because of who it might have belonged to."

"Who?"

"Nefertiti—wife of the heretic pharaoh, Akhenaten. Egyptologists have often speculated on what became of her—a woman who inspired a legendary love and who ruled during one of the most controversial times in ancient Egypt. Her husband abolished all of Egypt's gods except for the sun-god. He even built a city monument to his religion. A religion declared heretical and all traces of which were removed from monuments and records."

"Then how do we know of it?"

"The demolition crew missed some things when they razed the city of Amarna. They may have been stricken from the record and the sands of time may have covered their city, but what the winds cover they can also uncover. Tourists looking for souvenirs found some pottery fragments with names of the pair. Archaeology was a new science, but skilled enough to build on these clues. Much was learned of the royal pair and Ahkenaten's mummy was found. But Nefertiti's fate remains unknown."

"What makes them think the necklace was hers?"

"It bears her name. It was stolen within weeks of its discovery. I wonder how Dressler came by it!"

"Anything is possible concerning him. It sounds like Dressler and Fletcher might possibly operate on the same side of the law."

"I agree. He might not have engineered the theft, but he must have known the necklace was hot. He was too astute to purchase anything without knowing its history."

"Then why is he making it known he owns it, I wonder?" Mitch thought a moment and then came to a conclusion; farfetched but plausible. "The clue says it's been returned from where it came. Perhaps he thinks to clear himself with this gesture and whoever finds it can be liable for the legality of possession."

"True, or maybe he doesn't think anyone is apt to make the connection. The discovery and disappearance were a good fifty years ago."

Mitch studied her seriously. "Perhaps we should give this item on the agenda a pass."

"Not if we want first chance at the third clue."

"You're right. We can wrestle with our consciences when and if we find the necklace. I have to admit, I'm surprised at the items chosen for the hunt."

"And maybe a little disappointed?"

"If I'm honest—yes. I had hoped for the pearl or the sapphire. But a crudely made necklace . . ."

"Aren't you forgetting, Mitch, it's supposed to have been worn by a woman of legendary beauty?"

"What good is legendary beauty when I can't know the legend? Every woman becomes a beauty to the man who loves her—even the plainest of women. Love penetrates the exterior and locates all the true qualities of beauty."

"That was very lyrical. I'm finding out, Mitch, how little I really know you."

"I could have told you that. For all your good qualities you have a tendency to stereotype people. The most noted example is the category you lump everyone into who has any money at all. You have to give people the opportunity to stand and fall on their own merits—not their bank accounts."

Rena turned away, refusing to concede him his point, but being able to see it.

Mitch was very wise; he knew when not to push his advantage. "Where do you suppose the necklace is? In the remains of the city you mentioned?"

"No, it was discovered far out in the desert in an area onetime thought to be haunted."

"How could a stretch of desert possibly be haunted?"

"The sands make an eerie sound at times. You've heard of areas where the sands seem to sing or in the case of a beach on Kauai, bark like a dog."

"True, I've heard of singing sands, but I didn't really think they referred to an actual phenomenon. I thought the reference was more poetical than anything."

"No, it actually occurs in different places all over the world and legends have grown up around them. In fact there really is no completely logical explanation as to what causes it. Some sands lie placidly uncomplaining as the winds blow across them and others protest loudly like a ringing bell or booming drum."

"But won't one spot in a vast desert be hard to find?"

"Not if we can research where the necklace was found."

"You amaze me, Rena."

"Why's that?"

"I always knew you were an intelligent woman, but until now I never realized just how intelligent."

"Don't give me more credit than I'm due, Mitch. I just have a good knowledge of my field."

"Good is an understatement. I knew I was smart to bring you along. Well, when do you want to leave?"

"As soon as you can make arrangements. That I leave to you."

"Good, or I'd really begin to feel useless. Let's try for tomorrow morning —early."

"Okay—I'll be ready."

Rena was aware of how tired she was as she slipped out of the red dress and into a thin nightgown. Mitch might think she had a thumbnail knowledge of many things, but she knew how deeply she'd had to dig into her memory for information on the necklace. And those memories had already been activated by sight of the necklace at the exhibition. She'd already slipped under the covers when it crossed her mind she should give Shay a call and let her know they were leaving Hong Kong.

First, she'd ask Mitch if he minded her telling Shay where they were bound. She didn't bother to knock, but simply pushed the door open as it was already ajar. Mitch's back was toward her as she stood motionless in the now open doorway.

"Okay, Carmen, you'll look into the matter of Randy Fletcher and have a report ready for me the next time I call? Thanks, you're a doll. Good-bye."

He hadn't heard her open the door and Rena stood there for what seemed like hours before he turned and saw her. There was no way he could have missed the anger burning in her cheeks.

"You went back on your word! You promised you wouldn't have him investigated."

"Rena, some promises are made to be broken. Especially if they concern your well-being. Nothing I own would be worth much if I lost you."

"Then why are you trying so hard to do exactly that?"

"If you'd knock before entering all this would have been avoided."

"No, this could only have been avoided if you'd kept your word."

Cold discomfort, having nothing to do with the weather, filled Rena. She'd tried to shake her mood which was only aggravated by a sleepless night. She no longer felt angry over what Mitch had done, but she still felt betrayed, while he felt justified.

Wind rattled the corrugated metal of an old building beside the landing strip where she and Mitch waited for their plane. He had decided they'd be better off chartering a private jet than taking a commercial flight. He was taking every precaution to keep their destination a secret. His reasoning was that they were less likely to be spotted. Rena knew he suspected Fletcher of tracking their every move. And she had to admit it certainly seemed that way.

The dark circles beneath her eyes attested to a sleepless night. As soon as she'd glanced in the mirror that morning Rena had known it was going to be a tough day. She felt limp and lifeless, and her drooping hair reflected that fact.

If she'd begun to doubt the destructive influence of money, such doubts were behind her. It gave the people who had it power over others as well as the ability to poke and pry and manipulate. Rena could never agree to this. As far as she was concerned, a person had a right to their privacy. Didn't the Constitution guarantee that?

Her tote bag was an uncomfortable weight on her shoulder and she finally swung it to the ground. At this point, Rena didn't care that the ground was nothing more than dirt and weeds or that her white cotton blouse and khaki pants were covered with dust. She'd taken little care that morning with her appearance beyond neatness. Even her hair was only tied back with a beige scarf.

Rena watched as Mitch conferred with the owner of the plane they were chartering. It was new and shining, in sharp contrast to the dilapidated building that served as an office. Weary of standing and waiting, she wandered over to the office, walked in, and helped herself to a Styrofoam cup of coffee. One sip and she grimaced. It tasted even worse than it looked. As she watched from inside, a gust of dust whipped around Mitch and the pilot. Even Mitch was sensibly dressed in khaki—like some old "B" movie idea of an archaeologist or desert explorer.

No doubt the spot they were headed for was inhospitable enough and Rena found herself wishing again for Bryan Windsor's Kauai beach house. Rena had tried to reach her sister several times, but there'd been no answer. Considering the secrecy surrounding their flight, Rena wondered if anyone would even know where to begin looking should they go down somewhere. She'd logged an untold number of air miles with nary a mishap. No doubt this flight would be as smooth.

Rena poured her coffee down the sink and waited for Mitch and the pilot to reach an agreement. Finally, she saw them shake hands and Mitch started for the office. All morning he'd tried acting as if nothing was wrong between them, but it was a game Rena wasn't willing to play.

"We should be able to take off soon."

Prodded by the unease that had plagued her all morning and which seemed a bit heavy to lay at the door of her disagreement with Mitch, Rena answered, "Mitch, couldn't we forget all this cloak-and-dagger stuff and take a commercial flight? I don't think anyone will be watching the airport."

"No, this serves our purpose much better."

"But I don't like the idea of no one knowing where we're headed."

"I assumed you would call Shay."

"I've tried, but I can't reach her."

"Don't worry about it, there will be a record here at the office. If the pilot doesn't check in then someone here will alert the authorities. The pilot will have filed a flight plan."

"I still don't feel right about it."

"You don't seem to feel right about much of what I do." There was a resigned sadness to his voice.

"Would you prefer I just kept quiet and said nothing unless directly questioned?"

"Of course not. If I'd wanted a robot I'd have hired one. Really, though, that plane checks out fine and it's almost new. If we flew directly into Cairo we would simply have to charter a plane there. This way we're saving a stop and time."

Rena rubbed her arms. "If you say so."

"You're probably just tired and that's why you're reacting as you are. But if it would make you feel better, why don't you try calling Shay from here? They can add the charges to my bill."

Rena thought a minute and then responded. "Maybe I will."

It took a few minutes for the call to go through and then an eternity of rings before Shay answered the phone.

"Hello." The line crackled ominously. "Hello?"

"Shay, it's Rena. You sound so far away."

"And you sound like you're at the other end of a long tunnel. Where in the world are you calling from? It's been so long since I've heard from you that I'd begun to get a little worried."

"I've tried several times, but you're never there or I can't get through." And then she gave her sister the information on their flight. "I'll check in as soon as I can, but in case you don't hear from me after a reasonable length of time you might start checking."

"Rena," and Shay definitely sounded worried. "Is something wrong? You don't sound like yourself."

"It's a long story and I wish you were here so I could tell you all about it." She couldn't say much because Mitch was standing right there.

"I take it you're not free to talk. But answer this, is there trouble between you and Mitch?"

"Definitely. You know the old scenario."

"Oh, Rena, what have you done?" Her sister's voice was practically a wail.

Rena fought to hold her temper. Why did her sister have to automatically assume the problem was her fault? "I've done nothing. You'll have to wait until I get home to hear all about our adventures."

"As long as you promise to let me talk some sense into you."

"When you've never returned the favor?"

"That's because I know what I'm talking about. You don't."

"That's debatable."

"Take care of yourself, Rena, and hurry home. Oh, by the way, I read about you in the papers. Congratulations on finding the jade butterfly. Mitch must have been pleased."

"You're the one who got me started in the right direction. But I'll explain all about it when we get together. They're warming the plane up so I've got to go. Bye." She hung up and turned to face Mitch who was waiting by the door.

"Do you feel better now that someone else knows where we're going?"

"Yes." She couldn't explain the way she was feeling, but blamed it on her disagreement with Mitch and the sleepless night that had followed. At least she hoped that was all it was and not some awful premonition. Then an arriving taxi caught her attention. "Look, someone else must want to charter a plane."

They were some distance from the landing strip and yet there was something familiar about the figure—something Rena didn't want to believe.

Evidently, Mitch felt as amazed. "Damn!" With no further conversation he pulled open the door of the office and stalked angrily from the building. Rena followed hesitantly.

Mitch's voice carried on the wind. "What the hell are you doing here, Fletcher?"

"Hiring a plane—just as you are."

"Well, you're out of luck as we've taken the last available one."

Rena worried a strand of hair that had blown loose and waited. It was some seconds before she realized she was holding her breath.

"I don't suppose I could interest you in pooling our resources?"

"And how do you propose we share the treasure?"

"By selling it and splitting the profits."

"That isn't exactly what I had in mind." Contempt for Fletcher's plan was evident.

"Don't tell me you'd keep the thing?"

"I've never been interested in the Dressler Collection for its resale value."

"I see, it's the collector and not the merchant prince who enters the hunt. To each his own and I guess the first one to the treasure will reap all the benefits. But remember, I offered to share."

Rena wondered if Randy had figured out the clue or if perhaps he'd again followed them. At this point, nothing would surprise her. But, she couldn't help noticing, he never once referred to the treasure by name. Either he didn't know or he was being as closemouthed as Mitch.

"Tell me, Fletcher, what made you pick this place? They're not one of the better-known airfields."

"Let's put it this way, Johns, you're not the only one capable of a little detective work."

Rena couldn't believe it. While Mitch was having Randy investigated, he'd been tailing them. In disgust, she walked away and boarded the waiting Learjet. The sooner they were on their way, the sooner this would all be over. She chose a seat near the middle of the plane, sat down, and closed her eyes. She was more tired than she thought and they were in the air when she awoke.

Mitch was seated across from her and working his way through a stack of papers. "Don't you ever rest or take a day off?"

"I'd like to, but the captain's got to be at the helm, you know."

"But most captains have a first mate."

"I know, but I guess I've never had reason enough to train a lieutenant."

"Do you need a reason beyond your own well-being?"

"When you've no one to go home to, then you might as well be working. Why don't you give me a reason, Rena, to close up early and go home at night?"

"Because I doubt if I could learn to live under surveillance."

"If you expect me to be sorry I had Fletcher investigated then you have a long wait ahead of you. I feel Fletcher is dangerous, but you won't listen to me. So I decided to go for some proof. I did it because I love you; because you mean more to me than anything."

"I still can't condone or accept what you did."

He answered her with silence so she turned her attention to the window. "Where do you suppose we are at the moment?"

"Hard telling, but I could ask."

Rena shook her head. "Don't bother—it's not that important."

"It wouldn't be a bother." He reached over and, touching her arm, forced her to look at him. "Nothing concerning you, Rena, is too much trouble. You mean far more to me than you could ever guess. That's why I went back on my promise to you. When I was trying to salvage what I could of Pacific Imports, I learned to cover all my bases and to follow up on every hunch. Right now that same instinct tells me we should know everything there is to know about our adversary. Don't think he isn't doing the same thing. Why else do you suppose he keeps turning up everywhere? He's following us—making use of our expertise."

"Could we not talk about this anymore, Mitch? Hashing it over isn't going to change anything—least of all my mind."

"All right, I'll give in to you now, but don't think I'm about to let this go indefinitely." With a snap he straightened some papers and then put them away. "Well, shall we talk about the necklace and what we're going to do if we find it?"

"I assumed you would add it to your collection."

"If what you suspect about its origins is true, then it belongs to Egypt. Should we be fortunate to find it, then I intend to return it to them."

"Is this because you really have no desire to own it?"

"If the necklace was stolen then it really doesn't belong to Dressler or anyone. Even if he didn't know it was stolen. The value lies in its obvious antiquity and the probability of who it belonged to. It should be returned to the country it came from."

"I can admire that viewpoint."

"You'd admire it a lot more if you realized how badly I wanted to find it, keep it, and present the treasure of one beautiful woman to another even more beautiful."

His voice was so seductively soft, so sincere, that Rena couldn't help looking deep into his brilliant lazuli eyes. The man behind those hypnotic eyes loved her—as she loved him. But his wealth and his way of life frightened her.

"You're being very melodramatic."

"Try substituting sincere."

"I am not beautiful and it embarrasses me that you keep insisting I am."

"I should think you'd be flattered."

"I put you on a pedestal and you think I'm beautiful. Perhaps we need to recognize a couple of home truths."

"That people are as we perceive them? Well, nothing will ever convince me you aren't exquisitely lovely. Perhaps my feelings embellish the fact, but that certainly doesn't make it any less true."

"Mitch, why didn't you tell me years ago how you felt?"

"I had the mistaken idea I should have more to offer than myself and a company recently saved from floundering. If I'd had any idea of your aversion to wealth I would have let the damn ship sink and I'd have carried you off caveman style."

"It's too bad you didn't. At the time my ideas about stations in life weren't so firmly fixed. Shay and Bryan seemed happy and I was very much influenced by their life-style. I probably would have jumped at the chance to emulate it."

"Proving once again he who hesitates is lost. In this case, I'm the loser because all I had to offer you was the moon and I thought I needed the sun and the stars also."

"It doesn't matter, Mitch, we're too different and we would only have hurt one another."

"If I wasn't concerned the copilot might walk back and interrupt us I'd show you how wrong you are."

"Don't remind me of my past mistakes." Silently, she was pleading for him not to show her how vulnerable she was to him.

"You really know how to hit below the belt, don't you?"

"I do and say what it takes, Mitch."

"Then maybe we need to talk about your shortcomings for a while."

"What do you mean?"

"I see, you don't like it when you're on the receiving end."

"I don't go snooping into people's private lives."

"No, you don't. Probably because you're too bent on revenge to have the time. I hope you'll let me know someday if it's really as sweet as they say. Personally, I think it's a wasted emotion. It's certainly using up all the sweetness inside of you."

"Don't be hurtful, Mitch. You always seemed to understand even if you didn't approve."

"Your intentions are honorable, I won't argue with that. But your father's disgrace happened years ago. Most people have forgotten it."

"Well, I haven't." The bitter taste of her father's defeat was still with her.

"I know. But, Rena, are you so sure he even cared that much at the time?"

"He would have to."

"Then why did he give up so easily?"

"I can't answer that. Maybe because he didn't have the finances to fight public opinion."

"He gave up, Rena, because he wasn't a fighter. And I'm afraid I can't think very highly of him for allowing you to dedicate so many years of your life to clearing his name when he did very little himself." He didn't like hurting her, but somehow she had to be made to see the truth.

"How can you say that?"

"Because it's true. The other gemologist could just as easily have been accused, but no, your father assumed the blame on his shoulders even though there'd been an appraisal done years before that confirmed his appraisal of the stones. Your father was thought guilty because he acted guilty."

"Are you inferring he was?"

"I'm saying he should have hung in there. If he could afford to retire, then he could afford to ride out the gossips. I think he used the incident as an excuse to quit."

"I don't agree."

"I didn't expect you to."

"Even if we were to agree on that point, you can't deny my mother walked out on him."

"True, but did he ever try to win her back?"

"She wanted a more extravagant life-style."

"The money was there, Rena, whether she stayed with him or not. Did he ever try to meet her halfway?"

"What are you trying to say?" She wished he wasn't beginning to make sense.

"It seems everything had to be your father's way or not at all. He could have agreed to some of the things your mother wanted. He wasn't even being fair to you and Shay."

"We were happy. We had the life-style we wanted."

"Then why were you both attracted to men with money?"

His plainly logical question dropped into the conversation like a handful of ice down Rena's back. "I don't think money had anything to do with it. I think we were attracted to the men behind the money and power. It wasn't a lack of finances that made Shay file for a divorce, but a lack of Bryan's time. If she'd wanted money she wouldn't have walked away from a settlement. Remember she works for a living."

"She'd have to, wouldn't she, once she'd turned everything down?"

"What are you insinuating?"

"Are you so sure she meant to go through with her divorce? Maybe she hoped Bryan would chase after her and give her what she wanted."

Her voice was shaking as much as her confidence. "You will not endear yourself to me by attempting to shake my reasons for everything I believe in."

He tried to take her hand but she jerked it away. "I don't mean to do that. All I want you to do is see that rarely is anything all black or white. Knowing you're not perfect, Rena, doesn't make me love you any the less."

She fought to keep the tears from her voice that were rapidly misting her eyes and made him seem to swim in her vision. "Meaning I should be able to accept the fact that you're not perfect either?"

"Exactly."

"Well, I'm sorry. I can't condone prying into another person's private life. It's wrong!"

"Then I guess I've lost and there's no sense in arguing further." There was a finality to his words that broke the hold she had on her emotions.

Rena stumbled and almost fell as she tried to move past him. He reached out to steady her and she pulled away, running by instinct to where she thought the rest rooms would be. She fumbled with the door and then managed to lock it behind her.

Sobs shook her body as she leaned heavily against the small counter. The light was ghastly and did nothing to alleviate the misery she was feeling. Her complexion had a gray cast and her eyes seemed too large for her face. Mascara streaked her cheeks and stung her eyes, but she couldn't stop crying. And this was the face Mitch thought beautiful? A fact that made her cry all the harder because he seemed perfectly able to accept her imperfections while she condemned his.

The plane hit an air pocket and gave a sickening lurch. Unexpected, it threw Rena against the door. It was frightening, but it brought her back to her senses. She blew her nose, splashed water on her face, and took ahold of her self-control.

The lock stuck and for a moment she panicked. Then it gave and the emotion subsided. She made certain her blouse was tucked in, gave a fleeting thought to how drab it looked, smoothed her hair, and walked back out to her seat.

After fastening her seat belt, she closed her eyes with the determination to once again fall asleep. It was the best way she knew of to while away the journey. But sleep was as elusive as happiness and she was still very much awake some time later when the plane landed to refuel.

She felt, rather than saw, Mitch's presence beside her.

"I'm going in search of something to eat. Do you want to come with me?"

It would have felt wonderful to stretch her legs, but Rena honestly felt it would be better if they kept their distance as much as possible. "No, I'll stay here. I'm really not hungry." Which was an out-and-out lie. She was ravenous.

In an effort to clear her thoughts of food, Rena concentrated on what was happening outside the plane. Nothing looked familiar and she wondered exactly where they were. Looking around for some clue, she suddenly saw a figure that looked familiar. But it was impossible! Nevertheless, the man hurrying away from beneath their plane looked very much like Randy Fletcher. Next thing she knew, everyone was going to look like him. Suspicion was tampering with her mind.

"Still feeling troubled?"

"Oh! I didn't realize you'd returned."

"Evidently not. Your frown was too deep. Is it caused by something I can help?"

Rena scanned his features and wondered if he had forgiven her. Mitch's anger rarely lasted long.

As many times before, he read her thoughts. "No, I'm not still angry. What sense would it make? We're in this thing together and we're not even halfway through. So we might as well put aside any differences and get on with what we have to do."

Rena was not against a truce. "That sounds good." The aroma of whatever he'd purchased was tantalizing her taste buds. "Is there by any chance enough there for two?"

"Since I seriously doubted you weren't hungry—yes. There's some fruit, cheese, and mineral water. And a loaf of crusty bread."

"Sounds delicious."

Mitch sat down next to her and divided up the ample luncheon. It was delicious and Rena made no pretense of not being hungry. She ate her share and when she noticed Mitch grinning at her, decided maybe she'd have a little bit more.

She pleaded in her own defense. "Who knows when we may eat again?"

"True. I should have had the foresight to purchase extra food. I'm not usually so unprepared. But I believe the plane has something in case of an emergency."

Rena pondered telling Mitch of the coincidence of thinking she'd seen Fletcher. Then decided it would only unearth the can of worms they'd just succeeded in burying. Besides, it couldn't have been anything other than a case of mistaken identity. Randy was probably still fuming back in Hong Kong or stretched out comfortably in the first-class section of a commercial jet.

"You know, Mitch, it might almost be better if the necklace were returned to the sands—rather than a museum."

"You mean it was never meant to be found and we should honor that intention?"

She nodded, "Something like that."

"I see your point, but if that were the case we'd know nothing about the past."

"And I see your point. The necklace will do everyone a lot more good in a museum in Cairo. Then anyone who wants can enjoy it and speculate about who it once belonged to."

"Do you believe it might have belonged to Nefertiti?"

"I'd like to think so. She's always seemed as much myth as reality. I'd like to know for certain what happened to her."

"Even knowing the legendary beauty is now dust or worse, one of those ghoulish mummies museums delight in displaying?"

"Mitch, you surprise me. Where's your scientific curiosity?"

"Limited. Digging up graves, regardless of what science it's in the name of, does not and never has appealed to me. Maybe this prompts my desire to return the artifact to the people of Egypt. After all, Nefertiti was their queen."

"Whatever your motivation, I still applaud your decision. You could return it to the black market for a tidy profit—as Randy intends, should he find it first."

He studied her intently, seeming to read much from her expression and yet giving nothing away. "Then I'm back in your good graces?"

She was saved from having to reopen the argument by a jolt of the plane. It seemed to suddenly falter and then lose altitude. Rena couldn't hide the panic filling her.

"What's wrong?"

"I don't know, but I intend to find out."

Mitch hurried to the cockpit and again the plane seemed to lose altitude. The awful conviction filled her that they were in serious trouble and she wanted nothing more than to run to Mitch. But the plane was descending at such a rate that Rena knew it would be a poor idea.

She scoured her memory for anything she'd ever been told about surviving a plane crash. Grabbing Mitch's jacket, she bunched it into a pillow, folded her arms, and laid her head on it. While she acted, she fought panic and the plane plummeted earthward. All she could think of was Mitch and how badly she wanted him there beside her—not only for her sake but his own. Then she forgot everything as the plane plowed into the ground.

CHAPTER 11

The battered metal bird tilted at an odd angle, a fact Rena realized as soon as she revived.

Darkness was everywhere—outside and inside. And everything was quiet. The silence was as impenetrable and complete as the darkness, and as isolating. Her thoughts flew to Mitch and the pilots. They must be hurt or they would have come to her rescue by now. Frantically, she tried to recall where everything was, but things seemed turned around in her memory.

Rena made herself concentrate until she had formed a layout of the plane in her mind. Then she reached under the seat and located her tote bag. Her purse was inside and inside that was a lighted compact. Only recently she had tossed out a small flashlight because it had ceased working. She had intended to replace it, but had gone no further than the intention. Only chance had recalled the compact. Shay had given it to her for Christmas. She'd filled it with powder and then promptly forgotten about it.

Her fingers still shook as she tried to open the compact and then she realized she was trying to open the wrong end. Why did the darkness turn everything so upside down and inside out?

She tried using both hands and the clasp gave. With a flicker the light came on and with it a relief all out of proportion to the faint glow. She was no longer lost in darkness, but how long would the tiny light burn?

As quickly as possible she got her bearings, located the door to the cockpit, and then snapped the compact shut. It seemed essential she conserve her small light. With the direction she needed fixed firmly in her mind, Rena tried to get up and realized she couldn't. Then she remembered she hadn't released her seat belt. She had to do it one-handed for fear if she laid the compact down she might not be able to locate it again.

Finally she was able to move into the aisle and slowly up to the cockpit door. She banged her ankles and knees several times, but scarcely noticed the pain as she tried hurrying as fast as circumstances would allow toward Mitch. It was no irrational fear that made her think he might be hurt. If he were all right he would have come to her by now.

How stupid their arguments seemed now—how petty her objections to having Randy Fletcher investigated. All that mattered, all that would ever matter, should she have another chance, was Mitch's safety and the chance to be together with him.

Her hand hesitated on the door for a swift second as she steeled herself for whatever she might find. Then she opened the door and flipped up the lid on her compact. The cockpit looked as if someone had taken a giant can opener to it. Her stomach knotted in fear as her gaze searched for signs of survival.

Nothing moved as Rena inched her way around the scattered debris. Mitch lay sprawled across the floor and she knelt beside him. Her fingers trembled as she felt for and finally found a pulse. It felt strong enough, but then what did she know about such things? Give her a handful of gemstones and she was of some use, but she knew little about first aid.

"Mitch, can you hear me?"

There was no response. Tears dripped off the end of her nose and ran into the corners of her mouth. She wanted to smooth back his tousled hair, but thought she probably shouldn't disturb him in any way. After assuring herself he was still breathing, Rena moved on to the pilot and copilot. They, too, were alive, if slightly the worse for the ordeal.

Rena's knees trembled as she tried to see what to do. But all the knobs and dials were mind-boggling. She had no idea what any of them were meant to do. Never had she felt so totally hopeless. Almost frantically, she turned knobs but couldn't even raise any static. Her hands shook out of fear and helplessness. There had to be something she could do!

"Everything's dead—that's—that's why nothing works."

Rena jumped at the sound of a voice and then realized the copilot had opened his eyes. She was no longer alone! "Are you all right?" She knelt expectantly beside him.

"I've got a busted leg, but otherwise I think I'm okay. I'm glad to see you found a flashlight."

"No, this is my compact. It's all I had."

"Woman's ingenuity, huh?"

"I guess. If I hadn't had it I'd still be back in the plane trembling with fear."

"Then I'll never think them a frivolous item again. In fact, I'll buy one for every girl I date. But if you prefer, you'll find some flashlights over there."

Rena followed his pointing finger and found the lights without much trouble. "Is there anything I can do for you? Or anything I can do to help our situation?"

"Tell me how those other two are." The tone of his voice betrayed the fact Rena wasn't the only one afraid.

"They're breathing, but unconscious. I didn't touch them other than to locate a pulse. I remembered the old warning about not moving someone who was injured. It didn't seem like the plane was in any danger of blowing up."

"We jettisoned our fuel when we realized we were going down."

"Do you know what happend?"

"Only one thing could have gone wrong. Someone tampered with our fuel. And there's no way to know that until it's too late."

Rena was forcibly reminded of the possibly familiar figure she'd seen hurrying away from the plane. Why had she been so foolish as to keep quiet?

"We're damned lucky to have made it, considering we hit the ground at about one hundred and forty miles per hour."

"Don't." And Rena closed her eyes, for the thought made her sick. Then she moved back to Mitch's side. Dull, golden hair fell across his forehead and she brushed it back. She loved him so much and she had been so wastrel with that love. Would he forgive her? Would fate give her another chance?

Rena's tears fell unchecked and her body shook with sobs. She had no way of determining how badly hurt he was. All she seemed able to do was cry and feel sorry and helpless. It wasn't enough. There had to be something more—something positive she could do.

Scrubbing at her tear-stained cheeks, she fought to gain control of herself. Turning back to the copilot, she found he was watching her.

"He's a lucky guy."

"How can you possibly say that?"

"Because you obviously love him very much. Hell, I could disappear off the face of the earth and no one would even care."

"Well, I care. I care about all of us. Isn't there something we can do to help ourselves? We can't just sit here."

"You're right about that. We sent out a distress call, but I have no way of knowing if anybody picked it up. We're in some pretty remote country."

While they talked, Rena kept glancing over at Mitch, hoping he would stir. She couldn't let her fears for him take over, not when she appeared to be the only person at the time who was ambulatory.

"Do you know where we are?"

"Somewhere in Jordan. Things were happening a little fast there at the last."

"Jordan?" Hastily, she reviewed her geography and knowledge of the current political situation in that part of the world. As far as she knew they at least weren't down in possibly hostile territory. That in itself was a relief.

Rena clenched her fists and tried not to panic. It wasn't easy. "I'll have to go for help. I can't just sit here and hope someone will find us."

"You're not going anywhere in this darkness. Besides, we need to wait and see if someone comes along. That's the sensible thing to do."

"The only thing sensible about me is the way I'm dressed. We could wait days for help and I don't think we have that luxury. You have a broken leg, and who knows what's wrong with them." And she gestured toward Mitch and the pilot.

"Look, lady, the worst thing you could do is wander off. We filed a flight plan; somebody will come looking for us when we don't turn up."

"But they might not come looking in time." Her voice broke at the thought of help arriving too late. "As soon as it's light I'm going to see if I can locate some help."

"You should stay with the plane." The copilot's voice was weak with exhaustion.

"Yes, you're probably right, but don't you understand? I can't just sit here watching each of you grow weaker and do nothing."

"Just promise me you won't do anything before it gets light."

"I won't." Rena returned to watch by Mitch's side. His breathing seemed regular and as near as she could tell his color was good. A glance at her watch revealed only a little time had passed. How far away was morning?

Rena watched Mitch with a heavy heart. Finally, she could stand it no longer and bent down to barely brush his lips with hers. She hoped for some response but certainly not the one she got. Mitch's mouth returned the pressure of hers and one hand fastened around the back of her neck. The sweet unexpectedness of his kiss filled her with excitement.

When at last he released her, she couldn't help the tears of joy that slid from underneath her lashes. "You're all right!"

"If all right means I feel like a building fell on me, then yes, I'm all right." He tried to move and winced in pain.

"Hey, buddy, I'm glad to hear from you. Maybe you can convince your lady not to go wandering off in search of help."

Mitch's fingers clamped around her wrist. "How could you even think of such a thing?"

"We can't sit around waiting for help. What if it never shows up? And look at you. You can't even grimace without it hurting you. The copilot has a broken leg and heaven knows what's wrong with the pilot."

"They issued a Mayday. Someone will come along."

But it was soon well into the next afternoon and no one had rescued them. They hadn't even heard any planes fly over.

"Tomorrow, as soon as it's light, I'm leaving."

"Rena, you can't. You're more liable to get lost than you are to find anybody."

"I'm probably going to have to head out sooner or later—so it might as well be sooner."

Surprisingly, the copilot was in her corner. "She may be our only hope, Mitch."

Mitch wasn't convinced. "She'll be lost within five minutes."

"Not if she marks her way. There's some spray paint in that storage compartment over there."

"Rena, I don't want you to go."

"But you're in no condition to stop me. Every time you move you darn near pass out, Mitch."

"It's just a few broken ribs and a dislocated shoulder. Nothing that won't heal."

"Well, it will heal a lot sooner if we have help. I promise not to get lost and I promise to come back if I don't find any signs of civilization." But Rena's words sounded a lot braver than she felt the next morning as she shouldered a canteen of water, a backpack of other supplies, and set out. Never had she felt so ill-equipped for any task.

Some vague notion urged her to head west and she periodically checked the compass pressed on her by the copilot. The ground was rough, rocky, and everlastingly empty of any signs of life. Even a darting lizard would have been welcome.

The landscape she stumbled over was inhospitable. Perhaps she would have seen the beauty in it if the circumstances had been different. She could only hope and ask that she was headed toward help. With a forced calm, she made herself take inventory of her surroundings, giving identifying names to large rock outcroppings. Occasionally she sprayed some of the white paint to mark her way, but never a lot. You would have to be looking for them to find them. But she had to make certain she didn't get lost. The safety of three men counted on it.

If necessary she'd return and personally remove the paint. The thought conjured up a somewhat comical image of herself, and Rena straightened her shoulders and strode forward. If she could smile at herself then she would make it. And if she made it then so did Mitch and the pilots.

Two hours from starting she skirted a rock wall, looking for a break she could pass through. Morning was in all its glory now, touching the rocks with a rose gold. How hot was it likely to get once the coolness of early morning had passed? Her feet were already aching as she continued to look for a passageway through the rock barrier confronting her.

And then she found it. Dipping down and passing through the cliffs was a narrow trail. Pebbles rattled underfoot and rooks sailed overhead. Rena quickened her pace just a little and allowed herself to wonder if perhaps the path led anywhere. These were ancient lands and the trail could be hundreds of years old and worn deep by feet no longer alive. But she could hope. After all, it was emotion prodding her flagging footsteps on.

Stopping, she took a drink of her water. It was precious and she had already given in to thirst more than once. Probably more in anticipation of the heat to come than out of actual need. She tipped her head back to drink from the canteen and that was when she saw it. Water trickled unheeded down her chin and onto her blouse as she stared.

The passageway she'd been traveling had grown increasingly narrow, encouraging the walls to crowd in around her. The light had become so dim that it was almost as though the day had passed without her realizing it. Knowing she really had no choice had been the only thing pressing her onward. Sounds had echoed ominously and Rena wondered what kind of wild animals might stalk the area. Some vague Sunday school remembrance of biblical reference to lions surfaced. Were there any still around or had they long ago gone the way of the almost legendary figures who had hunted them?

Now all her tears were lost in the wonder of the sight before her. Mesmerized, Rena walked from the dim chasm into the full glory of sunlight. Before her rose one of the most spectacular sights she'd ever seen. Carved into the rock, silent and waiting, towered a stone monument that might have been waiting forever. It was only one of many that stretched outward, forming a city of silent stones. She couldn't help being lifted from the moment by its special and unexpected beauty. Only when she realized the path she'd followed led not to civilization but to this city, deserted sometime in antiquity, did Rena come down to earth. Beautiful as it was, she would find no help here.

With a thud, her soaring hopes landed only to dissolve in despair. Sitting on a flat rock, Rena gave way to tears. Was she anywhere near help? Or did all the desert roads lead only to the past? In frustration, she raised her voice in a wail that reverberated back to her with crescendoing echoes.

Her tears spent, Rena stood up, shouldered her pack and her courage, and turned in preparation of retracing her steps. Once help was found she would find out what ancient place she'd stumbled into and perhaps bring Mitch back to share it with her. But those were thoughts to be saved for after their rescue. Plodding on she once again entered the narrow passage that led back into the outside world.

Head down so she wouldn't stumble, Rena walked onward and then stopped abruptly—as unbelieving and speechless as she'd been at first sight of the rock city. The man striding toward her had seen her first. He wore a very official-looking uniform and fixed her with a very official-looking glare. Rena didn't care. He was real and he would help her. Only decorum kept her from throwing her arms around his neck.

Help had been relatively close all along. The man said very little except that he'd gone to investigate what sounded like a human wail. As far as he'd known there were no visitors in the area as yet, and he'd been prepared to find someone in distress. If he hadn't come searching, Rena wondered if she would have wandered off in the right direction or the wrong.

Rena stayed close beside him as he took her to the Government House and explained in heavily accented English that she had stumbled into the ancient city of Petra. She wondered that she hadn't recognized it, so well photographed were some of the ruins. She had even heard Burgon's oft quoted line, "A rose-red city half as old as time." Perhaps, given a different set of circumstances, she would have recognized where she was. No matter now, she was rescued, Mitch and the pilots were rescued.

Rena had half expected to do a lot of explaining in order to receive help. But her unexpected and disheveled appearance had been explanation enough. Within no time at all, she was back at the plane and this time with a rescue party.

As she sat beside Mitch in a helicopter, she explained where she'd been. "You've heard of Petra, haven't you?"

"I would think most people have; why?"

"Dressler should have chosen it for one of his treasure sites; it's spectacular. I wandered in by mistake, hoping I might find a village. It's not quite what I expected, but I did find help. Or rather it found me. I'd love to show it to you—maybe when you're feeling better."

"That may be all that's left to us. By the time we unravel the mess of the crash we'll be too late to find that necklace anyway."

"I'm sorry, Mitch."

"I'm just glad we all seem to have survived. I mean to discover who or what was responsible."

"The copilot told me the fuel had been tampered with. That nothing else could have caused the problem. I don't quite understand, but I'm sure he knows what he's talking about."

"When the fuel's been tampered with you don't know it until it's too late. And then the plane stops dead. If this had happened closer to Hong

Kong then I would have had my suspicions as to the guilty party. But the tampering would have to have happened at our last refueling stop."

Rena kept quiet about her own suspicions, but she vowed to locate Fletcher and make him admit to what she was sure he'd done. He would not walk away from the crash if he was responsible for it. She needed no one to tell her how lucky they all were.

Once they reached a fair-sized city, Mitch and the pilots were taken to the hospital. Rena was nicely taken care of at a hotel. Never had a hot bath felt so good or simple biscuits and tea tasted so delicious. She even allowed herself a short nap in a comfortable bed before taking a taxi to the hospital. More than anything she wanted to reassure herself Mitch was indeed all right.

As Rena rested comfortably in a taxi, she rehearsed what she would say to Mitch. And she wondered how much, if anything, she should say about Fletcher. They had both underestimated their adversary, that was for certain. And it had cost them the Egyptian necklace and darn near their lives.

Rena didn't have to wait to see Mitch, and she grinned when she found him sitting up in bed drumming his tanned fingers against the white bedding. "What's the matter, won't they let you have a telephone?"

"Not only that, they won't let me out of here. My diagnosis was correct. The shoulder's now back in place and the ribs are taped. And there's no reason for me to stay."

"It can't hurt to take it easy for a couple of days."

"We can't afford the time, Rena. Not if we're to be in on the third phase."

"Maybe we should just forget the hunt."

"That doesn't sound like you. What about Fletcher and the LaSalle diamonds?"

"He'll get his—one way or another. Seeing him brought to justice for the diamonds is no longer my primary concern." But seeing him caught for what he'd done to them was.

"To what do I attribute this abrupt change of attitude?"

"To the fact I had to discover the hard way what is really of value to me."

"Care to enlighten me?"

Rena perched carefully on the bed and took hold of his hand. "What if someone comes in to take your temperature?"

"They'd discover it was near the boiling point." Mitch's voice was husky with the desire she was feeling.

"Mitch, I went through all kinds of hell when I realized you were hurt. I knew then that everything else aside, all that mattered to me was you."

"Is that why you took the foolish chance of going for help?"

She nodded. "I understood then why you had broken your promise and had Fletcher investigated. You were concerned about me and willing to do anything to insure my safety."

"I explained that to you before."

"I know that, but I had to be in a similar position before I realized what you were getting at. I knew my chances of finding help were slim, just as I knew any expert would advise against my leaving the plane. But I had to do what I felt was right."

"Just as I did."

"Exactly. I'm sorry it took such a horrible event as the plane crash to make me realize I was being narrow-minded and less than sensible."

"I'd go through it again if it cleared the air between you and me. But tell me something, do you still feel as you did about my money?"

Her smile was almost apologetic. "I think I might be able to learn to live with it."

"If a few broken ribs can accomplish all this then maybe I should arrange to do it more often."

"Don't you dare."

"Don't worry—I don't intend to let anything keep me from enjoying your capitulation to the fullest."

"You know, Mitch, I really feel terrible. I've been so concerned with us that I haven't even asked about the pilots."

"They're okay except for some broken bones and a concussion in the case of the pilot."

"That's good."

"Now, if we can just discover who tampered with the fuel . . ."

Rena guiltily kept silent. She would decide what to tell Mitch once she knew one way or the other if Fletcher was responsible. She was sure that in light of their new understanding he would understand her hesitancy. But she wouldn't deny her thoughts were troubled and more so when she saw a look of worry pass across his face.

"Mitch, is there something you're not telling me? Is there more to your injuries than you're letting on?"

"No, I was only wondering if I should tell you a bit of news I learned a few minutes before you arrived."

"I take it I'm not going to like it." She could almost predict what he was going to say.

"The necklace has been found."

"Who told you?"

"We can't accuse Judson Kingsley of not being on top of everything. He wired the hospital as soon as he found out where we were."

"How could he possibly have known?"

"I think we made the news."

"Should I even ask who found the treasure?"

"Not if you've already guessed it was Fletcher."

"Damn!" Well, he'd made good use of the time they'd lost.

"I don't imagine it will be long before the necklace finds its way back to the black market."

"It certainly won't be donated to any museum. He was lucky this time, but he won't be again."

"That sounds almost threatening."

"Well—he's not a nice man. So how can I be happy for him?"

"Are you keeping something from me?"

"Would I do that?"

"Probably, if you thought you could get away with it."

"I'm not, so don't worry. If I sound unusual then I think you can blame it on the fact I'm tired and more than a little disappointed Randy was lucky enough to claim the necklace. I wanted to see it returned to Egypt."

He ran his thumb across the knuckles of her hand and then kissed the tips of her fingers. "The deed isn't entirely finished—yet."

She immediately perked up. "Do you know something I don't?"

"No, not at this point. But this whole event is receiving a lot of publicity. Don't think for a minute the right people aren't aware that necklace is out there."

"Good, if Dressler doesn't legally own it, then none of us have a right to it."

"Rena, your attitude about Fletcher seems to have changed. Care to tell me why?"

"I've always thought he was suspicious."

"Yes, but you weren't so vehemently against him."

"Let's say I've had time to think."

"There's more to it than that."

"I'm not very sure about anything at the moment, Mitch. When I am, you'll be the first to know."

"Statements like that make me worry. Promise me you'll be careful." Lines of concern creased his forehead.

"Aren't I always?"

"No, otherwise you wouldn't have gone off on your own into the desert."

"Someone had to go for help."

"You could have been lost forever."

"We all could have been lost forever, but we weren't so let's not worry about it." And she reached over to kiss him, to smooth some of the pain lines from his face. "I really learned the lengths one person will go for another. But I wish I could have learned in a gentler way."

Rena knew her eyes mirrored all the love she had for him and that she'd kept carefully hidden for so long. She blinked and cleared her throat. "Can you tell me how long before you're out of here?"

"The doctors have threatened me with at least a couple of days. I don't see the need to stay, but the doctors seem to think there is, so I'm humoring them."

"Good, you continue to do that." Was there a chance in the world he'd listen to those in charge and take time to mend? If he did, she might possibly have time to get to Cairo and back before he was any wiser. Once there, she could furnish the authorities with a description and all her suspicions concerning Fletcher. Just maybe they'd be willing to investigate the matter. Especially if the legality of ownership concerning the necklace was involved. But she suspected Mitch would be very angry if he knew what she was contemplating.

"Mitch, I want you to remember one thing. No matter what happens, I love you."

He studied her, his eyes and expression serious. "Should I feel threatened or warmed by that statement?"

"It's just something I want you to remember."

A nurse bustled in, an interruption Rena welcomed with enthusiasm, not even protesting when she was shown the door. Rena permitted herself to linger only a moment while she filled her gaze with the sight of Mitch.

As she tried unsuccessfully to relax in the taxi racing her back to her hotel, Rena reflected on the accuracy of that old saying—a little knowledge is a dangerous thing. Although she had no hard, cold proof, she did have her suspicions, and they were driving her toward a course of action that frightened her and certainly wasn't going to win Mitch's approval. If the Egyptian police didn't listen to her, then she was going to pursue Randy on her own. He might have gotten away with the LaSalle jewels, but he was not getting away with sabotaging their plane if he was guilty.

Rena was absently sorting out her thoughts when she entered the hotel. "Miss Drake!"

She turned and realized the desk clerk was trying to get her attention. "Yes?"

"Someone is looking most anxiously for you. They are in the dining room at the moment."

Rena frowned. "Did they give their name?"

"There were several people waiting when they arrived and I didn't think to ask. I'm sorry."

"That's fine. I'm sure they'll recognize me even if I don't recognize them." As she strode toward the dining room she wondered who in the world was waiting and if they would make demands that would keep her from leaving.

A voice heralded her as soon as she stepped down into the dining room. "Rena, over here!"

She couldn't believe her eyes when she saw Shay and Bryan. "What are you two doing here?"

"You don't think we'd stay away when you were in trouble, do you? Only it seems we got here a little late to be of any assistance." Her tone was scolding, but relieved.

"How did you know?"

Bryan answered, "The papers are following the treasure hunt pretty carefully and picked up on the disappearance of your plane."

Rena was thrilled to see the two of them together. "I won't deny I'm glad to see you."

"The Seattle papers especially played up your disappearance. I was frantic to do something so I called Bryan. I knew he could and would help me." Shay sat across from her sister and exchanged an affectionate glance with her ex-husband.

"I'm glad Shay thought of me. But by the time we arrived you'd walked out. I'm not sure I approve of what you did, but it certainly turned out to be right."

"I had no choice since it didn't seem help was coming. But you mentioned the disappearance of our plane being in the papers and you knew to come here. Why then weren't planes out looking for us?"

"I think they would have found you eventually, but they were searching farther north."

"Eventually can seem like forever when you're in a situation like that."

Bryan tapped the edge of his coffee cup. "I can well imagine. I've logged a lot of air miles, but so far I've been lucky to escape an accident."

"Mitch will be pleased to see you. He's rather a reluctant guest at the hospital."

"That doesn't surprise me. How is he?"

"He'll be okay, but he needs to rest. He has some broken ribs."

"Does this put you out of the hunt?"

"I hope not, but I suppose that could all depend on when they distribute the third and last clue. Mitch might be healed enough to tackle it and then again he might not."

"Would he let you carry on alone?"

"I doubt it, Shay. Mitch seems to think the game is a bit dangerous for that."

Bryan frowned. "Why should he feel that way?"

Rena let out a deep sigh. "It's all a bit complicated."

"Well, sis, would you go on without him?"

Under the watchful gaze of her ex-brother-in-law, Rena thought over how to answer her sister's question. How much should she reveal about her suspicions concerning the fate of their plane and Randy Fletcher's dubious background?

"I really don't know. I'm tempted to say yes, because a lot is riding on this. There's more than a prize to win, there's a debt to be paid." Rena remembered her father's shattered career and a wrecked plane in the Jordan desert where she could have lost the one person she loved more than anything.

Bryan had been mostly silent, letting the two sisters have their say, but now he interjected a question that put Rena on the spot. "There's more to this than you're telling us, Rena. What's going on?"

"I can't answer that, Bryan. Not right now anyway. Which isn't fair since I'd like you to help me."

Bryan smiled ruefully. "That's like asking someone to loan you money with only their word and a handshake for collateral."

"You're not far wrong there. But *will* you help me?"

Bryan evidently found his food undesirable and pushed it away. "What is it you want us to do?"

Rena's relief was great. She trusted Bryan Windsor as she had trusted few people.

"The doctors say Mitch must spend a couple of days in the hospital. During that time I must get to Cairo and back. Yet I've got to have some plausible reason for not going to visit him. So far all I can come up with is a feigned illness."

Bryan frowned. "You're pretty sure Mitch wouldn't approve of what you want to do?"

Rena nodded. "I'm positive he'd approve of the results."

Bryan was thoughtful. Shay, anxious and eager. "I think we should help Rena. She and Mitch are in this too far now to stop."

Rena realized Shay thought she wanted to fly to Cairo to pick up the third clue. A misconception that might work to her advantage. "I'm hoping the third prize will be a little more spectacular than the first." The grandest prize of all would be Randy Fletcher in handcuffs.

"Aren't there a lot of people competing?"

"Yes, but I think we stand a good chance. So will you help me slip away without Mitch knowing where I've gone?"

Rena and Shay watched Bryan weigh the decision in his mind. What it amounted to was what he thought they should do, balanced against what Rena wanted to do. "You're sure you can manage on your own?"

"Definitely, it won't be as much fun, but I'll manage."

"All right, we'll tell Mitch you're under the weather and then we'll keep him entertained. But you report in every evening—understand?"

Rena reached over to squeeze Bryan's hand. "I knew I could count on you."

Bryan's response was resigned. "And I know I'm going to regret this."

Rena ordered coffee when the others ordered dessert. After a couple of sips of the stout liquid, she excused herself and went upstairs to bed. Great weariness overtook her as she walked to her room. The key fitted stubbornly in the lock and there were a couple of uneasy moments when she wondered if it was even going to turn or if she'd have to go for help. Then the door swung inward.

Rena entered, pushed the door shut, tossed her purse on the bed, and walked over to the window. Pushing it open, she took a deep gulp of evening air. She was doing what she had to, but the decision didn't rest easy on her conscience. What if Mitch didn't understand and it shattered their newfound truce?

Sitting down on the wide window ledge, Rena surveyed the city spread out below her and pulled the pins from her hair, tossing them on the bed. Some of them made it, but others hit the bare floor. She was loath to move from her comfortable position by the window, for it was relaxing to survey the city in the gathering light of evening and to bask in the coolness of the night air. Her skin felt hot and a light wind brushed refreshingly against her.

A small insect flew in the open window and landed on her arm. Carefully, she brushed it back outside. How wonderful if she could as easily brush aside her troubles. As always, reality intruded on even the few spare moments of respite she allowed herself.

A firm knock at the door wasn't entirely unexpected. Rena had assumed Shay would come to call—not only to fill her in on her efforts to locate Rena, but also to scold her for not being more careful. There was a great deal of the mother hen in Shay. But it wasn't her sister knocking.

Bryan smiled back at her. "I take it you weren't expecting me."

"No, I had thought Shay would be by. But come in, you're certainly welcome. Have a seat."

He glanced around the room and seeing there was only the one chair, protested. "I can stand, this won't take long."

"No, take the chair. I was sitting in the window anyway, catching every breath of air I could. You know when this is all over with I'm going somewhere cool for at least a week. If I live to be a hundred I'll never forget what a bake oven that plane was."

"Both Shay and I were commenting on how thin you looked."

Rena managed a rueful laugh. "You're probably remembering those times when I was a little too round to be fashionable."

"It was always very becoming."

"You're sweet, Bryan. In fact, you're probably one of the sweetest men I've ever known. I want to thank you for being there for Shay when she needed you."

"If it wouldn't sound callous I could almost thank you for that plane crash. It brought us back together the way all the wishful thinking in the world could never do."

"Then it wasn't all bad. I can be thankful for that when I'm feeling more guilty than I can stand."

"Why should you be feeling guilty?"

"Oh, Bryan," and she pushed back her heavy, dark hair, all the while wondering why she had pulled the pins free. It was so much cooler when pulled up, but her head had been throbbing and each pin had seemed to be digging into her scalp. Maybe it was exhaustion and strain or maybe just good sense, but she decided to confide in him.

Briefly, she launched into an account of what had happened when they'd stopped to refuel. "I should have said something, but Mitch and I had been quarreling and as usual Fletcher was at the root of it. I wasn't positive and so I just kept quiet. I never once thought anyone would do anything to the plane. That kind of action is so—final." Her voice broke on the end of her explanation and she buried her face in her hands, grateful that her hair fell forward.

Bryan was beside her instantly, comforting and reassuring. But it helped only a little. "Rena, you couldn't have known. We have to accept some things on trust and you had no reason to believe Fletcher was that dangerous."

She pushed her hair back and wiped her eyes. "Mitch thought he was. That was why he was having him investigated. I should have listened to him instead of protesting we were invading Randy's privacy. I just couldn't help remembering how awful it was for Shay and me when Dad was suspected of stealing the LaSalle diamonds."

"You were both doing what you believed was right. You can't be faulted for that. Chances are that even if you had mentioned the instance to Mitch he would have dismissed it. For Fletcher to intercept your flight quite so soon was damned lucky for him. In fact, you have no proof he was to blame."

"They know the plane was sabotaged."

"Still, where's the proof it was him? Mitch would say that, any board of inquiry would say that."

"I intend to find that proof."

"That's why you want Shay and me to cover for you while you go to Cairo, isn't it? This trip has nothing to do with the Dressler treasure."

"That's right."

"You could be walking into a great deal of danger, Rena."

"But I'll be forewarned this time. I can't let this pass, Bryan. Randy could disappear without a trace. Once more proving that for him, crime does pay."

"Don't you think you should let the authorities handle this?"

"I intend to go to them, but if they don't believe me then I'm going to track Fletcher down and confront him."

"What would it take for me to convince you I should accompany you to Cairo?"

"Oh, Bryan, it isn't necessary, really." How would she accomplish anything with another watchdog?

"I can almost read your thoughts, Rena. You're wondering how you'd accomplish anything with me along."

She couldn't help looking sheepish. "Mitch has a tendency to be over-protective."

"Don't you think he has a right?" Bryan had very dark eyes that, like his questions, seemed to bore right to the heart of a matter. "Rena, when a man cares deeply for a woman one of his primary goals is to see she's taken care of."

"Even if she's unhappy as a result?"

He evaluated her remark and then thoughtfully rubbed his hand across his forehead. "All right, I'll make you a deal. Let me come with you. We'll do everything possible to convince the authorities to detain and investigate Fletcher. But you have to promise me no unscheduled heroics."

"I can't ask for anything more, thank you."

"What about your promise?"

"Okay, if there are any heroics I'll let you in on them."

CHAPTER 12

Morning dawned with all the brightness and vigor of an ancient battalion. Rena stretched, yawned, and wondered why she was so constantly reminded of the past in a country often in the news because it was very much a part of the brushfire-hot present. Perhaps because antiquity so breathtakingly survived in such places as Petra. Rena knew she would be back someday to explore and get in touch with this splendid land.

She felt more rested than she'd expected considering the time she'd had getting to sleep. Her brain had been too busy planning what she would do once she arrived in Cairo.

Was there any possibility she could locate the third treasure for Mitch? It would certainly serve as the peace offering she was afraid she was going to need when he found out what she was about to do. Her main reason for agreeing to Bryan's company was because she knew it would help her cause when Mitch found out about her unscheduled flight to Cairo. She could always point to Bryan as a chaperon. Rena threw back the covers and hurried into the bathroom to shower and shampoo her hair. Lately, it always seemed full of dust.

Mitch was in her thoughts as she dried her hair, nibbled some fresh fruit, and drank strong coffee. Then Bryan was knocking at her door and they were headed for the airport.

Bryan looked rested and impeccably dressed. "You look like you slept a bit better than I did."

"Were you having second thoughts?"

"Heavens, no! I passed second thoughts a long time ago. I just hope Mitch understands."

"He loves you, Rena. Men in love are willing to forgive a lot."

"Is that a promise?"

Nodding, he smiled. "A promise I can guarantee."

The flight, the landing, the trip through customs were as smooth as possible. They were in Egypt and, everything else aside, Rena felt excitement grip her as she set foot on soil she'd long dreamed of visiting.

Rena pulled Bryan aside. "You go on to the hotel and I'll catch up with you later. I'm going to make inquiries and find out where I can contact the police. Surely someone here in the airport can tell me."

"I'm going with you. I think I might be of some use."

"In other words, you're not sure how serious they might take a woman alone with a somewhat wild tale to tell."

Ever the diplomat, Bryan simply repeated, "I think I might be of some use."

"But shouldn't we be booking a room?"

"My dear, don't you know me well enough by now to know I go nowhere without a reservation? We have rooms—very nice ones I hope—at a well-known hotel. We'll send our luggage on and then we'll get down to business."

Business started as an encounter with a very polite and knowledgeable tourist policeman. He in turn directed them to the main police station downtown.

Rena began to relax as their taxi sped them expertly, if sometimes hair-raisingly, through traffic. "This is turning out to be easier than I thought."

"Don't get too comfortable. I suspect the easy part is behind us."

And Bryan was right. No one at the police station seemed to take them seriously and Rena was close to tears of frustration.

"Bryan, why can't we make anyone understand?"

"Do you really blame them? We have no facts, only speculation. We're asking obviously busy people to help us solve a crime that might not have been committed."

"Then that means we might have to figure out how to proceed on our own."

They were turning to leave when one of the policemen they had talked to pointed them out to a well-dressed man who could easily have moonlighted as a movie star. His dark eyes took them both in but lingered for a fraction of a second longer on Rena. Then he approached.

"I understand you have a rather interesting tale to tell. Let me introduce myself. I'm Ahmed Bey and I think I can help you. Shall we step into my office?"

He listened with an attentiveness that was almost unnerving. But at least he was listening. It was Rena's story so Bryan let her do most of the talking. "I know it probably all sounds terribly farfetched."

"On the contrary." He stopped tapping his fingers together and opened the top drawer of his desk, withdrew a picture, and passed it across the table to her. "Is this the man in question?"

It was and it wasn't. Rena frowned as she tried to place the blond-haired, mustached man in the photograph.

"His name is Martin Dankin."

Suddenly it all came together for Rena. She handed the picture back to the inspector. "He is also Randy Fletcher."

"But you've known him as Dankin?" The dark gaze probbed along with the question.

Rena nodded. "He was apprenticing with my father at the time the LaSalle diamonds were in question. However, he didn't have a mustache."

Bryan was plainly surprised. "Did you make the connection before?"

"No. But you have to remember that's been years ago. And he looks so different now since he has dark hair. I never suspected it wasn't natural. Or maybe the blond hair wasn't natural." Then she cast her attention back to the policeman. "You must be suspicious of him since you have his picture."

"The man in question has had a long and profitable career. Then he dropped out of sight a number of years ago about the time I would imagine Randy Fletcher surfaced. He had made several careless mistakes before he changed identities. Nevertheless, there were enough similarities to make certain people suspicious and the evidence has built up. What you've told me has helped immensely. And we have been on the lookout for this necklace. It did not leave my country legally and we want it back. Now," and he pushed back his chair and stood up. "Why don't you return to your hotel and enjoy yourselves? You can safely leave the detective work to us."

It was a polite, encouraging dismissal. But a dismissal nevertheless. Rena and Bryan were back outside and looking for a taxi. The sun was hot and the competition fierce, but Bryan was soon helping her into the backseat of a cab.

As they sped toward the hotel, Rena voiced a vague concern. "Do you really think the authorities will do anything?"

"I don't doubt for a moment they'll do what they can. And I think what you had to tell them will help. It's another link in their chain of evidence."

"Well, I don't know. I still feel like I should be doing something."

"Rena, leave the detective work to the professionals."

She said nothing more, but Rena knew she would slip away as soon as possible and give some time to trying to locate Randy's hotel. She had a score to settle, although she wasn't quite sure how.

Their hotel was suitably elegant and Rena looked forward to a hot bath, a soft bed, and a light meal. But most of all she looked forward to a night of trouble-free sleep. She just wished she felt entirely confident the local police were going to do everything possible to trap Randy—or at least prove his guilt.

The door to her room opened easily and as she pushed the door shut behind her she dropped the room key in her purse. The room was dark and she wondered why the draperies were pulled. It made the room cool, but it also made it gloomy. She was halfway across the room when a voice stopped her.

"You certainly took your time. If I hadn't been on the same plane with you I would have begun to wonder if your plane had been hijacked."

Mitch lay comfortably stretched out on the bed. After jerking open the curtains and filling the room with sunlight, Rena rounded on him. "What are you doing here?" Then she added, "I didn't see you on the plane."

"What I'm doing here is waiting for you. And I took great care so you wouldn't see me. I sat well back in the tourist section, lost in a wreath of cigar smoke from the man next to me."

Rena kicked off her shoes and sat down on a chair near the bed. "How could you? You're supposed to be taking it easy."

"Don't I look like that's what I'm doing?"

"You look like you're rumpling my bedspread."

He feigned a look of hurt surprise. "You mean it isn't our bedspread?"

"Most definitely not!"

"One room's cheaper than two."

"But not nearly as restful." Darn it! Why did her heart have to race so? "You have your health to consider."

"It was my health I was thinking about when I suggested we share expenses." He leered teasingly and Rena threw her shoe at him. Catching it neatly, he tossed it back. "Is that any way to treat an invalid?"

"You're about as invalid an invalid as I've ever seen."

"Then since you don't feel you have to spare my feelings, how about telling me what you and Bryan think you've been up to."

"Believe it or not, we've been at the police station all this time, trying to get someone to listen to us."

"Any luck?"

"Finally. At least the man was aware of Randy's identity. Perhaps I should say other identity. Mitch, you'll never guess who he really is."

"You sound like you know him."

"I do, but I never made the connection until the inspector showed me a picture. It took me a bit to recognize him as Randy Fletcher."

"Rena, if you don't tell me soon who he is, I'm going to wring your neck."

"His name was Martin Dankin and he was apprenticing with my father at the time of the LaSalle fiasco."

"And that's Fletcher's real identity?"

"I would assume so. It was the one he was using at the time anyway."

"How come you haven't made the connection before?"

"Because his hair was longer and quite blond."

"No wonder he was a little skittish around you at first."

"He probably wondered if I was going to recognize him. Then when I didn't it probably became a game with him."

"How is it the Egyptian police are on to him?"

"Apparently his career has not been without error. By the way, they have a dossier on each and every person involved in the Dressler hunt, and someone at their headquarters with a very good eye for faces linked Fletcher's picture with Dankin's. They only needed me to confirm it."

"Why the dossiers?"

"They don't intend to let that necklace out of the country again."

"Nice little mess Dressler pitched us into."

"He might not have known."

"You go ahead and give him the benefit of the doubt. I don't feel much like it. Being in that plane crash was bad enough, but then you went off and left me with every intention of going it alone as I thought we'd agreed you wouldn't do again."

"I'm not alone. Bryan's with me—as I imagine you well know."

"When you're not with me, Rena, you're alone. And I'm not about to let another man take my place."

"Bryan could scarcely do that."

He had moved to run his fingers along the back of her neck and the curve of her jawline. As always, his touch did crazy things to her equilibrium. "I'm glad you realize that."

"Mitch?"

"Hmmm?" His lips lightly touched only the most sensitive places on her neck, but they left a wake of fiery desire.

"Mitch . . ." and Rena ran her tongue over very dry lips. "I don't think we should be doing this. We've business to attend to . . ."

He interrupted her with a frown. "I thought the police had everything under control?"

"I'm sure they do, but . . ."

"But nothing. You and I are both free to indulge ourselves. And what better way to do that than in loving."

"Someone should be seeing to Shay."

"What about Shay?"

"She remained behind to keep you company. You didn't by any chance bring her with you?"

"No, I wasn't aware I had a guard dog."

"How did you know we were leaving?"

"Just say a little bird told me."

Rena frowned and drew back. "Shay told you—didn't she?"

"Okay—I didn't want to get her in trouble, but yes, she did. I don't think she thought I'd do anything about it. But she did think I should know."

"Darn her!"

Catching her face between his hands, he forced her to look at him. "She was worried about you and Bryan, afraid you might have taken on more than you could handle. Like all of us, Rena, your sister's good intentions sometimes go awry. I, for one, am glad she told me."

"Why? There's nothing you can do."

"Oh, isn't there?"

Mitch might have several broken ribs, but he gave Rena every reason to doubt it as he pulled her to him in an almost suffocating embrace. "Mitch, there are a lot of things I should be doing other than dallying with a man who should be taking care of himself."

"But I am taking care of myself—and you at the same time."

"Mitch!"

He gently massaged her back while he nuzzled the most vulnerable part of her neck.

"You have a very unfair advantage, Mitch."

"What's that?"

"You can make me want you so easily."

He drew back and his blue eyes wove a spell around her. "Don't you think that works both ways? Why do you think, with all advice to the contrary, I followed you?"

"To be in on the last leg of the treasure hunt?"

"You, dear lady, are all the treasure I could possibly want."

The words were so lovingly spoken that all of Rena's resistance fled. Mitch was right—there was nothing more they could do for a while.

Somehow her hair tumbled lose and fell forward. Mitch buried his face in its thickness and murmured, "You always smell so sweet."

"Mitch?" And she spoke against the softness of his shirt and the hardness of his chest. "What if what we have doesn't last?"

"It will."

"But what if it doesn't? What if our differences get the better of us?"

"Rena, everyone takes that chance when they love somebody. We just have to trust what's between us will always be. There are no guarantees in love, only the pleasure of the moment and the hope for tomorrow."

Still she was afraid of losing him—of not fitting into his world. All the while he talked, he brushed her face and neck with kisses. They lay together on the bed now and Mitch held her the length of him. She couldn't help being acutely aware of every contour and need of his very masculine body. His fingers easily unbuttoned the top button of her blouse just as his lips easily tasted the swelling curve of her breast above a lacy scrap of bra.

Rena was lost then. She yielded to his kisses, his caresses. Finally, it was her lips that sought his with demands echoed by her body. They weren't just two people meeting in passionate love, but a mirror image of the needs of a world.

Some time later she lay resting in his arms. "Was that so bad?"

"You know it wasn't."

"Then why do you always waste so much time arguing against it?"

"Well, for one thing, Mitch, I really do think you should take care of yourself. And for another, I don't like feeling that I give in too easily."

"Just like I prefer to finish the treasure hunt—not let Bryan do it for me. No matter how casual I might be about it, I'm not in the habit of throwing around half a million." Then his voice dropped intimately. "Besides, I'm not used to letting the woman in my life go off with another man."

"Bryan? Bryan is not another man. He's like a brother to me."

"But how does he feel about you?"

"He's as in love with Shay as always. I think there's the possibility our little mishap may get them back together."

"Then I guess it wasn't all bad—not if it brought four people together where they belong." The look he gave her was both loving and possessive. "You will be mine, in spite of all your objections."

"As long as you let me be myself."

"Do you think I'd allow anything else? I should think by now you'd realize I wanted an equal partner."

"Partners don't try to tell each other what to do."

"Maybe because partners don't like to see each other make mistakes."

"It's impossible to go through life without making mistakes."

"Yes, Rena, but some can be much more far reaching than others. Perhaps even fatal."

He couldn't possibly know what a knife thrust of guilt his words carried. He couldn't know that Randy Fletcher might have tampered with the fuel for their plane, and that if she had only said something their crash might have been avoided. Talk about mistakes, she had a lot to make up for as far as that one was concerned. But make up for it she would. Randy Fletcher would not walk away if he was guilty.

"Your thoughts have taken you away from me."

"No they haven't. They were very concerned with you."

"Where are you going to run off to once I leave here?"

His question surprised her. "I'm not going anywhere. I intend to order up a light supper and get a good night's sleep."

"Probaby not a bad idea since the third and final clues will be handed out tomorrow night. So it could be a late one."

"That's why you left the hospital?"

"Partly. I had already decided I was going to follow you when I received a telegram from Judson Kingsley."

"Well, I guess I should buy something suitably exotic to wear then. So that takes care of tomorrow." *That and trying to find where Randy is staying, in case the police aren't doing their job.* "Does this mean Fletcher's gone public with the necklace?"

"Not necessarily. Dressler had someone present at the site as he did in Hong Kong with the butterfly."

Rena wondered if she should ask him to accompany her while she shopped. It would make it hard to check up on Randy, but Mitch might think it odd if she didn't invite him along. "Do you want to go bazaar hopping with me tomorrow?"

"I don't think so. I think I'll take it a bit easy. I hate to admit it, but I'm a little weary. So, if you'll excuse me."

He didn't look all that good either, but then Rena was certain the doctors had never intended he fly to Egypt and make love to her as if there was no tomorrow.

"Would you like me to get you a room?"

"No, I suspected you wouldn't let me stay here. I already have one down the hall." His hand on the doorknob, he hesitated before leaving. "I left Shay a ticket. I imagine she's here by now. I didn't want you to think I abandoned her in a strange country."

"Then she and Bryan will soon be together again."

"Where they should be. Where all lovers should be."

"I hear you, Mitch."

"Good, then don't forget what I said."

"I won't."

Alone in her room, Rena turned out the light to enjoy the cobalt-shaded evening sky and the shadowy images of those most intriguing of ancient mysteries: the pyramids. They were as awesome as the guidebooks promised and Rena longed to stand beside them and to touch their ancient stones.

She longed to play the tourist in this land of incomparable sights, shop the bazaars, and return to her hotel room laden with exotic treasures. It would be fun to play tourist for a day.

The sun was already hot against her linen blouse and Rena was glad she'd decided on a cool, loose-fitting skirt and low-heeled shoes. Even with sunglasses the brightness was intense and she wondered how anyone ever became used to it. What would it have been like to be born in this land that sprawled along the life-giving Nile and stretched back to ancient times? Her fascination for the country was such that she wondered if at some time she hadn't walked the golden sands and worshipped Osiris.

A stop at the hotel desk before starting out had served a dual purpose. She'd left a note for the rest of her party and also asked directions to the shopping district. They had asked her if she wanted modern shopping or the old bazaars. Naturally she had chosen the bazaars. Now a wild taxi ride presumably took her in that direction. Soon she was walking the length of the Muski, what her enthusiastic taxi driver had assured her was the oldest commercial street in Cairo.

Picturesque lanes were lined their narrow length with little shops, each one with a wooden awning. Rena gratefully ducked under cover and got a little relief from the burning sun. The proprietor quickly brought her some coffee and invited her to browse as long as she wanted. The shop was rich with the mingled scents of spices. Every item was appealing if not immediately useful and she knew it was a good thing her funds weren't unlimited. She wasn't sure how she would have gotten everything home if they were.

Several hours later she emerged from the Khan El-Khalili bazaar with an assortment of treasures. Some blue hand-blown glass she hoped was carefully packed and a gold cartouche with her name written in phonetic hieroglyphs were special finds. She'd redeemed these extravagances by purchasing a galabia to wear that evening.

It was a full-length cotton garment traditionally worn by men, but another woman in the shop had assured her it was very popular with female tourists. Rena had chosen one with gold thread embroidery and wondered if women tourists weren't in mind when it was made because she couldn't imagine a man wearing it. Although there was always the possibility she was wrong. What did she know, after all, about Egyptian dress?

She supposed she should get started scouting the hotels in hopes of finding where Randy was staying. But she was reluctant to get started. So it wasn't difficult to let a goldsmith at work distract her. She was just marveling at the man's talent when the sound of raised voices caught her attention.

Glancing around, her breath caught and her heart raced. She hadn't been wrong in recognizing the voice raised in anger. Having mistaken him once, she'd never do so again. Rena was positive she'd know Randy Fletcher anyplace, anytime.

If his speciality was keeping a low profile, then he was certainly blowing it now. In fact, he was far from setting a good example for fellow tourists with his voice raised in angry argument. There seemed no need to disagree with any of the shopkeepers since they were more than ready to bargain amiably.

She glanced around anxiously for a policeman, but saw none, so when she saw Randy stalk away from the shop, shouldering his way rudely through the crowd, she decided to investigate the shop he'd so recently vacated.

Smiling at the dealer who'd been showing her some gold jewelry, Rena made her way to the shop in question. It was typically dark inside after the bright Egyptian sun and she had to wait a moment for her eyes to adjust. The shopkeeper was grumbling and as they were alone she decided on a hunch to approach him. Angry people sometimes talked too much.

"There was a man in here—just now. I think he's a friend of mine."

"Then you should make some new friends."

"Oh?" Would he respond to the unspoken question in her one-word reply? She really had no idea what to expect.

"He would cheat me if he could. But I am too smart for him."

"Randy did always try to get a good deal."

"Randy? I know no one named Randy. I am speaking of Martin Dankin —a thief among thieves. Once, many years ago, I helped him dispose of some diamonds he couldn't sell."

Rena's heart did double time, but she was afraid to speak for fear of breaking the chain of information.

"Now he assumes I will help him steal one of our national treasures. A smart thief never would have touched that necklace. Anything that well-known is bad luck, because the authorities can't be far behind. The police have been everywhere questioning and showing pictures. Have we seen this man; have we seen this necklace."

Perhaps Randy's public show of anger was because he couldn't find any-one to take the necklace off his hands and he knew he'd never be able to leave the country with it. "Can you tell me, do you have any idea where that man was going?"

The shopkeeper shrugged eloquently. "Who knows? Somewhere in the bazaar probably."

"He gave you no indication where you might be able to reach him if you changed your mind?" Was this man as honest as his indignation suggested?

"I told him I wasn't interested. Minor artifacts are one thing—many people deal in those. But this necklace is too big. It would mean big trouble to be associated with it."

"Then you think the necklace belonged to somebody important?"

His eyes narrowed meanly. "I think you ask too many questions. I'm busy and I know nothing."

"But you know enough to interest the police."

"And I shall tell them what I know when they arrive."

"You contacted them?"

He drew himself up to his full height which was an inch or two below Rena's. "As soon as he left I phoned the police. They should be here very soon."

Before Rena had time to reply the shop was indeed swarming with Egyptian police and she found herself caught in the middle. She wasn't under suspicion, but of course she was expected to stay around. Especially after the shopkeeper informed the police that she claimed to be a friend of the thief. In no time they were deluging her with a barrage of questions—some of them in such heavily accented English she couldn't have answered if she'd wanted. But at least they could speak her language, which was more than she could do with theirs.

It was a relief when she recognized the inspector who had listened to her so politely the day before. Unfortunately, he didn't look quite so glad to see her.

"What are you doing here, Miss Drake?"

"I was shopping . . ." He interrupted before she could continue.

"Are you sure that's all you were doing? You weren't by any chance playing detective?"

"No, I wasn't." And she hadn't been, not yet anyway. She'd been too caught up in the variety of the bazaars to go tracking Randy as earlier planned. Pure coincidence had involved her in this mess.

"Then this is a chance encounter?"

She looked him directly in the eye in an effort to give leverage to her answer. "Yes, it is."

The official was darkly handsome and totally unreadable as he fixed her with a penetrating, no-nonsense glare and she wondered how much of the truth he believed. "I hope, Miss Drake, you are telling the truth, for you are far too lovely, and I expect too innocent, to be involved with a man of Martin Dankin's reputation."

The words were meant to be flattering and that's exactly how Rena felt. If she weren't in love with Mitch, she knew she would be more than flattered. But even that much response made her feel disloyal. "I'm having far too good a time shopping to be chasing thieves."

"So I see." The man smiled for the first time, revealing even white teeth and almost gothic good looks. Rena reasoned he might even be fun when off duty.

"It seemed to take you quite a while to get here. Do you think you'll be able to pick up his trail?"

"We are not as slow as we seem. As soon as this good citizen notified the police, an officer in the vicinity was contacted and began following the suspect. I don't think Dankin will get very far. My men are extremely good and we don't like antiquity thieves. Now, I would appreciate it if you would come to police headquarters. I would like you there when he's brought in."

The request was phrased as politely as possible, but Rena knew she had no choice but to accept. A glance at her watch made her wince. She had lost herself in shopping and time had gotten away from her. As it was, there was barely time to leisurely get ready for the party if she were to start now. The gatherings were not fashionably late and the distribution of the clues waited for no one. Mitch would not appreciate her being late, especially if he found out it involved Fletcher in any way.

Glancing up from her watch, Rena found the detective watching her. She would have to do what he asked and hope that Mitch understood if she was late. But the ride to the police station and the subsequent wait were fraught with anxious tedium. They kept her waiting forever, then apologized profusely for doing so. Then it seemed all they wanted her to do was identify Fletcher and confirm his other identity as Martin Dankin. She supposed such identification was necessary, but couldn't they have had her do it to start out with?

She was waiting for the car that would take her back to her hotel, when someone called her name. She turned to find a handcuffed Fletcher regarding her somewhat sadly while Inspector Bey watched.

"Well, Rena, I guess this is good-bye."

She supposed she should hate him, all things considered. For in true mystery story style, he had confessed to everything; although he had not been the mastermind behind the theft of the LaSalle jewels, he had replaced the originals with clever fakes. As gemology was a profession handed down in her family, so was jewel theft in Fletcher's.

"It looks that way." She felt more sorry for the way of life he'd chosen than anything. He certainly had the intelligence to have made it big on the right side of the law.

"I'm glad you survived the crash. In fact, I'm glad you all did."

"I find that most hard to forgive, Randy. Why did you do it?"

"I was in a hurry and I got careless. Frankly, I didn't even think the plane would get off the ground."

"You mean you did something like that without even knowing the consequences?"

"I thought I knew what would happen. Believe me, Rena, when I say I would never have done it if I'd known the plane would be airborne when the contaminated fuel hit the tanks."

"I'm probably a fool, but I believe you."

"You will probably never know how much that means to me. Well, good luck. I hope you're the one to find the third and final treasure."

As he walked away, it was still with a confident swagger.

Several hours later than she should have been, a police car deposited her in front of her hotel. Date palms swayed in the evening air and stone lions looked on disapprovingly as if they guessed how angry Mitch was going to be. Repeated attempts to reach Mitch or Bryan and Shay had met with failure. She had no difficulty in imagining the anger and fear they must have experienced.

The clock in the hotel lobby confirmed the time on her watch. She hoped Mitch had gone on without her.

Rena didn't have long to wait for an answer; Mitch had once again gained admittance to her room. He looked fantastic, doing very sexy things to a three-piece suit. It was impossible to tell if his icy calm disguised anger or concern. No doubt he'd soon enlighten her. A small voice inside reminded her that Mitch wasn't unreasonable. Then another voice reminded; unless they were dealing with Randy Fletcher.

"Where have you been? I didn't know whether to be mad or worried."

"I'm sorry I'm late, but I've been at the police station for hours."

"Don't they have any telephones there?"

"I tried, Mitch, believe me. But I could never reach you."

"You could have had me paged."

Rena felt instantly foolish. "I didn't think of that. All I could think of was reaching you and explaining I would be late and why." Then she added as if an afterthought, "I'm sorry if you were worried."

"Worried! That's putting it mildly. I envisioned you with your throat slit in an alley or locked inside one of the national monuments. My God, Rena, what would I do if anything happened to you?" Then he fired a question at her as if he'd just heard her earlier explanation. "What were you doing at the police station?"

She tossed her purchases on the bed before she remembered some of them were fragile. "Randy Fletcher is no longer a part of the competition. The Egyptians have him in custody for dealing in stolen artifacts, among other things."

"No doubt he'll plead ignorance of the necklace's background."

"No, I don't think so." And she recalled the clean breast he'd made of everything.

"Then we're finally finished with him?"

"I hope so."

"Not as much as I do. He was very much a presence in our relationship, proving two's company and three's a crowd."

"He's never been a threat to you, Mitch."

"I know I want to believe he never meant anything to you other than a means to an end. But you wouldn't leave him out of your life."

"Because I wanted to be finished once and for all with the LaSalle business. It was an old obligation I was committed to but weary of." Did he understand? How she wished she knew. "You look tired and I know I've let you down. You should never have attempted coming to Egypt. Not after what you'd been through."

"Well, you certainly behaved as if I weren't here."

"Mitch, that isn't so. I didn't plan on being caught in the middle of Fletcher's capture."

"I really want to believe that. Maybe it would be easier if I didn't feel like I'd been stepped on by a herd of elephants. You know, it's almost ironic. You saw the treasure hunt as a means to finally settle the business of the LaSalle jewels. I saw it as a means for you and me to be together so maybe we could really get together."

"And we did." She wanted so badly to reach out and touch him, but there was an invisible barrier newly erected between them.

"If you call snatched odds and ends of moments being together. The beautiful woman I wanted to call my own has proven time and again that her feelings for me, as well as mine for her, have to be fit in whenever it's convenient."

"I know it looks that way, Mitch, but . . ."

"I don't want to share you, Rena. Here," and he tossed the third clue on the bed. "I no longer give a damn about priceless baubles. Like memories, they won't keep a man warm at night."

He was gone from the room, slamming the door behind him. There was nothing she could think to say tonight that would change his mind. Perhaps tomorrow when they'd both had a chance to rest. She loved him more than anything.

Tired as she was, she would spend a while trying to solve the third and final clue. Mitch would see she could be dogged at something other than tracking thieves.

CHAPTER 13

Hours later and far deeper into the night than she had expected, Rena still hadn't solved the entire riddle of the third clue. She did know what she was looking for but the location escaped her. Again she smoothed the crumpled note, again she read it aloud.

"The oldest and only surviving member of a prestigious group. Like this gem, they're beyond price. Now what," she asked the unresponsive hotel room, "is the location?"

Her legs ached from sitting cross-legged on the bed so Rena stood up, stretched, and walked around the room. It was by now monotonously familiar to her, as was the ritual of circling the room to relieve her cramped muscles. She had ordered up a huge pot of strong coffee, which was stronger than she expected. In fact, she wondered if she'd ever be able to sleep again.

A gem beyond price could only be a pearl—at least as far as popular thought was concerned. And there had been a massive one on display with the Dressler Collection. But the first part of the clue had her stumped.

Several times she'd reached for the telephone, ready to call Mitch for help, but each time she'd withdrawn her hand, stopped by her pride. At five in the morning she decided to shelve her pride.

The hotel operator answered promptly, which helped keep her from again retreating at the thought of confronting Mitch. Several times the phone rang before a sleepy voice answered. Rena was unable to respond to the groggy-sounding hello, for it definitely wasn't Mitch who answered, but someone female. Quickly, Rena hung up the phone. Then she decided the hotel operator had obviously rung the wrong room. Again she called Mitch's number. This time there were only three rings before a decidedly less groggy, but definitely annoyed, female voice answered. Rena knew there could be no mistake a second time and she replaced the phone on the hook.

She sat there chewing her bottom lip and fighting tears. While she'd been worrying about the clue and overloading her system with caffeine, he'd been with another woman. Well, so much for caring on his end.

The truth of her sobering thoughts made her suddenly weary in spite of the gallons of coffee she had consumed through the long night. In despair, she curled up on top of the bed and cried herself into an uneasy sleep.

When Rena awoke three hours later her pillow was wet and her mouth tasted as if she'd been chewing on old socks. It was only her desire to escape her room that prodded her from bed. Yet she dressed carefully, perhaps because her spirits were more often raised by wearing something feminine than they were by anything else. It wasn't the end of the world just because Mitch had discarded her, and people would not see her going around in sackcloth because of it.

Carefully, Rena shook out a gauzy peach skirt and blouse she'd never worn before. She'd taken them along because the material had a slightly rumpled look whether pressed or not. Therefore they seemed the perfect garments to withstand the wrinkling of being packed in a suitcase. The color did nice things to her complexion, touching it also with a tint of peach. Carefully, she applied her makeup and brushed her shining hair until it glowed. Then she pinned it into a loose knot that had a faintly Victorian look to it. Tiny pearl earrings seemed just perfect to complete her appearance.

Only after she fastened them in her ears did she realize they were miniature symbols of the treasure she sought. With slightly shaking hands, Rena gathered up her purse and headed downstairs to the hotel restaurant. She had to eat no matter how little she felt like it. How she hoped she didn't run into Bryan and Shay who would ask uncomfortable questions. Or Mitch and whoever had answered the phone. But if she did, at least she wouldn't look jilted.

The maître d' gave in to her request to seat her at a small table well screened behind a luxuriant potted palm. The only thing that saved the situation for Rena was that she felt somewhat like a two-bit spy, a fact that added a bit of dash to an otherwise depressing situation. With a barely suppressed grimace, she ordered more coffee, fruit juice, and muffins. It would be a breakfast she could linger over, especially as coffee was served at the table in individual silver pots. Dining was slow as she kept an eye on the entrance. She was loath to meet Mitch face-to-face, but she would like a look at his last night's companion.

Her leisurely breakfast paid off, but not in the way she had hoped. She was just sipping the last of her chilled and luscious-tasting juice when she saw Inspector Bey who had listened to her suspicions about Fletcher. He paused in the entrance, spoke to the maître d', and was directed to her table. Today he was dressed in casual clothes, but was no less official-looking and no less handsome. Really, Rena thought, he should be in the movies carrying nubile young maidens to striped tents on the desert. A giggle arose at the thought and she had to quickly disguise it as a somewhat trembly cough.

He stood across the small table from her and smiled. "I hope this is not an intrusion, Miss Drake, but I wanted to inform you that the troublesome Mr. Dankin will find no way of escaping justice this time. Your evidence, along with what we had and what's been trickling in all night, will provide him with free room and board for some time."

"I'm glad, vindictive as that might sound."

"It doesn't sound that way at all. The man is a criminal, a thief who has caused untold grief to many people."

"And the necklace?"

"Placed in the hands of those who can appraise it properly."

"But it will be for everyone to enjoy?"

"As soon as it has been identified and authenticated."

Rena frowned; she could see the necklace as lost to the enjoyment of museum lovers as it had been in Dressler's private collection.

"Don't frown, Miss Drake. I know what you must be thinking, but I can assure you it will go on display before long even if there is reasonable doubt about whether or not it really belonged to a certain lovely queen. It is old and valuable regardless of who wore it and the public will be allowed to view it."

"I'm glad to hear that."

"You are a lover of antiquity?"

"I'm in love with the history of your country."

"As are a good many people. Sometimes it is wearying to be revered more for your past than your future."

"But how bleak to have had neither."

"You're right, and even as familiar a sight as they've become I find that each time I view the pyramids near sunset I, too, marvel at their beauty and ingenuity. Would you mind if I shared a cup of coffee with you?"

"Oh, please do. I didn't mean to be rude."

He pulled out the chair opposite her and snapped his fingers for the waiter.

After he'd taken the policeman's order, he left. "He is wondering if the fact I'm not in official dress means you're in any less trouble."

His tone was so sincere and conspiratorial that Rena couldn't help laughing.

"There, that is much better. Your lips were meant for smiling—remember that." His gaze lingered overlong on her mouth and for a moment Rena wondered if he wouldn't have brushed her with a kiss had they been alone. It was the boost her ego needed, to think he might find her attractive.

He sipped his coffee when it was brought, all the time watching her over the rim of the delicate cup. "Are you enjoying your stay in my country?"

"Yes, although I regret I've had little time for sight-seeing and what I did have I spent shopping."

"And how is the treasure hunt going?"

"Not too well at the moment. I sat up all night, drank probably lethal quantities of coffee, and still I can't decipher where the third treasure is hidden.

"I wish I could help you as you helped me yesterday. I hope the delay didn't cause you any trouble?"

She hesitated, remembering exactly how much trouble it had caused, then decided it would be rude to say so. But Ahmed Bey was too quick for her and too used to reading the truth lurking in people's eyes and behind their smiles.

"I can see that it did and for so serious a frown I would say the trouble is with a man. Would it be the gentleman who accompanied you to the police station?"

Did she imagine the regret in his voice? "You're very good at ferreting out the truth."

"I am paid well for it. But you are quite good yourself at answering a question with one of your own."

"Yes, it did cause me trouble with a man, but not the one you met, who was just a friend. My employer was not too happy that I missed a rather important function last night."

"This employer is important to you?"

"Very."

"Perhaps I could explain."

"No, he has to trust what I tell him."

"Sometimes that isn't so easy when you care for someone."

"But it's essential to a relationship."

"Caring—loving—isn't always reasonable or rational."

Rena thought of her years of resistance to Mitch simply because of his fortune. "No, you're right."

"If you won't let me make things right with him, perhaps you would let me show you some of the wonders of my country—those close to the city, that is."

Rena was surprised at the invitation, but knew it was sincere. Would it hurt to spend some time with this very charming man? After all, Mitch wasn't brooding in isolation—if he was brooding at all. She could worry the third clue as easily in Ahmed's company as she could on her own. "I think I'd like that, particularly if you'll take me to see the Sphinx and the pyramids."

"I see you are going to be easily pleased. But if you'll consent to spend the day with me I would like to show you these wonders at sunset. For they are unsurpassingly spectacular then."

"That sounds very agreeable. Will you give me a few minutes to let someone know where I'll be?"

"Ah-h-h," and he smiled knowingly. "You wish to tell your doubting employer."

"No! I don't imagine he'll even know I'm gone. I was thinking of the other two people making up our party."

"Certainly, tell them. I will eat that very delicious-looking roll you left and drink some more of this very good coffee." Then, as she would have brushed past, he caught her wrist and his hand was as warm as the desert sands. "Don't be too sure you won't be missed. Perhaps it will do your employer good to know that you don't need to sit and suffer his displeasure."

Rena wished he were right. And even if he weren't, what better way to see Cairo than in the company of a very handsome and congenial Egyptian. Luckily, she ran into Shay in the elevator.

"I was looking for you, Rena. Where have you been all morning?"

"I've been enjoying a leisurely breakfast."

"Is Mitch with you?"

"No, I've been entertaining the very efficient policeman Bryan and I met our first day here."

"Are you in some kind of trouble?"

Her sister sounded so aghast, Rena had to laugh. "I think it's purely a social call. He's asked me to spend the day with him."

"What will Mitch say?"

"Oh, Shay, does everything have to be okay with Mitch?"

"No, of course not. It sounds like the two of you have been disagreeing again."

"You might say that. I spent a good part of yesterday with the police and he seems to think I did it deliberately."

"He was really quite worried when you didn't show up. I think he had visions you'd been kidnapped by terrorists or something equally dreadful. Couldn't you at least have called?"

"I tried, but I couldn't reach any of you. Unfortunately, Mitch didn't seem to understand."

"Only because he'd been so worried. Plus I don't think he's feeling quite as recovered from the crash as he'd like us to think."

Rena remembered the sound of the woman's voice answering his telephone in the early morning hours. That certainly didn't make it sound as though he was under the weather. "He has a funny way of showing it."

"What are you talking about?"

"Nothing, forget I said anything."

"Where are you going with your handsome policeman?"

"How do you know he's handsome?"

"Because I know you, dear sister—and you have a way of attracting good-looking men."

"Well, I don't know where we're going, but he has promised to show me the pyramids at their peak."

"When's that?"

"Sunset. So don't expect to see me very early."

"I don't really expect to see you at all. At least not for a while."

"Why, where are you going?"

"Bryan and I are flying back to Seattle. That's why I was looking for you. I didn't want to leave without saying good-bye."

Rena couldn't disguise the joy that filled her. "Does that mean things are better between you two?"

"It means we're going to start seeing each other again. We're going to take each day as it comes."

"It sounds promising, Shay."

"I hope so. I've never loved any man but Bryan."

"You have all my best wishes."

"Well," and there was an awkward pause as if Shay was trying to think of something encouraging to say. "Have you made any progress on the final clue?"

"I have a good idea what to look for, but that's not much good since I don't know where."

"Perhaps Mitch could help."

"I tried to get hold of him, but I couldn't. So I figured I'd think and enjoy the sights at the same time."

"Especially with a local tour guide. Well, little sister, keep in touch, will you?"

"Of course, and, Shay, I'm really glad things are looking better for you and Bryan."

"So am I. I was awfully tired of wearing socks to bed to keep my feet warm, and looking at an empty chair across the table. I've grown up a lot, Rena, and I think I could make Bryan a good wife if given another chance."

"You're lucky. Not everyone gets a second chance."

"Really, I have you to thank. If you hadn't gone off and gotten lost in some forsaken desert I wouldn't have found the courage to call him. But I needed help so I grabbed hold of my courage and dialed his number. I don't know what I would have done had a secretary answered. And yet I'm surprised one didn't." Shay hesitated and then plunged onward. "I don't know what's wrong between you and Mitch, but don't wait until a tragedy happens to make things right. Life is too short for that."

"And sometimes the opportunity is lost."

"What have you been talking around all through this conversation, Rena?"

Rena raised eyes that brimmed with unshed tears. "Early this morning— very early, after I'd pondered that damned third clue through the night—I called Mitch's room. I thought perhaps he would have some thoughts on the subject that might be escaping me."

"Did he?"

"I don't know, I never talked to him. A woman answered—a sleepy-voiced woman."

Shay was speechless for the moment. "Are you sure you had the right room?"

"My first thought. But when I had the hotel operator ring again I got the same woman. I didn't ask to speak to Mitch. She might have put him on the phone and I simply couldn't have talked to him, Shay. Not knowing he had someone there with him."

Shay was full of sympathy. "I don't blame you—and I didn't realize the situation, but it still surprises me. It seems so out of character for Mitch."

"How do we know that, Shay?"

"But he wouldn't even know . . ."

"He could have run into an old friend."

"Too coincidental, Rena."

"Regardless of the circumstances, he wasn't alone." Then she admitted to her vigilance of the morning. "I even had hopes of seeing him this morning when I spent a leisurely hour and a half at breakfast. But if he ate, he ordered room service."

"I'm sure there's an explanation we're overlooking."

"What could it possibly be besides the fact Mitch felt the need for a little female companionship?" Then she added bitterly, "Maybe he called room service for that, too!"

"Rena, don't make it any worse than it is. Don't do that to yourself. Look, enjoy your day. This is a beautiful and fascinating country; make the

most of the little time you have to view it. And make the most of being
with another man."

"This is not a romantic encounter."

"Who knows what it will turn out to be?"

"Shay, I'm no more able to easily replace Mitch than you were Bryan."

"Okay, I get the point, but it doesn't mean you can't have a fun day. For
pity sakes, the man was nice enough to ask you out. Don't spoil it for him."

"Would I do that?"

"I don't know. Your spirits are sagging so low I'm not sure you can get
them up before the day is over."

"Don't worry, Ahmed will enjoy my company. I'm wondering though if I
should change."

"Don't, you look very romantic that way."

"But I'm not going to a garden party."

"Nor are you going on a voyage of discovery. You look just fine."

Rena felt doubtful, but didn't really want to change. "Well, if I'm forced
to crawl into the pyramids on my hands and knees you'll hear about it."

"I don't think you'll have to, so don't worry. Bryan's waiting for me, so
I'd best be off."

"Take care now and keep in touch."

"You too."

The sisters embraced and Rena watched Shay walk away. At least there
was the chance of a happy ending. Stopping by a mirror at the end of the
hall she smoothed her hair and repaired her lipstick.

Ahmed was waiting in the hotel lobby with a dark-eyed look of appreciation that almost gave Rena second thoughts. What did she know of this
man, anyway, except that he was a policeman? And what did he know of
her except she was nursing a bruised heart? Would he try taking advantage
of that?

Deciding not, she summoned a warm smile in return for his. Ahmed
linked his arm with hers and they walked out into the Egyptian sun.

"You don't look like the typical tourist."

"This is—to quote someone dear to me—my garden party look. Actually,
I've been grubbing around in grubbies for what seems like forever. And I
decided to dress the way I enjoy today."

"I'm pleased I'm the one to benefit."

Rena felt a trifle uncomfortable. This was a casual afternoon for her, a
chance to forget for a short time the problems confronting her. Surely,
Ahmed wasn't reading more into her friendly acceptance of his invitation
than there was meant to be?

He ushered her into a small black car and moved expertly into what seemed a confusion of traffic. "It isn't often I get to spend a relaxing day away from work."

"I would imagine in your line it has a way of following you home."

"You're very perceptive. And if it doesn't, then my children keep me occupied."

Rena was glad of her dark glasses for she knew they hid the wide-eyed stare of surprise she couldn't help. Was she spending the day with a married man? "Oh, you have a family?"

"Three children. They live with my sister and her family because I'm gone so much and keep such irregular hours. I've been a widower for three years now."

"Oh, I'm sorry to hear that."

"I suppose I will cease to miss her in time. We were children together and our marriage seemed inevitable. Destiny perhaps."

"I think you loved her very much."

He smiled ruefully. "I still do. I want to thank you for agreeing to let me show you my city. It's not often I get to spend time with a woman who isn't either a criminal or assessing my possibilities as a husband." He gave her a sideways grin and continued, "And that isn't ego talking."

"I understand. It is pleasant to spend an uncomplicated day with someone."

"Now, do you have something special you care to see or will you place yourself in my capable hands?"

"Other than the pyramids, which you've assured me are best seen at sunset, I don't have any preferences."

"Good, then shall we be off?"

Rena saw ancient and modern Egypt through the eyes of a proud Egyptian. Then they went somewhere for a cool iced drink.

Lazy ceiling fans stirred the heavy air and Rena sipped her lime-flavored drink. It was tart and refreshing and had been Ahmed's recommendation. So far he had not steered her wrong the entire day. She poked her straw at a piece of ice as she spoke. "You know, I thought you were rather official and somewhat ruthless yesterday."

"I do my job. And I have little pity for criminals."

"But you wouldn't let me go home."

"Because I needed you."

"So did someone else."

"Ah-h-h, I sense by detaining you at headquarters I not only caused trouble with your employer, but with the man in your life."

"I can't deny you rather fanned the embers of an existing problem."

"My offer to explain is still good."

"You're a very kind man. No wonder the ladies in your life consider you speculatively. But it wouldn't help, I don't think."

"Perhaps if you explained, or have you already tried that?"

"I tried, but it didn't work out."

"Wouldn't he listen?"

"I couldn't reach him." She wasn't going to go into the humiliation of explaining there was another woman in Mitch's bedroom. Some embarrassments were best not shared.

"Then perhaps you should keep trying—that is if the relationship is worth fighting for."

"It is, but I think I came to that realization a bit late."

"Sometimes we go looking for love and aren't aware it was there all the time."

"How right you are. In my case I knew I'd found it, but I didn't really know or understand how rare and precious it was. Which is strange."

"Why do you say that?"

"I'm a gemologist and I'm used to assessing the worth of things. Shouldn't I have been aware of the value of love in my own life?"

"Being an authority on one thing doesn't automatically make you an authority on all others."

She smiled at her newfound friend, and although she might never see him again, she would never forget this day spent together. "You are somewhat of a philosopher, Ahmed."

"People who know me well tend to think I'm too much of one. But in my work it seemed necessary to be one or else I'd become jaded and spoiled by the things I saw. My country's crime rate is low, but unfortunately it isn't nonexistent. And then there is the fact that these are uneasy times in much of the world. We cannot ignore them, but neither can we let them govern our lives. Being philosophic about what I see in my work and what I read in the papers definitely helps." He sipped his drink, his obsidian eyes never looking away from hers. "Would you like to tell me about the problem?"

Rena laughed. "I imagine you're very good at wringing confessions from people, because somehow you do give one the feeling you can help."

"I'd like to think I might be able to make things better."

"I'm afraid it might be too late for that in my case."

"It might not be as late as you think."

"When you've abused a person's love as much as I have, well, there's not much you can do about it."

"I can't believe you would ever do that."

Rena knew he meant what he said. "I was afraid of that love. And so I made cruel and senseless mistakes. I was always trying to be in control of the situation."

He nodded. "Which doesn't always work when people are romantically involved." Ahmed took her hand, now cold from clutching the icy lime drink, and held it in his, which was as warm as his smile and as encouraging. "Why should you have been afraid? You don't strike me as a fearful woman."

"I loved Mitch so much I couldn't stand the thought of losing that love. And I'm afraid I don't come from a family with much luck at making marriage work. Somehow, too much money on the part of one of the partners seemed to always be the culprit. And Mitch is very, very rich."

"And you objected to that?" His hoot of laughter turned several heads in their direction. "That's certainly a first."

"Hardly that. But I guess I was afraid we were too different—that I could never adjust to his wealth and background. Ahmed, Mitch comes from very old money. The way he acts is well-bred, instinctively. What if I were to embarrass him?"

He studied her with a look of incredulity. "You can sit there looking like a Dresden figurine and suggest you might embarrass someone? Rena, you are the very essence of good breeding and manners. I can't believe you would ever be anything but an asset."

"Perhaps not. But we've had so many differences of opinion. For instance, he became very impatient and almost distrustful of this whole business concerning Randy Fletcher. It's like I couldn't accept his wealth and he couldn't understand my single-mindedness in pursuit of a cause I believed in."

"Isn't someone special to love more important than all the differences in the world, whether they're real or imagined?"

"Yes."

"Real love is rare, Rena, and not to be abused or pushed aside. It's to be snatched and savored and shared with the one we love." His words were from the heart. "For we never know when that love might leave us. Happy memories are infinitely better than bitter regrets."

Her tear-stained voice was barely a whisper and he leaned forward to hear. "I'm still so afraid of failing."

Ahmed snatched a tear as it quivered and dropped from her lashes. "But you'll never know unless you try. We fail only when we don't try. And if we give in to fear, then we walk away from life."

"Do you really believe that?"

"I do indeed. Fear can keep us huddling in a cave or hiding in the dark. We need to be bold. For if we succeed then the world is ours."

"Then you're not afraid of failure?"

"It is there, but it is only truly real when we learn nothing from a situation. Besides, my dear lady, I don't think you need to worry over much. What man alive could resist forgiving you?" Then he grinned almost devilishly. "Especially since I would imagine the making up is quite sweet."

"I want to believe you, but . . ." And she told him about the woman who had answered Mitch's phone in the early hours of the morning.

He smiled gently in return. "There are a lot of explanations for that. When someone has made an indelible mark upon our life and then hurt us, we often seize upon rather drastic measures to erase the imprint they've made."

"But with another woman?"

"Unfortunately, that's very often the way. One thing you have to realize is that because you know how you feel doesn't necessarily mean he does. I would imagine his ego is a little fragile where you're concerned."

"Perhaps Mitch shouldn't forgive me. Maybe I don't deserve it."

"Rena, guilt is as wasted an emotion as fear. Don't substitute one for the other."

She took a deep breath, looked into his dark eyes, and understood the wisdom of his words. "I'll try—really I will."

"That's all I ask. Now light is leaving the sky, shall we drive to the pyramids or would you prefer to return to your hotel?"

"No, I need time to absorb all we've discussed and I really have been looking forward to seeing them at sunset."

"Good, then let us be on our way.

"I'm going to take you a route not usually used by the tourist. I think it's a vantage point even the ancients might have envied."

"It sounds very intriguing, but how do people usually travel?"

"By the Pyramid Road directly to the Giza Plateau."

"And we will be going?"

"Through Mena village. But hush now, and watch. You will soon see a sight with few rivals."

Rena sat silently and waiting anxiously, for Ahmed had aroused her awareness and she was prepared for something spectacular. Her impatience grew as they drove past a hodgepodge of shops and private homes.

Not even his warning or her sense of eagerness was preparation for the sudden splendor and power of the Sphinx appearing on the horizon. And then to the west loomed the pyramids. "Oh-h." She could think of nothing else to say for anything would have been inadequate. They were beautiful, timeless, and they took her breath away.

For the second time that day, her eyes misted. But not out of sadness.

Rather she was so touched by the scene before her that she could think of no other response. She sniffed and turned a sheepish smile toward Ahmed. "I feel somewhat foolish, but they bring tears to my eyes."

"Why feel foolish? Even Herodotus was impressed."

He stopped the car and they got out. Rena waited while he purchased their tickets. When he returned she tried to explain what she was feeling. "I've read about them and I knew they were magnificent, but nothing prepared me for this view. Thank you for this."

"You're welcome."

"They look old. And I know that seems silly to say, but I can remember when the Tutankhamen treasures toured the United States I waited anxiously to see them. While I was thrilled and they were beautiful, I was just a trifle disappointed because they didn't look old. Do you understand what I'm saying?"

"I think so. But those treasures were protected from the elements. The pyramids have been abused by the sun, sand, time, and vandals. And they are some four thousand five hundred years old. Of the Seven Wonders of the Ancient World, they are the only surviving ones."

His words dropped as if pebbles on the calm surface of a pool. Their rippling effect spread throughout her and she grabbed his arm while demanding, "What did you say?"

He was justifiably surprised. "They're the only one of the Seven Wonders of the Ancient World still surviving."

"Oh, Ahmed, you're wonderful!" And she gave him a quick kiss.

"That's nice to know, but what did I do?"

Knowing he was completely trustworthy, she explained. "I have not been able to figure out the location given in the third clue of the treasure hunt. Until now and thanks to you."

"What was the part of the clue you couldn't decipher?"

Rena quoted the words burned into her consciousness by a sleepless night. "The oldest and only surviving member of a prestigious group. Now I know what that means I wonder how I could have been so blind as not to understand. Probably everyone has figured it out."

"Sometimes we overlook the most obvious."

"You know, Ahmed, you're very good for me. Like a breath of fresh air in a closed-up attic."

He laughed heartily until he had to wipe his eyes, but all he would say is, "It's nice to be appreciated."

They stood for a moment and surveyed the scene before them that had been awe-inspiring thousands of years ago. Rena wondered what it would have been like to see the pyramids in their just completed glory. She decided she wouldn't trade then for now. She was sure nothing could compare with the luster of their antiquity. Ahmed's hand against the small of her back recalled her to the moment.

"Would you like to go inside now?"

"Yes, I only wish I knew where to go from there."

"What do you mean?"

"I know I'm looking for a pearl and a very large one. And I know it's somewhere in the vicinity of the pyramids, but any more than that I don't know."

"Something so small to be found in something so large. Are you certain?"

"Yes, not that it's much help."

"Well, let us go inside; perhaps just as my chance remark suggested a solution to a part of your puzzle, there will be something inside that will lead us to the pearl. Come."

Rena gladly took his hand as he led the way. A railing had been added and steps cut into the stripped core blocks. There were several in their party and they were well to the back, which suited Rena fine. She wanted to experience the awesomeness of the structure without a constant babble of voices. Ahmed seemed to understand without being told. But then he seemed to understand a great deal, and she knew—as she suspected he did —that in another time they might have been more than friends.

"I'm missing what he's saying," she whispered. "Is it important?"

They stopped for a moment, falling even farther behind, while he explained. "This is not the original entrance, but a forced one used because it provides the easiest access."

"Was it forced by thieves?"

"I suppose it depends on your definition of a thief. The Caliph of Cairo in the ninth century, al-Ma'mun, could not find the true entrance and so he had this one forced."

"What was he after—treasure?"

"That depends on the story you hear. He left no written record, but some say he was after treasure, others that he was after the lost knowledge of the ancients. Come, we're going to fall too far behind and the guides don't like that. As a policeman I must set a good example."

Rena knew he was teasing her, but she hurried to catch up with their group. The guide said something to Ahmed in their language and she wondered if her escort had suffered a rebuke or if they were exchanging a joke. Whichever, Ahmed didn't look upset.

Before long he was forced to release her hand as they began to scramble up a steep passage where they were obliged to hunch over. It was impossible to stand up and before long a dull ache had overtaken Rena's back.

As if sensing her discomfort, Ahmed turned to her. "Try imagining this passage encrusted with bat dung and the accompanying stench, as well as the smell and smoke from the torches used for illumination. You would have definitely wanted your grubbies, as you called them."

Rena shuddered. "I might have been able to stand it as long as the bats were long gone. They have got to be among the most loathsome creatures. What is this passage called, by the way, or does it have a name?"

"The Ascending Passage."

"How novel." Somehow she had expected something a little more original for a structure of this kind. She had also hoped for a hint to the treasure.

"As opposed to the Descending Passage. But that's another story."

Eventually, the passage leveled out and they had their choice of routes. Their guide took the stairs and so did they. The room they entered was in its way almost as inspiring as her view earlier of the Sphinx and pyramids. The room was huge, spectacular, and without the adornment she had somehow expected. Confined as they were inside the pyramid, there was yet a sensation of openness.

She leaned over and whispered to Ahmed, "Where are we now?"

"The Grand Gallery."

"How appropriate."

In their guided exploration of the pyramid, they passed a sealed entrance or what looked like one. Rena tugged on Ahmed's arm. "Where do you suppose that goes?"

"It closes off the entrance to what is known as the Well or the Grotto."

Instantly, Rena's senses became alert. "Wait a minute. What do both names suggest to you?"

"Water?"

"Exactly! And where do you find pearls?"

"In oysters."

"Well, yes, but where else?"

"In the water. But there isn't any water around here."

"It could be symbolic. I know it's way-out, but so far this whole adventure has been."

"All right, but where would the pearl you seek be hidden?" His tone was kind, but Rena suspected he felt she was reaching desperately for a solution to the site of the treasure.

"In other words, wishful thinking doesn't make it possible?"

"It just doesn't seem practical. Still, it won't hurt for us to search."

It took only the briefest of explorations to prove their efforts were futile. Rena felt disappointed all out of proportion to the possibility of their finding anything.

He took her hand and began leading her toward the outside. "Come, we both need some fresh air and some light, although the sun has probably left the sky. I imagine we caught the last tour of the day and our guide is undoubtedly wondering where we are."

As they walked along, Rena wracked her brain and her imagination for where the treasure could possibly be.

"Don't let the fact we couldn't find anything spoil your memories of the Great Pyramid."

"I won't. Nothing could do that." With her attention on him, she was late to find their passage blocked. She turned, stepped backward, and felt Ahmed bristle protectively—every inch the policeman.

Then recognition replaced fear. "Mitch!"

"I knew you'd have to show up here sooner or later. Everyone on a sight-seeing expedition in Cairo usually does. But I must admit, I've grown weary of waiting and bribing the guides to let me remain inside." He looked questioningly at Ahmed and then back at Rena. "I expected you to be alone."

Ahmed had been right, there was little light left in the sky, but what there was seemed to gather in the gold of Mitch's hair while casting his face in shadow. Rena was glad they were no longer inside the pyramid for she would have hated to desecrate the memory of it with the anger Mitch's accusation generated. All of Ahmed's good advice seemed forgotten.

"Why should I be alone? You certainly haven't been wanting for company."

Mitch didn't answer. Was he phrasing a plausible lie he hoped she'd accept? Her heart thudded in her chest and she realized how desperately she wanted him to deny there was anyone—past or present—except her.

"I suppose it was very unreal of me to hope my memory might linger a little." She willed her voice not to break, reminding herself they were not alone and that Mitch appeared in no mood for apologies. Seeing how stubborn he could be and hearing his cold accusing anger, would Ahmed still counsel her to try again for an understanding?

A wind had risen with the setting of the sun and blew her skirts around her. The same wind brought with it the smell of desert sands and times long past. And still Mitch didn't answer her. His silence confused her. "I'm waiting for an answer, Mitch. Or didn't you think I knew?" Ahmed stirred behind her and she remembered his urgings to try and try again, because love was worth it.

"I called you this morning, Mitch. To make peace, to tell you what I'd deciphered of the clue, to see if we couldn't finish together as we'd begun. But you didn't answer your phone, a strange woman did." Her voice lowered so it could scarcely be heard above the wind crying eerily from the desert, much as she cried inwardly for him. "Who was she, Mitch?"

He found his voice then, but he had not lost his anger. "I have no idea who she could have been. I vacated my room after our latest disagreement and only a sense of fair play kept me from abandoning you and boarding the plane I'd bought a ticket for."

Rena's spirits soared like the wind. He had not replaced her so cavalierly as she had feared. Then they as quickly plummeted to earth. How could she justify being with another man when he had committed no such indiscretion? A pleasant afternoon, a harmless interlude, suddenly became something shadowy and clandestine.

Ahmed was no less sensitive to the mood swings of their conversation than he had been to hers. He had let them each have their say, as he had let them try to solve their differences on their own. But he was far too astute not to realize what a poor job of repairing things they were doing.

Stepping forward, he extended his hand and, after the briefest of hesitations, Mitch shook it. "I am the wretched policeman who kept Rena so late yesterday. I apologize, but Martin Dankin, alias Randy Fletcher, was far too big a fish to let swim away. I needed everything Rena could tell me. I am sorry if our official inquiry caused some delays in your own business matters."

Mitch had no opportunity to be anything but reasonable. "It doesn't matter. I was worried about her more than anything. But I see she's being well taken care of. Her sister left Cairo and a note that Rena was sightseeing. As the day progressed I began to worry. But I see I needn't have. Rena is, as always, in good hands. I was a fool to think she might be needing me." He turned into the shadows.

Rena started to protest when someone careened into her. Caught off-balance, she fell against Ahmed and then against the steps of the pyramid. He helped her up and made certain she was all right. But as they both realized they were unhurt, they also realized Mitch was gone. Everything had happened so quickly, so silently, that he couldn't have known.

Rena broke away from Ahmed and hurried down the steps to the sands. "Mitch, Mitch!" But only the wind answered and there was no movement to be seen—not from Mitch, nor the careless person who had tumbled into them.

Ahmed caught up with her. "I fear he is gone. I'm sorry. Again I have come between you—and for the most innocent of reasons."

"Don't worry about it. It wasn't—isn't meant to be. Not years ago, not now."

"How can you say that when the man is so obviously hurting?"

"Hurtful, you mean."

"Why didn't you fly to him today when you discovered all he had done to be certain of intercepting you? It takes not only a patient man, but a very loving one to wait as he did."

Rena sagged in despair. "Because I never thought of it. I was surprised, and then angry, and . . ."

"I noticed. Anger is not the most productive of emotions, Rena."

"I think I might finally have learned that—but as usual, a little late."

"As long as you're both alive it is never too late. Now I think I need to get you back to your hotel and use a little of my official capacity to locate your Mitch."

They hurried back to the car and he expertly turned it around and headed back into the city.

"Who do you think ran into us?"

"Probably someone caught inside the pyramid after dark. They panicked, I suppose."

"But how would they know whether it was dark or light?"

"Some say the pyramid takes on certain characteristics once the sun sets."

"Surely you don't believe that."

He smiled reassuringly and patted her hand. "No more than I believe you and your lover are finished with one another."

Rena blushed and wondered if their relationship was that obvious.

"Only the hurt anger you both display gives you away, Rena. It is my experience that when love carries that much hurt it also carries that much closeness."

As they pulled up outside her hotel, Rena reached inside her purse and felt for her room key. Instead, her hand fastened on a small leather pouch. "What's this? It certainly isn't mine."

"Let us go up to your room and examine the contents." His voice was once again official. "No doubt we have our recent collision to thank for it."

She turned to him. "Then you think it was deliberate?"

"It suddenly looks that way."

As they entered the hotel and crossed the lobby, Rena scanned the crowd for a familiar face. There wasn't one and they had the elevator to themselves.

Her room was stuffy and she hurried to open the windows. Then with shaking hands she opened the small leather bag. Emptying its contents into the palm of her hand cleared up nothing, for it contained only smooth pebbles. Glancing up at Ahmed, she let her puzzlement show. "This means nothing to me."

"Let me see the bag."

She handed it to him and he felt down inside. Then a smile crossed his face and from inside he pulled free the large pearl Rena sought. "It was caught inside the lining."

She hardly had a chance to look at it before the telephone rang. Rena, hoping it might be Mitch, ran to answer. But it wasn't. Instead a voice she didn't recognize spoke in her ear. "Congratulations, Ms. Drake. You are again the clever one, or should I say lucky?"

Before she could answer, before she could even think of any response, the receiver clicked in her ear.

CHAPTER 14

Rain—soft, comforting, and very wet—streaked down the windshield of Rena's borrowed Jaguar. In spite of the adequate car heater, Rena shivered. Would she ever acclimatize and forget the warm sun of Cairo? It had been weeks now since the day she'd stood alone at the Cairo airport waiting for the plane that would wing her to Scotland. Ahmed had planned to be there, he'd even sent a car to pick her up at the hotel, but at the last minute he'd been detained by official business. So she'd picked up the ticket he'd reserved for her and waited alone for her plane. She'd been surrounded by people ever since, but hadn't ceased to feel alone inside.

She had tried to locate Mitch. But even though he hadn't checked out, she couldn't find him. Once again she had left a valuable package for him in a hotel safe and a sealed note in his box.

She'd heard from Ahmed since arriving at her destination. She had promised to wire him when she arrived and she supposed he had called in response. No, she amended that thought. He had called because he cared—because they both suspected a relationship would have grown between them if Mitch had not stood in the way. But Rena could no more stop loving Mitch than she could stop the rain spotting the windshield of the car. It was there, it was a fact, and she had to deal with it. How she didn't know. Tucked away in a special corner of her memory would always be the hours she had spent with Ahmed.

Rena had made no attempt to further contact Mitch. The hurt of his rejection was still too raw. And she had heard nothing from him, but then, unless he was having her followed, he wouldn't know where she was. Not even Shay had known until three days ago. Then Rena had broken down and called her sister and received a well-deserved tongue-lashing for her negligence in not getting in touch.

So far things had been going well in Scotland. The castle where she was staying was beautiful, old, and remarkably well kept. It was a full-scale renovation project that had brought to light the cache of jewels now occupying her time. They'd been found in a small, sealed room and were providing Rena with a challenge. At some time in the family's history fakes had been substituted for many of the real stones. But the replacements weren't consistent. A real emerald might be surrounded by paste diamonds and vice versa. There lay the challenge—no stone, no matter what size, could be assumed to be either real or fake.

The road wasn't much more than a wide lane and although there'd been precious little traffic, Rena still had to concentrate on what she was doing. For the narrow, twisting road was rain-slick, and the night a classic example of stygian darkness.

Rena shivered and wished she hadn't made the comparison in her mind. Alone as she seemed to be in the night, she didn't need to conjure up visions of scary stories and unsolved murders. Her imagination—as Mitch had often said—was a little too active. Damn! Would he never stop popping up in her thoughts? She was determined to forget him as apparently he'd forgotten her.

No, that wasn't fair. How would she know if he'd forgotten her or not? He had very little way of knowing where she was, especially since they'd quarreled over the fact he'd kept tabs on her in the past just to make certain she was all right. It was highly unlikely he would make that mistake again. Yet Rena knew she wanted him to find her and make everything all right. She wanted to be a part of him; to sleep in his arms; to relax in the fact he made her world seem so right. Why had it taken another attractive man to make her realize how precious true love was?

Driving along, she passed hedges, winding country lanes, and an occasional cottage tucked back from the road—but no other cars. Which wasn't surprising, since it really wasn't a night to be out. Now ahead in the ever-increasing rain was a car, its hazards flashing to alert any other traffic. Which was a good thing, because the road was scarcely big enough for two. And in this weather and without warning, she could easily have plowed right into him. As it was she had to swerve to go around him.

Rena considered stopping and then thought better of it. It was a dark night with no one else around. If the driver had wanted help he would have flagged her down. Anyway she was almost at the estate and could see about sending one of the men back to assist if her hosts and employers thought it necessary. Even those good intentions couldn't keep her from feeling a trifle guilty over leaving someone stranded in the rain. It was a night to spend cozily tucked away with a good book, not to be broken down on a little-used country byway. Anxious to be out of the weather and to ease her conscience, Rena stepped down on the accelerator. At last the lights of Highland House appeared on the horizon.

It was a three-storied structure with two wings. A handsome house surrounded by lavish and well-kept gardens, with just a glimpse of the sea. During her free hours, Rena had found a somewhat overgrown but enchanting route to the rocky beach below. Here she was able to be by herself and forget, at least for half an hour, that there were such things as duties and personal problems. However, her hosts were spoiling her with hospitality and the most exquisite food. When she discovered some of her waistbands getting tight she'd added a walk after dinner as well as after lunch. Walking was much easier than refusing dessert worthy of a gourmet.

Rena parked the car placed at her disposal and hurried through covered passageways to the main part of the house. There Ian and Nell Kirkpatrick were waiting for her while enjoying the comforts of a well-tended fire.

"Rena, we were beginning to think you'd taken the wrong turning." Ian was a delightful man, if a little overconcerned with everyone's comfort.

"The road was unfamiliar, and I didn't want to drive too quickly in the rain." She held out her chilled hands to the fire and then accepted a glass of brandy. She took a sip, abhorring the taste but enjoying the accompanying warmth, and was about to mention the stranded motorist when Nell interrupted her thoughts.

"Did you pass any cars? We're expecting another guest and he's late."

A look passed between her hosts that Rena was at a loss to understand. "I was about to mention that a couple of miles down the road a small car was pulled off to the side with its hazards flashing. I didn't stop, thinking they would have flagged me down if they'd been in much trouble. And now I feel guilty that I didn't."

"Ian, that must be him. He should have been here some time ago." Nell's voice was definitely anxious and she again glanced at Rena in a sidelong manner.

"I'm sorry, I should never have passed him by."

Ian hastened to reassure her. "No, you did the right thing. One can't be too careful these days. I'll take a car and see if I can be of some help. Nell, see if dinner can wait a bit longer."

"Everything's on hold as it is. We may be eating cheese and crackers if Cook has to wait much longer."

The minutes passed slowly, with Nell and Rena mainly discussing Rena's work with the family jewels.

"I suppose Ian has told you the family had wondered for years what had become of the gems written up in past journals. It was assumed they'd all gone by the way until we started this remodeling project of the east wing. It's been boarded up for so long that we'd almost forgotten it was there."

Rena wondered how you could simply forget a wing of fourteen rooms. "What's interesting is that the substitutions made on the jewels were done so haphazardly. Not one single piece is wholly fake. The larger stone might be, and then all the accompanying stones will be real."

"Are any of the stones of size real?"

"There's a ruby that will pay for all your renovations if you care to sell it."

Nell sighed. "I don't know what Ian means to do. I suppose if the collection were untampered with he would feel obliged to keep it. Part of the family history, you know. But where it's been so randomly altered, I don't know."

"I don't think what was done was random, Nell. I think someone was very clever about it. If all the stones had been replaced, then someone at some time might have become suspicious. As it was, I doubt anyone ever knew—except the culprit. And who knows, maybe it was done over succeeding generations."

"In other words, when the family fortunes were at low ebb they'd sell a jewel or two?"

"Exactly."

Their conversation ceased when the hearty sounds of male laughter reached them. Ian had returned and evidently Rena's stranded motorist was the Kirkpatricks' awaited guest. Nell rose to greet them and Rena waited with a smile of apology that quickly died.

It was apparent now why Ian and Nell had exchanged meaningful glances. And also apparent was why they hastily excused themselves with murmurs of dinner and wine to be brought up from the cellar.

Rena was conscious of every sound from slanting rain to crackling fire as the awaited guest closed the drawing room doors and walked across the carpet to greet her. Her hands shook so badly that she placed her snifter of brandy on the mantel and clasped them together.

Eyes the color of Nordic skies questioned her and she was unsure how to respond. Then she could almost hear Ahmed's voice urging her not to let differences matter—only love. Never had she been so unsure of her welcome and so uncaring. Throwing doubt to the wind she ran to meet Mitch. He never hesitated as he folded her into his embrace and kissed the warm nape of her neck with willing lips.

"My God, I've had a time finding you! Don't you ever disappear like that again."

"I won't if you don't want me to." Her words were muffled against his broad chest and woolly sweater.

"I don't want you out of my sight, Rena. Ever!"

They held each other tightly and then stepped apart, although their hands remained joined.

"How did you locate me? Did Shay tell you?"

"Shay, the last time I talked to her, didn't know any more than I did and was equally as worried. Rena, how can you do that to the people you love and who love you?"

"I'm sorry. I don't need anyone to tell me how thoughtless it was. My only excuse is I was so hurt and confused I didn't know what to do. So I buried myself in work and let myself heal to the point where I felt like reaching out to people again."

"Then why didn't you reach out to me?"

"Because I thought if you wanted to see me you'd come looking for me."

"I didn't know where to find you."

"Couldn't you have inquired at the airport?"

"When your friend reserved your ticket it was in his name—a fact I didn't know at the time. Not until I talked to him."

"You talked to Ahmed?"

"Only when I decided I'd have to track you down whether you considered it an invasion of your privacy or not."

"What did Ahmed tell you?"

"Where you were staying."

"Then you and the Kirkpatricks aren't really friends."

"On the contrary, Ian and I went to college together. Therefore it was very easy for me to call up and invite myself for a long weekend. Especially when the situation was explained. I'm afraid they find this all very romantic."

"Oh, Mitch, I've never been so glad to see anyone. I've so much to explain, so much to apologize for. I've held conversations with you in my head over and over again, but my reasons for the crazy way I acted didn't even make sense to me."

"Shush! It doesn't matter now. Anyway, I think I understand. I had quite a talk with your Egyptian friend. He certainly got close to you in a short span of time."

"I doubt if Ahmed has much trouble getting confessions."

"Whatever the reason, I understood you a lot better by the time I boarded a plane for Scotland."

"I love you so much, Mitch. I didn't want to lose you."

He took her hand and kissed it. "Everything's all right now."

Sometime later they were still cuddled together on the sofa when a tentative knock came at the door.

"Come on in."

Ian presented an apologetic front. "Sorry to bother you, but your companion is getting a bit impatient to join you."

Rena drew her brows together in puzzlement. "You're not alone?"

"No, I brought a friend. Well, actually he's your friend as much as mine."

"Who?" Rena could think of no one save Ahmed. But she couldn't imagine Mitch bringing him to Scotland.

"You'll see."

A bounding and exuberant ball of fur propelled itself across the floor toward Rena. At first she was uncomprehending and then her eyes misted over with tears of joy. "Cookie!"

Dropping to her knees, she embraced the wriggling, joyful bundle that squirmed, licked, and whined with happiness as Rena hugged and petted the misbegotten animal she'd met in a Hong Kong alley. Unashamed of the tears streaking her face, Rena questioned Mitch. "I thought you gave him away?"

"I found a home for him while all the red tape was cut to get him out of the country. The two of you were so taken with each other and he so obviously deserved a loving mistress, how could I keep you apart?"

"Mitch, this is the most wonderful of gifts, and you're the most wonderful of men."

"I won't deny I enjoy hearing such praise and I won't deny how glad I am my gift pleases you. But talking of gifts, that jade butterfly and outsized pearl were pretty spectacular. Shouldn't I have done something in return?"

"You hired me to obtain those, Mitch. I was only doing my job. I just wish I had something as thoughtful as Cookie to give you."

He reached out to touch her, to brush back a wayward lock of hair loosened by Cookie's exuberant greeting. "Rena, don't you know you have given me the greatest of all gifts? You have given me your love."